W9-AHE-489

MINNESOTA STRIP

MINNESOTA STRIP

A DAN FORTUNE NOVEL OF SUSPENSE BY

MICHAEL COLLINS

DONALD I. FINE, INC.
NEW YORK

FOR GAYLE

The harlot's cry from street to street
Shall weave old England's winding sheet.

WILLIAM BLAKE
Auguries of Innocence

The girl ran among the shadows near the river on the first cold night of a New York September. She looked behind her through the light of a solitary street lamp. A street of dark tenements and windowless warehouses. She stumbled as she ran, her ankles turning in black high-heeled pumps.

A tall girl of nineteen or twenty, with black hair and pale skin, an aquiline nose and brown Oriental eyes. A face from two worlds—Eurasian. Slim-hipped, she had large hands and full breasts. Foreign and exotic, yet oddly American. Almost boyish as she stopped in deep shadow to remove the high-heeled shoes. She breathed hard, looked back along the silent street as she struggled with the shoes. Hampered by her blue Chinese dress with its high neck and long leg slit. Alert to run again at the smallest movement along the late September street.

Shoes in hand, she waited in the shadow of an empty doorway, watched the street in the cold river wind. She saw nothing, heard nothing. Only the wind. She lit a cigarette, continued to watch the dark street. She waited for some time. For three cigarettes. When she did step out, barefoot, she walked to the corner and turned into the broad riverfront avenue under the silence of the closed West Side Highway.

She moved in the shadows of the abandoned elevated roadway, passed by a single car and one cruis-

1

*ing taxi, until she reached a lighted all-night diner
with neon beer signs and a xeroxed menu in its window. Inside, she took the counter stool farthest from
the door. The counterman wiped the counter.*

"Late to be over this far alone, Miss," he said.

"Coffee," she said. "Okay?"

*The counterman drew her coffee from the large urn.
He looked at her thin Chinese dress, the shoes still in
her hand, the thick black hair ragged from the wind.*

"Cold out there," the counterman said.

*"Yes, cold." She searched for words. "Warm here.
Coffee good."*

*Her voice had a heavy accent. Her English was stiff
and poor. She seemed to realize where she was, bent
to put on her shoes. She smiled, shivered even in the
warm diner.*

"Good coffee, sure. I mean, warm, yes?"

"You okay, Miss?" the counterman asked.

*"Sure." She held the heavy coffee mug in both
hands. "You bet, okay? Hey, don't ask, right?"*

*Don't ask: a New York joke in broken English. She drank
her coffee. At the long counter three other night people sat
absorbed in themselves. The girl watched each of them in
the long mirror behind the counter. She watched a skinny
youth who came in and ordered coffee, used the telephone
booth, left without drinking his coffee. She drank three cups
of coffee. After each cup she looked toward the door as if to
leave, then ordered another.*

"You sure you're okay?"

*"You hear like . . . sirens?" the girl asked. "Like
police, you know? Couple hours ago? I mean, tonight?"*

"Not even a ambulance," the counterman said.

"Yeah," she replied. "Hey, what the hell, okay?"

*The counterman thought that was an odd reaction
and watched the girl look again at the door. Even*

inside the diner she seemed cold. He decided the odd words had been just her poor English. He took a danish pastry from under a plastic dome on the counter, picked up one of the diner's advertising buttons.

"One more coffee and a danish on the house. All you got to do is wear one of these buttons."

He put the pastry on a plate, drew another cup of coffee and pinned the button on the high collar of the thin blue dress. ALDO'S DINER—On The River—GOOD FOOD. The girl ate the danish. She drank the fourth cup of coffee. When she left she was carrying her shoes again.

On the deserted riverfront avenue she walked north beneath the closed highway. Past abandoned shops with dusty merchandise still in their windows. Boarded doorways, padlocked window gratings, the neon entrance of a tavern without windows. It was just beyond the saloon that she stopped and looked into the alley between the tavern and an empty store. She stepped toward the alley. A single shot from a 9-mm automatic killed her instantly.

1

WE ARE A SPECIES that preys on itself. We live on our own kind, hunt each other. That's what I wanted to tell the girl who faced me across the desk in the office part of my one-room loft, but I didn't. I told her what the police had told me.

"No witnesses," I said to Julia Lavelle, "but that's what the police say happened. People remember her running along the street in the high heels and Chinese dress. The police found her cigarette butts in the doorway, talked to the counterman at the diner. They found one motorist and a cab driver who saw her on the avenue. The bartender in the tavern called the police almost an hour after she was shot. The saloon was empty by then, of course. The bartender didn't hear the shot, just happened to look out his door and see her. By the time the police arrived she was naked. Looters took it all: watch, shoes, jewelry, Chinese dress, underwear. No identification at all."

"Dead? Jeanne-Marie?"

Judy Lavelle was a small girl. ("Most people call me Judy, I never did know why. I mean, Judy should be short for Judith, not Julia.") She'd come into my Chelsea loft early that morning with two photographs and a hundred dollars. I hadn't the heart to tell her my per diem had gone up to three hundred, even if most of the time I don't get it. She wanted me to locate the two people in the photos: Roy Carter and Jeanne-Marie Johnson.

"Jeanne-Marie left Pine Dunes two weeks ago, Mr. Fortune. She had a fight with the Carters and ran off. I think she called Roy three days ago because he told me he had to find her in New York. He said he'd call me, but he hasn't and I'm scared."

She had no other leads. If she had she wouldn't have needed me. I asked her where Pine Dunes was.

"It's a little town out on the Island, north of Bay Shore. We all live around there."

I took her hundred, told her three days wasn't long to be missing, but that I'd look around. She could have checked the hospitals and morgue herself, but she was too scared to think straight and a hundred was a hundred. I found Jeanne-Marie Johnson in the morgue.

"The police think she could have known the killer," I told Judy Lavelle now. "From the location of the body, marks on the sidewalk, it looks like she walked right into that alley."

A shade heavy in a gray corduroy skirt and blue turtleneck sweater over low-heeled black half-boots, Judy Lavelle had large brown eyes. A rectangular face under neck-length brown hair that fell across one eye every time she shifted nervously where she sat facing me. She shifted now, shivered. She wasn't listening to me or thinking about a killer. Most people don't when you hit them with sudden, unexpected death—they think about death.

"She couldn't be," she said. "I mean . . . she . . ."

Telling the concrete facts sometimes helps them. "Your Roy Carter went to the police early this morning to report her missing, that's how they identified her. He gave an address in Pine Dunes—142 Hickock Drive—and a hotel in town. The hotel address was a phony, and now they can't find Carter. They contacted Pine Dunes—a Mr. Jerry Carter didn't know where Roy was but he said he'd come for the body. Why would he do that, Miss Lavelle?"

"What?" She was having a lot of trouble handling it.

"Why would Mr. Carter come for Jeanne-Marie's body? Are they related?"

"No." It took her a moment to realize she needed to say more. "Jeanne-Marie lived with them. When she wasn't away someplace. They're the only family she had here."

"Here?"

"She came from Vietnam. Her father was an American soldier. Eller's wife sent her to the Carters. Eller was Roy's brother, he got killed in Vietnam. His wife's still over there, she sent Jeanne-Marie here maybe three years ago."

"And Jeanne-Marie became Roy's girlfriend?"

"No," Judy Lavelle answered, raised her head and brushed the hair out of her eyes. "I'm Roy's girlfriend."

The steady stare of her brown eyes challenged me to deny that she was Roy Carter's girlfriend. But it wasn't only me, it was anyone, the world. I was beginning to see the picture, the relation of Judy Lavelle, Jeanne-Marie Johnson and Roy Carter. To see what really scared Judy Lavelle, what had scared her when Jeanne-Marie and Roy disappeared from Pine Dunes.

"The police," I said, "want to find Roy because they think he knew Jeanne-Marie was dead before he came 'looking' for her. When they asked him what she was wearing the last time he'd seen her, he seemed surprised at first, then quickly described her clothes in detail. Later they realized he must have known she was naked when she was found. If he did, he had to know she was dead, and reporting her missing was an act."

Pale, she looked toward my door, then at my windows. She listened to the early evening traffic on Eighth Avenue. The sound of late-twentieth-century America—screeching brakes and blaring horns getting nowhere and going nowhere. She was trying not to think about what she was thinking about.

"When he came to ask about her, he told the police where she'd been living. It's a brothel, Judy, on West Forty-first Street. In the Minnesota Strip. Did you know about that?"

"Prostitution." She stared at me. "Jeanne-Marie?"

"Roy Carter said nothing about that when he told you he was coming to New York to find her?"

She shook her head, her eyes down.

"The owner of the brothel told the police that Roy had described exactly what she'd been wearing when she left the brothel about eight last night."

Brakes screeched louder than usual on the avenue below. I waited for the satisfying crunch of steel against steel.

"Did he have a reason to kill her, Judy?"

"No!"

It was too quick, of course, too certain. She couldn't really be sure one way or the other. But she was as afraid Roy Carter had killed Jeanne-Marie as she was sure he hadn't. Fifty-fifty between fear and hope. Unless she knew the truth.

"The police want to see you. I had to give them your name."

She nodded.

"You want me to go on looking for Carter?"

"I guess not. I mean, the police will, won't they?"

"They will," I said. "And they'll want to know where you were last night."

"Me?" She brushed her hair from over the one eye. "Here in the city. I got in around six, stayed at the Y. I went out to look around and eat, you know? Trying to decide who to go to about Roy. There were so many detectives in the phone book. Your name sounded like good luck: Dan Fortune. Your address sounded cheap. I didn't know about your arm."

"It doesn't show in the yellow pages."

She smiled at the joke, then, unable to think of anything more to say or do she got up and walked out. I had no reason to stop her. I'm not the police, sometimes a case walks away. A lot of times. If she didn't want me to go on, that was the end of it for me if not for her.

2

THE RESTAURANTS AND CAFES of a resurgent Chelsea were crowded in the late evening. Diners sat behind elegant dinners and three-dollar cups of coffee. The affluent visitors to the city, the solidly successful, the rich and the rising young who spent more money than they could really afford as the eager young have always done. On the corner of Twenty-fourth Street a drunk lay on the sidewalk, like a rock in the river of privilege. At Twenty-fifth a narrow-hipped youth in a black plastic jacket waited for anything he could steal.

Bogie's was on Twenty-sixth Street. I had a Beck's, ordered the fish of the day: fresh salmon. They broil it nicely. With my last bite of chocolate walnut pie and second cup of coffee, I saw the man in the archway between the dining room and the bar.

A big man, thick through the chest and neck. The heavy belly of a weightlifter, and a flat, Indian face under stiff black hair. Eyes as unblinking as a jungle animal waiting with infinite patience for its prey. His hands opened and closed like claws waiting for a victim to stumble into their grasp.

His eyes fixed on my empty sleeve as he walked to me.

"You're Fortune."

"Why not?"

"He wants to see you."

"Who?"

"My boss."

"Give me his name and number. I'll call him."

"Come on." I was wasting his time.

I left a tip. He wouldn't care what he had to do to bring me to his boss. This was his work. It paid the rent, bought the good times, gave him his reason for getting out of bed each morning. The Puritan ethic is part of everything we do, even our violence.

On the street an illegally parked Mercedes waited. We rode in the back. A small, silent Latino youth drove. Up to West Forty-first Street and an address I already knew: the brothel where Jeanne-Marie Johnson had been living before she died last night, a few blocks away, in the first cold wind of winter.

It was an old brownstone with windows shuttered even on its upper floors. Across the street another brownstone proclaimed itself: The Rescue Mission. Its windows were shuttered too. Neither the damned nor the saved were going to escape.

We went around the front steps to a narrow entrance below street level. Through an iron gate and along a passage with a low ceiling in what had been the kitchen, pantry and servant work area in more elegant days. My hulking escort took me into an office, vanished into the dingy old brownstone's depths. I heard the distant laughter of females.

"You asking about Jeanne-Marie Johnson?"

He was seated on a desk, one foot on the floor, one foot dangling. A lanky man with a long, weatherbeaten face.

"You telling about Jeanne-Marie Johnson?" I said.

He slouched where he sat, rubbed one hand back and forth along the thigh of his dangling leg. A rough hand that had worked in the sun, but not recently. He wore tailored gray slacks, his black oxfords had the soft sheen of gloves. His blue striped shirt was the best Egyptian cotton. His regimental tie looked authentic, and the diamond in his tie-clip was. An expensive blue blazer hung over the back of the office chair.

"I want to know why you're asking, mate."

His accent was lower-class British—Australia or maybe South Africa.

"I was hired to ask."

He continued to rub his hand along his thigh. Everyone has some aid to concentration. The yellow stain between his fingers said he'd been a smoker. Fingers that flashed with rings. Something was paying him well. His blue eyes were pale and sunk in creases as if he'd looked across a lot of distance.

"Who hired you, mate?"

"A girl from her hometown. You know her hometown?"

"Stateside?"

"Out on Long Island."

"No." And his manner changed. He leaned toward me, friendly and confidential. "Look, mate, sorry about the dustup, but we had to know about you. We all want to find the bastard that killed her."

"Any idea who that could be? Or why?"

"Not a frigging clue, you know?"

He didn't know and didn't care, already thinking of other matters.

"I'm asking about Roy Carter too," I said. "You interested in Roy Carter?"

He wasn't. "Never heard of him, mate."

He walked out of the office. The big man with the Indian face appeared to escort me out. On the street it was dark now, the light and noise up on Eighth Avenue, the gaudy and violent Minnesota Strip. I lit a cigarette and watched the faint sign of The Rescue Mission across the dark street. The Englishman, or Australian, or whatever he was, didn't give a damn about Jeanne-Marie Johnson, only about my connection to her. Concerned not about her, but about me.

I saw the shadow on the steps of the next building. Someone standing in the feeble street light. A pale face like a reflection of the moon. I walked toward him. Well over six feet and skinny, his hands and wrists lost in the sleeves of a thin, black nylon windbreaker two sizes too large, he wore glasses that reflected the glow of my cigarette, army camouflage pants and scuffed jump boots. His collar-length hair looked brown in the dark. A small nose and a full mouth. I couldn't see his eyes behind the glasses, but the boyish face seemed familiar.

He spoke before I did. "You work for that Evans, mister?"

"Why do you want to know?"

"I want to know about him."

His voice was light and toneless, yet determined, almost threatening. He wasn't outside the brothel by accident.

"He asked about a girl who was killed last night. Is that what you want to know?"

He knew what I was talking about, and I knew why he was familiar. I'd seen his boyish face in a photograph that morning.

"You're Roy Carter."

His hands went into the slash pockets of his over-sized windbreaker shell. There was something besides his hands inside the voluminous nylon.

"I don't know you."

"I know you," I said. "You came into New York to find a girl. You found her dead. What are you doing now?"

"I still don't know you."

"Dan Fortune. Judy Lavelle hired me to find you and Jeanne-Marie. I found Jeanne-Marie, now I've found

you. I found Evans too. Or he found me. He doesn't
give a damn about Jeanne-Marie's murder, but he does
about my interest in her. What is he worried about,
Roy? Something else about Jeanne-Marie and—"

I saw his eyes the instant before he hit me. Brown.
His shoulder drove me against something that caught
my legs and threw me backward over a row of garbage
cans. I sprawled among the cans in a clatter and clang
as loud as an alley cat digging for food. When I untan-
gled, I was alone on the street.

3

THE AUSTRALIAN, OR WHATEVER he was, had
wanted to know about me, now Roy Carter wanted to
know about the Australian and wanted no part of me.
Technically I was still on Judy Lavelle's hundred, and
it looked like I had a case. Or it had me. I also had
someone in this brothel I knew.

In the vestibule there was a different name under
each mailbox, as if it were just another apartment
building. As if every policeman in the precinct, if not
the city, didn't know what was inside. The bouncer at
the door grinned at my empty sleeve.

"Come on in, friend. Our kinky chicks gonna love you."

"I'm looking for Georgia."

"You'n General Sherman."

"Georgia Dumont. Blonde, about thirty, nice body."

"Business hours. Get lost."

I dug a twenty out of my wallet, held it out for him.

"Tell her Dan Fortune wants a half hour."

He took the twenty, tucked it away. "You got a nice face."

The parlor floor was still laid out as it had been in its glory days as a Victorian townhouse, but that was all that was left of that proud, opulent time. The ragged hall carpet was a dingy red, the stairs to the upper floors carpeted the same shabby color. Battered sliding doors on the right were closed. On the left the doors were open into a living room of small sitting areas around old coffee tables with shadeless lamps and chipped saucer ashtrays. Two johns sat in the room.

"Nice place," I said.

They looked at me as if I were insane.

A slim black in a gray silk suit herded three women into the room. Two were maybe sixteen. One had on a see-through blouse and short skirt with running shoes, the other a basketball shirt and net stockings. The third was an older Oriental in a Chinese dress who folded her arms under her breasts to raise them.

"That all you got?" one of the johns asked.

"Most have regulars," the owner said. "Take or pass?"

The men looked at their watches, at each other.

"Okay," the first one said, "gimme the Chink."

"The kid in the running shoes," said the other.

The girl in net stockings walked out of the room, her face a mask. The chosen two led the men out with the same lack of emotion, except that the Oriental took her john's arm. The dapper owner turned to me.

"You waitin' special?"

Besides the gray silk suit, he was wearing a pale gray shirt and dark gray tie, gray suede shoes and gray silk socks with black clock faces on them. He had a strong face, pale brown with a narrow nose broken more than once, small torn ears and scar tissue above both eyes. His hands were large for his size, bent and scarred. He'd put in his time in boxing rings or alleys or both. Broad in the chest and shoulders, going to belly now under the gray silk. A diamond pinky ring dazzled on his left hand.

"Georgia Dumont," I said.

He walked out. For a small man he moved heavily, flat-footed. I could see where he'd gotten the scarred face. A hard hitter, but a slow mover and easy cutter. Not a manager's dream. So he'd taken his bruise money and bought a business he had the talent for, knew how to handle.

I listened to the female voices, that weren't as distant now as they had been when I was in the office on the floor below. The windows were so thickly curtained that no sound penetrated from the street. The bordello could have been in the underbelly of any city in the country.

"What the hell you doin' here?"

Once plain Stella Fanelli, Georgia Dumont was a short blonde with a thin smile and the eyes of a plastic doll. Eyes as dark as her hair had once been.

"Just some talk, Georgia."

"You don't love me no more?"

She took me up to the second floor into a room furnished with drab but durable furniture. She sat on the iron double bed.

"How long?"

"Fifteen minutes, maybe less."

"Fifty minimum, Dan. Sorry."

She got an hour almost what I got a day. The owner took most of it, but she still made more faster and easier than any other way she could. A good business for both of them. Except for what it did inside. I'd watched her grow up on the Chelsea streets, a child of the perpetual poor. If you asked her why, she'd tell you she'd been giving it away since she was fifteen to a no-good husband twenty years older, and, after he had the grace to get killed in an alley, to a series of assorted losers who came and went, so why not get paid for it?

"How is it, Stell?"

"Warmer than the streets and dry when it rains. MacKay runs a fair shop. We even got medical insurance."

"MacKay's the owner? The man in gray?"

"Mr. George MacKay. He likes the 'mister.'"

"A solid citizen. Tell me about Jeanne-Marie Johnson."

She took a cigarette from a package on the bare bed-table, offered me one. I lit both. She blew slow smoke.

"How'd you get mixed up in that?"

I told her about Judy Lavelle and Roy Carter. "How long was Jeanne-Marie here?"

"Week or so. Never saw her much. She was up on the fourth floor, didn't talk to us working girls."

"Who did she talk to?"

"Evans, I guess. Most of the girls figured she was his private stuff waitin' to be set up somewhere permanent."

"What did you figure?"

She shrugged. "MacKay lets a john stash a private tootsie sometimes. Some important john."

"Is Evans important?"

"I guess." She smoked, thought about what was or wasn't important. "Name's Coley Evans. An Aussie. He brings girls for the place, Orientals. MacKay likes 'em, they do good business."

"He has an office down on the pantry floor?"

"That's MacKay's office. He lets Evans use it."

"Like letting him stash a tootsie," I said. Noblesse oblige in the trade. "You have any ideas about why Jeanne-Marie Johnson was killed?"

Georgia let the smoke drift around her head, seemed to enjoy it. "Someone didn't want her around."

I waited for her to go on. She didn't.

"That's all?"

"That's all, Dan."

Sudden death was as ordinary on the Minnesota Strip as whisky and heroin and pimps' Cadillacs. I left her smoking alone on the stripped bed. On my way out the bouncer gave me a wink and a smile. Twenty dollars' worth. I walked up through the dark of the side street to the sprawl and glitter of Eighth Avenue, caught a cab downtown. In my loft I opened a Beck's, sat and thought about Jeanne-Marie Johnson.

Just another murdered runaway? Almost two million kids ran away each year. A hundred fifty thousand never returned, ended up selling themselves to stay alive on the Minnesota Strips, the Combat Zones, the Tenderloins. Four to eight thousand died each year. Most were never even reported missing. Unwanted and forgotten.

I drank my Beck's. Jeanne-Marie Johnson had run away, had lived, if briefly, in a brothel, and had died on the street. But she had not been unwanted or forgotten. A lot of people were interested in Jeanne-Marie Johnson—and in me. Maybe I could call Judy Lavelle and get rehired. Give her a cut rate.

4

THE BEEFY MAN WAS waiting in front of my door when I got back from breakfast next morning. He had that thick build men who work with their hands get early: heavy chest, no waist, girth as full as the chest. An inch under six feet, two hundred thirty pounds. Thick neck and arms. When he was nineteen he'd weighed a hundred ninety and drank more beer than anyone.

"You Fortune?"

His blue suit shined in the morning sun. An old suit worn uneasily by a man who did not wear suits. A white shirt, blue tie with large gray fish, stiff black Sunday shoes. Short hair almost white. Large hands not used to hanging at his sides.

"She said a guy with one arm. How'd you lose it? The war?"

"Samurai sword. Chopped it right off. Never even felt it. Who told you I had one arm?"

His blue eyes were confused. He heard the tone I use when I tell the thrill-seekers lies about how I lost the arm, didn't understand how I could be flippant. Then he forgot about it. He wasn't a man who thought long about what he didn't understand.

"Judy Lavelle. I'm Jerry Carter."

Up in my loft I sat behind my desk, waved Carter to the seat facing me. The detective and the client in their proper places. The comfort of ritual.

"Why did Miss Lavelle tell you about me?"

"The New York cops called me about Jeanne-Marie, about Roy identifyin' her and then sort of disappearing. I asked Judy if she knew anything about Roy, where he was. She told me she hired you to find him and Jeanne-Marie. She says you think maybe Roy killed Jeanne-Marie." His hands looked for something to hold, to work with.

"Miss Lavelle thinks Roy could have killed Jeanne-Marie," I said. "I don't think anything."

"They sure fought enough." The big hands seemed to get in the way as he talked, as if he couldn't think of anywhere to put them. "Hey, not that he could of done it, you know? No way."

"Why did Roy and Jeanne-Marie fight?"

"About her buyin' everything in sight, runnin' through her money, droppin' out o' any school we got her in. She never fit in over here. Eller's wife never should've sent her. Sure, she wanted to come to the States, but, hell, who don't?" He waited for my agreement, but when it didn't come he seemed confused, then went on. "She never oughta have come over here. Eller never oughta have married one of them."

"Your older son married a Vietnamese woman?"

Jerry Carter nodded.

"She's still in Vietnam?"

He nodded again. He wasn't interested in his Vietnamese daughter-in-law even if she had sent Jeanne-Marie to him. Or because she had sent Jeanne-Marie.

"If Roy and Jeanne-Marie fought so much, why would he come to New York to help her?"

"Hell, she did live with us, you know. When she wasn't off in New York or California or somewhere."

"What made her run away this particular time?"

The big hands went on groping at emptiness. "She'd come back broke again, you know. We was gettin' tired of supportin' her, told her she got to learn a trade, somethin'. She got mad, her and Roy got to really yelling at each other." He stopped, and I had the sudden impression he didn't know what he was saying about anything until he heard it himself.

"The police think he knew she was dead before he went to them."

He heard that. "It don't mean he killed her!"

"No," I agreed. "Only that he was there when she died. It would help a lot if we knew what made him come after her."

Jerry Carter shook his head. "She went and he went. Didn't say nothing to me or his mother. Cut his college. I always wanted a boy of mine to go to college. Eller up and joined the army. Only Roy's harder to talk to every day. Twenty-one, and I don't know what the hell he wants. I mean, it's great he came home and wanted to go to college, only he never says nothin' about what he's learnin', what he's studyin' for."

"Why did you come to me, Mr. Carter?"

"Jerry," he said. "Everyone calls me Jerry around the plant. Forty years with the company. I say to him, Roy, so what's after college, and he don't say nothing. I say—"

He had a rambling mind, easily turned into side paths, responding to the sound of his own words.

"Did you come to hire me, Jerry?"

He looked past me out the windows above Eighth Avenue. "If you could sort of, I mean, find him and ask what the hell he's doin'. His mother's worried, you know?"

"You're not worried?"

"I guess." A man doesn't worry like a woman. A man is cool, calm, firm. "I tell him college is great, but then what? What's he gettin' ready to do? He never tells me. He was an easy kid, happy most of the

time. Up to high school anyway. Maybe it's 'cause he
never really got to know Eller. He come along a lot
later, you know? I mean, Roy he was kind of a accident, you know, and he . . ."

*Roy Carter grew up idolizing an older brother he never
really knew. Nineteen years younger than Eller. An accident. The result of a wife with no further interest in sex
after the proper number of children for a young Italian-
American matron. When passion is rare it's hard to be
careful. More children are born of bad sex than good.*

*In uniform, Jerry Carter married Debbie DeVasto in
St. Ignatius Roman Catholic Church, Brooklyn, on June
24, 1942. Their first son was born in March 1943. That
day Jerry was in North Africa with the Fourth Infantry
Division, which had more total casualties than any
other U.S. division in World War II. In Normandy, Jerry
Carter became one of those casualties, but he survived,
with no permanent damage, to return to Debbie and
Eller and a semi-detached in Bay Ridge.*

*The young Carters shared the building with the
elder DeVastos. Papa DeVasto was an old-country
patriarch who commanded a street repair gang and
his family, so Jerry got a job operating a drill press in
an aircraft parts company on Long Island, moved
Debbie and young Eller into one of the mushrooming
tracts of cheap houses, Pine Dunes. There Debbie Jr.
and Melanie were born and, finally, Roy. After that
Debbie moved into her own bed, Jerry took up bowl-
ing and Eller went into the army.*

*Roy Carter was two years old when his brother
enlisted. It meant little to Roy then, but a lot to Jerry
Carter. He had not understood—he still didn't. He had
planned for Eller to be the first Carter, or DeVasto, to go
to college, had saved the money since the day he returned
from war.*

Eller made different decisions. He dropped out of high school, went to work in a factory in Brooklyn. Involved in a strike, he was fired, came home to Pine Dunes to get his high school diploma and go, briefly, to a community college on the North Shore. In 1964 he joined the army. Germany, then England. Reenlisted, and in 1968 reached Vietnam, where he won a Silver Star and two Purple Hearts.

When Roy was eleven the war ended for most Americans, but some troops remained to advise, and Eller was among them—because of that yellow ass he married was Jerry Carter's opinion. Eller was killed when Roy was thirteen, one week before the final debacle of the Thieu government and the exit of the remaining Americans. A time of the emergence of the Vietcong from their tunnels into the center of the city. A time for those who had cast their lot with the Americans to take what they had and escape to the safety of Europe and America, the comfort of Paris, the warm sun of California. In that final melee, Eller Carter died. No one in Pine Dunes ever knew exactly how.

Roy became moody. He stopped playing sports, stopped going to American Legion functions with Jerry. When he was sixteen he stopped going to Mass. He read a lot, began to go into New York city on weekends. At eighteen he graduated from high school and left for a two-year wander across the country and around the world. When he returned some six months ago he got into Hofstra University and Jerry Carter finally had his college son. Roy did well, majored in history. Jerry wanted premed or prelaw, Debbie favored business administration, but they counted their blessings and kept their mouths shut. Until last week.

The year before Eller's death, he and his wife found a half-American orphan living in a cardboard carton and took her in. Saigon, then and now, was full of these children. Forgotten by the Americans, an unwelcome problem for the Vietnamese, they were pieces of debris washed up on the shores of a mistake.

After Eller's death, the girl continued to live with his widow until there was no place for her in Vietnam. She wanted only to come to the country she had dreamed of all her brief life. So when Roy Carter was nineteen and somewhere in Europe, Jeanne-Marie Johnson came to live in Pine Dunes.

She entered the local high school and took private English lessons. A Hollywood company heard about her and wanted to film her story, make a TV Movie-of-the-Week, even a series about her life. They gave her a five-figure advance, she immediately bought a fur coat and a silver Porsche. A magazine paid her a large fee to write her views and impressions of the Vietnam war and what it had meant. She found it hard to learn English, was unpopular in high school, so she dropped all her classes, moved out of the Carters' house and got an apartment in New York.

She soon ran out of money. The magazine didn't like what she wrote and asked for its advance back. Jeanne-Marie drove to California, told the movie company she needed more money and wanted to play herself in the film. They had lost interest and dropped her entirely. She got an agent to sell her story to another company. He took what money she had left and then told her no one was interested. She had to sell the Porsche to get back to Pine Dunes.

Roy had returned by then. Jeanne-Marie sold her story to another magazine, was going to pose as the centerfold. She promptly moved back into New York. This magazine lost interest too. She tried to get a real job. She had no skills, no education, still spoke poor English with a heavy accent. She had to return once more to Pine Dunes. Barely nineteen, with no real prospects, Debbie and Jerry told her to go back to school, study English and learn a trade. She refused to do any of that, argued a lot with Roy and ran off two weeks ago. Three days ago Roy Carter also left Pine Dunes.

Jerry Carter listened to the passing voices and traffic noise below on Eighth Avenue. He was supposed to do something besides worry, go out and fight, but he'd lost one son and he was worried.

"What's he doin', Fortune? You know? What's he done?"

"I don't know, but I saw him last night." I told him about the encounter outside MacKay's brothel. "It was dark, but he looked like the photo Judy Lavelle gave me."

"What the hell was he doing around a place like that? He never had to pay for it, for Chrissake!"

"It's where Jeanne-Marie was the last two weeks."

"You mean . . ." His awkward hands moved in the air as if looking for a throat to grip. "Jesus."

"You want me to investigate, Mr. Carter?" If I was going to snoop, I might as well be paid.

"Jerry," he said. "How much?"

"Three hundred a day plus expenses. A week in advance."

"Three hundred?" he said. "A day?"

Inflation and the years were hard on him. He'd probably gone from sixty dollars a day to seventy-five over the last ten years and thought he was a great success.

"I got laid off couple o' months ago. I mean, it's okay, they'll call us back soon, only . . ."

"How much can you pay?"

The wallet in his big hands was fat with photos, membership cards and cash.

"A couple of hundred, run a tab on the rest, okay?"

If I'd wanted to be a good businessman I'd have found a different line of work.

"Five hundred," I said, trying to sound firm.

He paled, but counted it out. In tens. The money was crisp. He'd gone to the bank before coming to see me. Spending savings. He was more worried than he admitted, or had something more on his mind than he'd said.

"Tell me anywhere Roy would go in New York. Where he'd get a room, who he'd visit or contact, where he'd eat, anything."

He shook his head. "All the time he been comin' into the city, I don't know nothin' about where he goes or who he knows." He thought about that, his face bitter. His son didn't talk to him. Or didn't say what he wanted to hear.

"What if he did kill her?" I asked.

"Then he gotta have a reason."

He didn't mean a reason, he meant an explanation, a justification, an exoneration. All killers have a reason.

5

ON THE EIGHTH AVENUE sidewalk a scar-faced black sold sweaters from a flat cardboard box on folding legs. *"Ten dollars! Pure cashmere. Take home two, check 'em out. Ten bucks steals a real cashmere. Money-back guarantee."*

At the brothel door the same bouncer looked me over.

"More talk or some action?"

"I'm too old for the action."

"If you was, you wouldn't say it so easy."

An expert opinion.

"Can I talk to MacKay?"

"*Mister* MacKay ain't here."

"When will *Mister* MacKay be back?"

"When he gets back."

A joke on me. A little fun. Guarding a door was a boring job. He grinned, said, "Try over to the mission."

Georgia must have told him good things about me, and everyone needs a friend. Even the guard on a brothel door. Especially the guard on a brothel door.

At the Rescue Mission the same brownstone steps led up to a front door open to admit anyone. Inside, the hall and living room had been turned into a kind of gameroom/library/spiritual center with tables, game boards, books and uplifting posters, some religious, some not. To the right, the dining room had become a dining hall of narrow tables and straight chairs.

Three skinny, cat-eyed kids watched me from the game room. A girl and two boys, all in jeans and T-shirts. The oldest, a boy with a pack of cigarettes rolled up in the sleeve of his T-shirt, looked maybe fourteen. I smiled at them.

"Anyone else around?"

Crouched over the game tables like alley cats over the garbage, they stared at me. Somewhere toward the rear I heard voices. I walked back with my head turned to be sure I saw any movement behind me.

The voices were in a small windowless office under the stairs. George MacKay held a tiny woman by the arm, talked to a taller woman. MacKay was all in white this time, from vested suit to patent leather shoes. The women were drab in comparison. The one in his grasp wore a dark blue sweater, a light blue skirt half way up her toothpick thighs, no stockings and black high heels. The taller was in beige slacks, a red wool turtleneck and sensible walking shoes. She listened to MacKay.

"... her man caught her holdin' out on the take so she run to me. I don't hold with violence, but no girl works for me ain't sixteen, see? So you send Jackie home, I pay the tab. I been meaning to help you folks anyway."

"I thank you for bringing the girl," the woman in the sensible shoes said, "but I don't think we can take your money."

"It's okay, honey," MacKay said. "I got a good business, I likes what you do. You send Jackie home."

The girl said, "Rags ain't gonna like this place."

"I handle Rags," MacKay said.

"Can't make no money here," Jackie said.

"Do you want to go home, Jackie?" the woman asked.

"Rags never lets me go nowhere," Jackie said to MacKay.

"Rags doesn't own you, Jackie," the woman said.

"Rags he come for me," Jackie said to MacKay.

"I told you," MacKay said. "I handle Rags."

"Rags beat the shit out of me," Jackie said. "You got to take me in. I make you good money."

Rags or MacKay, nothing else made sense to her. Nothing else was real, true. Her *man*. Father and mother. Home.

"You do what these folks tells you," MacKay said, nodded to the mission woman. "God bless you, sister."

He saw me when he turned. Jackie retreated into a corner. The woman smiled at me.

"I'm sorry, may I help you?"

"I came to find Mr. MacKay."

MacKay looked puzzled. "I know you?"

"Last night. I wanted Georgia."

"Yeah, sure. Okay, walk me out."

Jackie tried to follow. The mission woman held her arm. She didn't struggle.

On the street MacKay said, "Cop? I'm sweet downtown."

"Private," I said. "Dan Fortune. Working for Jeanne-Marie Johnson's family."

"Thought she was a Nam orphan."

"Adopted family. Out in Pine Dunes, Long Island."

We reached the steps up to his door.

"Some young guy come today askin' my girls. He family?"

"Roy Carter?"

MacKay shrugged. "Didn't talk to me. Wanted to know what she was doin' in my place, what was she up to the night she got wasted."

"What was she doing in your place?"

Takin' up space. Favor for an associate."

"Coley Evans?"

"You got it."

"What else does he do besides supply Oriental tricks?"

"Ask him."

"I can find out."

"Not from me."

"What was Jeanne-Marie doing the night she was killed?"

"I just loaned the space."

"She could have said where she was going."

He started up the steps, stopped. "She was out of my place." His eyes considered me as if making up his mind about me. "The girls say that young guy never asked about who maybe killed her. Just what she was doin' before she got killed, who she was with."

"Anything else?" I said.

"That lady over at the mission, name's Woollard. Her and that Jeanne-Marie talked some."

He went on up the steps into his establishment. He didn't hurry. A substantial man, owner of his own business.

6

THE MISSION WOMAN LOOKED up her stairs at the twelve-year-old hooker, Jackie, being escorted by two other scrawny girls.

"I hope she'll let us help her. I hope we get lucky this time. We don't often get lucky, Mr. — ?"

"Dan Fortune," I said. "It's Miss Woollard?"

"Anne Woollard, yes."

She continued to look up the stairs.

"It can get you down," I said.

She walked back to her windowless office under the stairs. I followed. She sat behind her desk. "When I came to live in this neighborhood the people wouldn't walk on the same side of the street with me. They were sure I was an undercover police agent. When they finally realized I was only a college girl from Connecticut come to 'help' them, they proceeded to steal everything I had. Even my textbooks and my Persian cat. Not mean or vindictive. I simply had things and they had nothing. Then the stealing stopped and now I'm more or less accepted. There are small victories."

She was a nice-looking woman in her late twenties with auburn hair and a round face without special features except bright, alert eyes. An intelligent face that had seen few troubles. A middle-class suburban girl who, in the orderly progression of life, should never have been where she was.

"You want to talk about Jeanne-Marie, Mr. Fortune?"

"Why do you think that, Miss Woollard?"

"I heard you mention her name to Mr. MacKay. He knows she spoke to me a few times."

"When was that?"

"I go over there to talk to the girls, see if they need any help. Mr. MacKay lets me. Jeanne-Marie seemed particularly anxious to talk to someone."

"About what?"

"Are you a policeman, Mr. Fortune?"

"A private investigator."

"Working for whom?"

"The family she lived with," I said. "Jerry Carter hired me to locate his son Roy. Roy Carter came to New York supposedly to help Jeanne-Marie, now he seems to be after something. Maybe her killer, maybe not. Why was Jeanne-Marie anxious to talk?"

She nodded to a chair. "I think she was bored, waiting for something to happen, something exciting. She talked about her plans, how rich and famous she was going to be. She was going to get her Porsche back, live in Hollywood and Malibu."

"Any idea how she was going to do it all?"

"No. They never have any real plans. Only naked longing, pipe dreams. Raw and desperate, because they know that for most it's never going to happen. Suburban kids have plans because for them the dreams are possible, even probable, but not here."

She was probably right, you learn a lot about reality in the slums. Only Jeanne-Marie Johnson wasn't from the slums.

"Did you see her with anyone in particular?"

"A tall man. I don't know his name."

"Had you seen him over there before?"

"I don't think so."

"The name Coley Evans mean anything to you?"

"No."

"She said nothing about what she was doing the night she was killed?"

"No. She was secretive about anything personal. Just talked about her dreams."

I got up. She stood with me.

"Who is this Coley Evans, Mr. Fortune?"

"I don't know who he is," I said. "Not yet."

"Let me know what you learn, would you? I liked the girl."

On the street I headed up to Eighth Avenue. Maybe Anne Woollard had liked Jeanne-Marie. But to have heard me mention Jeanne-Marie to MacKay she had to have followed us to the front door and listened. George MacKay had volunteered information, and Anne Woollard had wanted to know what MacKay and I said. It wasn't what I would have expected from either of them.

7

THE CITY NIGHT LAY on the silent alley half a block from the East River. Abandoned warehouses stood dark on both sides, doors and windows boarded on the ground and first floors, the upper ones broken or gone.

A crooked sign proclaimed that the warehouses would be torn down to make way for a low-rent housing project, the proud achievement of a borough president whose name was barely discernible and the mayor of two administrations ago. Half its supports had already gone for firewood, and all the funds had gone for more important projects, leaving the sign to fade like the hollow promise it was.

I knocked at the last dim, boarded doorway. A cracked female voice spoke from nowhere.

"What you want?"

"The Chief."

"What you bring?"

"Cigarettes."

"Four packs."

"Two."

The blackness behind the boards moved. The boards themselves swung outward. I stepped through into a deeper black, waited for my eyes to adjust. Somewhere far off in the cavernous interior there was flickering light. An old woman wearing thick layers of dresses and shawls held out a bony hand. I gave her two packs of cigarettes. She scurried off.

The vast dimness was broken only by shadowy pillars and silent shapes. Along the crumbling walls and around the pillars winos sprawled unconscious, bag women slept among their carts and shopping bags, ragged youths sat with violent eyes torn between anger and sleep. None of them watched me. Since I'd been allowed in I was probably no danger, and since I'd come voluntarily I probably had nothing worth stealing.

"Okay."

I followed the old woman through the gloom to the stairs. Any elevator had been sold or stolen years ago. Even the stairs ended at the second floor. The top, where the privileged of the alley lived. The strongest. Those who had the most.

"What you got, Dan?"

He was at the top of the stairs, an electric lantern in his hand. In his late twenties, stocky and swarthy. His thick black hair in two heavy braids like Gall, the Oglala warrior chief who had kept Major Reno in the rocks while Crazy Horse wiped out Custer. A single eagle feather straight up and arrogant. A buckskin vest heavily beaded with the intricate patterns of the Comanche. High-booted moccasins like the Apache. Torn jeans and dark glasses even at night.

"I need some help, Chief."

In the far corner of the empty second floor, blankets hung from pipes and beams to form a kind of tepee. Inside, more blankets covered the floor and a raised platform. A Coleman camp stove stood in the center with pots and cooking utensils. There was an old refrigerator powered by a long extension cord that went out the window. Painted shields, feathered lances, beaded quivers and parfleches hung everywhere. The Chief took down a peace pipe, sat cross-legged on the platform. I sat with him. He lit the pipe, puffed, handed it to me.

His name was Kevin Canizarro. A runaway Irish mother and a vanished Italian father and he'd wanted to be an Indian as long as he could remember. Anything except Irish or Italian or the ward of an aunt with seven kids of her own and no time for an unwanted mistake. Where the aunt lived in Brooklyn there had been Mohawks. They worked high on steel beams above the city. They had a tribe, were different, special. Kevin read books about Indians. When he was twelve he ran away into Manhattan and became an Indian. Washing dishes, running messages, sweeping floors, taking welfare was no way for a warrior. So he became a hustler and a booster, a thief and a burglar, a raider and a trader. The Chief.

"I need to know about a man named Coley Evans."

"What for?"

I filled him in on the murder of Jeanne-Marie John-son and everything else. "Coley Evans had her stashed at MacKay's, maybe playing with her, maybe not. He's not worried about her killing, so he's probably covered. But he is worried about people asking questions. I want to know who he is, everything he does."

"Sells Oriental pussy to the cat houses. Lotus Blossoms."

"What else does he do? Where does he do business?"

"Cost you a little one. 'Flation."

Nothing is free in the Chief's world.

"Fifty tops," I said. "There's a muscleman too."

"Femio Rivera. You got him."

"And Roy Carter."

"That's the whole C-note."

Roy Carter was an outsider, not in the normal underworld where the Chief knew every cranny, had his web of connections. It would be a lot harder to learn what Roy Carter was doing, even to find him, and the Chief hustled all he could all the time.

"I'm glad I'm a friend," I said.

It was a joke. The Chief had no friends. He walked me out of the blanket tepee and down to the first floor. With-out him I might not make it to the street. On the ground floor a wino shuffled up with a scrap of paper.

"Lady she call, want one all day tomorra."

The Chief took the paper, gave the wino a buck and sent him back to the pay phone a block away where the Chief got calls. He walked back through the gloom to a smaller room lit by candles. Ranged along the walls on sleeping mats were ten or twelve small dark people. They had cookpots on stoves in front of the mats, their other possessions tied in bundles. They were mostly women.

"Who wants all-day job?" the Chief asked.

They all looked up at him with large, expectant eyes. None pushed forward, but all waited. The Chief pointed to a woman in blue jeans, an orange silk turban on her dark hair.

"Six in the A.M. Pick up bus money 'fore you goes."

The woman nodded. I followed the Chief back to the outside door.

"Who are they?" I asked.

"Indonesians. Smart operator sent 'em over to work for rich folks. Like, they can't hardly get no good help these here days, right? Rich folks got to do their own cookin', cleanin', ever'thing. A cryin' shame. So this cookie worked out a scheme. Told 'em they get high-payin' jobs in the States, paid 'em show money, forged phony tourist visas, gave 'em one-way tickets from his own travel agency. A partner met 'em, sold 'em to rich families for three thousand dollars a head. They got no ticket home, they works for no pay, sometimes got slapped around 'n locked in the houses. A lot of 'em ran off, got payin' jobs. Sometimes the richies tracked 'em down, tried to get their three grand back from the new folks hired 'em. Immigration got into it, raided the houses, got a case 'gainst the operator. No case 'gainst the rich folks, o' course. Only a lot of 'em don't want nothin' to do with INS, right? They wants to stay over here, so they's hidin' out. I let 'em crash here, get 'em work whiles they waits for INS to forget about 'em."

"What do you get?"

"Fifty percent."

"They'd do better to just go home."

The Chief grinned. "Ain't no uptown game. We got different rules."

I went out through the door and the hinged boards, up the alley to the dark street with the East River half a block away. The Chief was wrong. The game might be different in the alleys, but the rules were the same.

I walked to the nearest subway, rode uptown, walked across to Bogie's for a few Beck's before I went to bed.

8

Coley Evans sat on a dusty packing crate under a single bare bulb. Across the dim cellar Roy Carter stood at the foot of the narrow wooden stairs.

"Why was Jeanne-Marie killed?" Roy Carter said. Bone thin, his long arms swallowed up in the sleeves of the loose black nylon shell made for a larger man. He still wore his army camouflage pants and jump boots. His brown hair hung limp over his college-boy face behind the horn-rimmed glasses.

"Who's Jeanne-Marie?" Coley Evans said.

The Australian sat on the edge of the dusty packing crate under the hanging light. One leg swung free. His right hand stroked the hard cloth of his light-brown cavalry twill slacks. Expensive slacks with leather-trimmed pockets.

"A girl you used," Roy Carter said, "fooled and got killed."

The third man in the cellar leaned against the encrusted wall to the left of the stairs and Roy Carter. Eufemio Rivera, thick through the neck and chest. The heavy belly of a weightlifter. His flat, almost Indian face watched Roy Carter without expression. One massive hand in his pocket, the other at his side. The hand at his side opened and closed rhythmically.

"Your girl?" Coley Evans said.

"No," Roy Carter said. "Just a girl who believed too many lies."

"Don't we all, mate. Name of the game."

"A rigged game."

"Well then, mate, you got to make sure you're on the side doing the rigging, eh?"

"I'm not your mate," Roy Carter said.

Coley Evans laughed. The hand on his thigh rubbed faster. His other hand began to drum a rhythm on the packing crate. An impatience in his quick glance toward Eufemio Rivera.

"Tell me why Jeanne-Marie was killed," Roy Carter said.

"Now how can I do that, chummie? Don't even know who the lady was."

"You know who she was. You know why she was killed."

Coley Evans moved on the packing crate. Leaned with both feet on the stone floor of the basement. Both hands moved slowly, repeatedly, back and forth along his thighs.

"I say you're out of a loony bin, mate."

Roy Carter took a step away from the stairs. Eufemio Rivera stepped toward Roy Carter. They both stopped. Evans watched them both, his leg no longer swinging in the dim cellar light, the birdlike singing of rats coming from somewhere in the dark corners. Roy Carter looked only at Coley Evans.

"I was there," Roy Carter said.

Coley Evans said, "Where?"

"Where she was killed."

Coley Evans said, "Then maybe you killed her yourself, mate." The Australian's voice was soft, soothing. "Maybe you just don't remember. You're all mixed up, Carter. You don't remember —"

"I was at the other place too," Roy Carter said.

Coley Evans stopped moving altogether. "What place?"

"Where you sent Jeanne-Marie."

The silence of the cellar was broken only by the faint sound of water running somewhere. Eufemio Rivera breathed thickly through a broken nose. Coley Evans again began to rub his hands along the hard cavalry twill of his slacks.

"What do you want, Carter?"

"I want what Jeanne-Marie wanted. What she came for."

Evans' nod was almost imperceptible. A small quick nod to Eufemio Rivera. The muscleman's free hand pointed at Roy Carter as if to pin him in space like a butterfly to a wall. Rivera's other hand came out of his pocket with a Colt Magnum.

Roy Carter held a short stubby automatic weapon. No more than a foot long with its stock retracted, its magazine extended down from a pistol grip he held in one hand. A single burst in the legs knocked Eufemio Rivera down. The Colt Magnum bounced off a wall to the floor.

Coley Evans never stood up. Roy Carter swung the square little submachinegun and shot him with three short bursts. Shot him again where he lay in his blood. A long, slow burst.

Carter let the gun fall back inside the nylon shell where it hung around his neck on a narrow black cord. He zipped up the jacket, walked past Evans into the shadows. He returned with a large brown paper bag, walked up the cellar stairs.

9

CAPTAIN PEARCE EMERGED FROM the dream of his own voice. "Evans was dead before we got there. Rivera told us the story. He's in the hospital. Three in the legs, not too serious."

He stood beside the bed as I came out of sleep, a shape outlined against the dawn breaking over Brooklyn outside my windows. Telling me about someone being killed.

"You sleep well," Pearce said.

"Sorry about that."

"I need the picklock practice. Just don't make me come through a window. You still looking for Roy Carter?"

I lit a cigarette, lay back in my bed. "I guess. Why?"

The captain straddled the straight chair he'd carried from my office area, told me the whole story of Roy Carter and Coley Evans in the cellar somewhere on the Lower East Side. "When the kid walked away, Rivera crawled up the stairs and banged his head on the door until Evans' Latino driver found him and called us."

"You're sure it was Roy Carter?"

"Told them his name right up front, description matches."

"He has an Ingram?"

"Model eleven, from what Rivera says. Efficient and simple. Less than a foot long, a shade over seven pounds. On a cord inside an oversized nylon jacket. He went there prepared."

"They didn't search him?"

"No one ever said crooks were smart," Pearce said. "Anyway, if they had tried to search him, he'd have pulled the Ingram and asked his questions that way. Or shot them then and there. I'm not so sure he even wanted answers."

"Revenge?"

"Looks like it, but he was after something else too."

"Could Evans have killed the girl?"

Pearce shook his head. "Covered all the way. Five witnesses. He could have had it done by ten other guys, but I don't think he did. And where did Carter get an Ingram? Automatic weapons are out in every state, they don't come easy or cheap."

It was a good question. We both thought about it while I got up and put my clothes on. Pearce is a trim, compact man in his late thirties who used to look younger than his age. Now he looks his age. Homicide captain in New York isn't a job that keeps a man youthful. When I was dressed, he stood.

"Let's go down to that cellar. Maybe you'll see something."

Pearce is mellowing every year. When he first took over from old Captain Gazzo he wouldn't let a private detective in his office. Maybe it's just that for most of us there comes a time when we'll take any help we can get. We rode his car downtown into the heart of the old ghetto. The upper Lower East Side beyond First Avenue around Tompkins Square. Where the newest immigrants live, or exist. First the Jews in the eighteen-eighties and -nineties, then the Poles and other Slavs, now the South Americans. We stopped in front of a dilapidated old-law tenement within smell of the East River. It was cordoned off. A uniformed patrolman gave us that vague touch of the cap that passes for a salute among New York cops.

In the vestibule, corroded mailboxes hung open and broken, a pool of urine covered half the grimy tile floor. Inside, the floor was gouged and splintered to bare wood. The walls were disfigured with leaks and filth and violent graffiti. The apartment doors had no paint, and the hall toilet had no door. The stairs were broken and the banister gone. The stench was overpowering.

"People don't live here?" I asked.

"People have to live somewhere," Pearce said. "Standard slumlord operation. Buy up buildings in such bad condition it's better for the former owner to sell at a loss than fix them up, then run them down even farther. Never spend a cent on them, overcharge the tenants who are poor, intimidated or can't speak English—usually all three. Bribe the building inspectors and fight condemnation."

"You can't charge the landlords?"

"Squeezing the poor isn't a crime, it's business. If Housing cites them and they don't comply after repeated citations, we can arrest them. They get out in an hour on low bail or their own recognizance. I mean, after all, they aren't criminals, they're businessmen. Then the lawyers take over and nothing happens. If a landlord has enough buildings, lawyers are cheaper than repairs."

We went down the steep wooden cellar stairs. The usual odor of earth and damp, the encrusted stone walls, the dusty floor. After upstairs it was an improvement. A silent detective from the precinct waited in the light of a single bare bulb that hung over a packing case. He pointed out the relevant locations:

Where Coley Evans had been found shot up near the packing case. "Fifteen slugs in him."

Where Eufemio Rivera had fallen against the wall near the stairs. "His Magnum was halfway across the cellar."

Where Roy Carter had stood a step or two from the stairs. "He could watch them both, back up and out if he had to. He knew what he was doing, Captain, only he didn't finish Rivera. That don't figure."

"No," Pearce said.

"Take a look back here."

We went back past an ancient coal furnace renovated into an oil burner half a century ago and unchanged since. There was a solid wooden door. The detective opened the door, flipped a light switch.

"Get that landlord the hell down here!" Pearce said.

The small room behind the furnace had no windows but good indirect lighting. A thick rug on the floor. A couch, three armchairs, glass and chrome coffee table, a wet bar with plenty of bottles, a refrigerator. Wooden filing cabinets—the best—two of them with the drawers pulled open. Steel shelves full of TV sets, stereos, videorecorders.

"Enough H and C in the cabinets to keep the streets happy six months," the detective, whose name I now remembered was Tancredi, said. "We figure half the H should be here ain't. Looks like the kid grabbed maybe ten kilos. Stuff on the shelves is stolen, we checked out some of it already. We been smellin' some big operation we couldn't find. Here she is."

We all stood and stared around the plush hidden room of Coley Evans. I could see where the heroin had been taken from a cabinet drawer still crammed with the plastic-wrapped, green-tied packages, white powder spilled all over the floor. It had to be what Roy Carter had taken away in the paper bag.

A patrolman led a tall man in a dark blue suit down the cellar stairs. A man with gray hair and a homburg, carrying a navy-blue topcoat and wearing a white shirt without a tie as if he had been pulled out of bed. An angry man. His face was deeply tanned from somewhere far from a New York October, and furious.

"Doctor Roscoe L. Millar, M.D.," the patrolman announced. "Of the Port Washington Millars, and who do we think we are bringing him here by force at this hour."

"Are you in charge here?" Dr. Roscoe L. Millar raged to Pearce. "You listen to me! I have friends—"

"Shhhhhhhh," Pearce put a finger to his lips. "You own this sewer and there's been a murder. The man from this nice office that doesn't show on your rent rolls. Probably doesn't show on your income tax. So now you'll tell me all about the man."

"I'll tell you nothing! Damn you, who do you think—"

Pearce reached, covered the man's mouth. "I told you, shhh. Evans is dead. This office is illegal. A secret tenant who dealt in drugs and stolen goods. *Your* tenant. How's that going to look in court when I close you down?"

Dr. Roscoe Millar glared. Another precinct detective, Alex Callow, came down the stairs. He nodded toward Millar.

"We just got the check on the good Doc. He's under a thirty-eight-count indictment out in Nassau. Defrauding the state medical-aid program. Seems he collected about a half a million for services he never performed, prescribed Valium, Preludin, Seconal and 'Ludes for state-aid patients didn't need 'em. Looks like most of 'em was addicts."

"I'm completely innocent of those ridiculous charges," Dr. Millar declared. "Anyway, it's not your jurisdiction."

"This is, Doc," Pearce said. "Murder, narcotics and stolen goods. Talk."

Dr. Millar shrugged. "All I know is that he rented the space. He furnished it himself, ran his own wiring and plumbing. He wanted privacy. I didn't ask questions. I don't believe there's a law that says I must."

"You didn't have any idea what his business was?"

"I did not."

"You don't know his associates."

"I don't live here, Officer."

Pearce said, "You just let him do what he wanted."

"He paid enough to do anything short of blowing up the building. Even that would have been all right. I'm insured."

"Take the money and run," Pearce said.

"I rent apartments to anyone who can pay the rent."

"Where do you live, Doc?"

"In Port Washington. Out of your area, I'm glad to say."

"Got a big house?"

"My house is adequate for my needs."

"I'll bet they're some needs."

"Is there anything else you want, Officer?"

"In court, Doc," Pearce said. "Some people call me Captain."

"I have lawyers . . . Captain."

"Get them ready for the building inspectors."

"I hope they don't close the building. Where will all these poor people live?"

"You do a real community service."

"As much as anyone does," Millar said. "May I go?"

Pearce nodded. Dr. Millar walked up the dusty stairs. As I watched him go I saw the faint glint at the foot of the stairs. Pearce and his men were busy inspecting the files, the shelves of stolen goods. I picked up the small, silver-colored metal disk from under the bottom step of the stairs. Clean and shining, it hadn't been there long. I slipped it into my pocket as Pearce came back to me.

"Tell me what you know about Roy Carter, Fortune."

I told him everything Judy Lavelle and Jerry Carter had told me, and about my meeting with Roy Carter outside the brothel.

"If Evans wasn't worried about the girl's killing, what was he worried about?" Pearce said.

"People asking questions about Jeanne-Marie."

"Because he used her?" Pearce asked.

"For what?" I said. "His own fun? His private tootsie?"

"Whatever he used her for, it wasn't that," Pearce said. "We got the autopsy results yesterday. Nothing special except one little detail. Jeanne-Marie Johnson was still a virgin. M.E. says, given her history over in Vietnam, it's not so surprising even at nineteen. Whatever she was doing in that cat house, she wasn't Evans' private stuff, and she wasn't working for MacKay."

And whatever had brought Roy Carter to New York to help her, it hadn't been sex.

10

ON THE SUBWAY I studied the small silver-colored disk. An inch across, it was some kind of brooch with a pin at the back but had a broken loop at the top as if it had been worn on a key ring or watch chain. The design was a twisted belt and buckle that circled a hand holding a dagger straight up, with the Latin words *Manu Forti* in the circle of the belt.

In my office I put the pin into one of my plastic evidence bags, checked my answering machine. There was no message from the Chief. There was one from Jerry Carter. How was I doing? Had I found Roy? Would I call him? For all his macho cool, I had an anxious client, or a nervous one.

I was thinking about a late breakfast—make it here or go out and buy it—when there was a knock on the door.

Julia Lavelle stood in the doorway in jeans, running shoes and a baseball jacket.

"I want you to find him."

"Come in."

She came in with her head down. To hide that she had been crying. I pointed to a chair at my kitchen table. My decision about breakfast had been made for me.

"I've got dry cereal, eggs and yogurt."

She shook her head. "Nothing, thanks."

"Eating helps, Judy."

"No it doesn't." She looked up. "I had doughnuts in Penn Station anyway."

"Coffee then."

I made the coffee, poured a bowl of bran flakes, cut up a banana. When the coffee was ready I got the milk, poured two cups of coffee and sat down. Eating helps me. Sometimes. She sipped at her coffee. I ate my breakfast.

"His father already hired me," I said. "He's afraid Roy killed her too."

Her head snapped up, red-eyed but fierce, violent in denial.

"I don't think Roy killed her!"

"Yes you do. At least you're *afraid* Roy killed her. You have been from the start."

She met my gaze for a moment, strong and furious, then looked away. When she spoke again it was more a question than a statement.

"He couldn't have killed her."

"Why not?"

"He just couldn't have! He couldn't kill anyone!"

I told her about Coley Evans. She was young enough to want to cry, so young she had to try not to in front of me, drank her coffee to hide any tears. I refilled her coffee cup.

"Why would he kill Coley Evans, Judy?"

Her voice was low now. "He wouldn't."

"He did. He left a witness."

"He's lying."

"I don't think so, Judy."

She sat there. Still awkward and even innocent, a country girl. As close as we get to that nowadays, with movies and television, when high school girls in Iowa know all the same things girls in New York or Beverly Hills do. She was still from a certain place and a certain house and a certain family she could count on to be there. Had a certain boyfriend. Only the boyfriend wasn't there anymore—or wasn't her boyfriend anymore—and maybe had killed people.

"He never mentioned a Coley Evans? On those trips of his into New York? He never told you anything about what he did in New York, who he saw?"

She shook her head.

"Had Jeanne-Marie ever talked about Coley Evans, or New York, or maybe the brothel and George MacKay?"

She looked up at me, the tears close to the surface of her eyes. "I don't know, Mr. Fortune. About any of it. I don't know if Roy knew Coley Evans. I don't know if Jeanne-Marie did. They both came to New York a lot, so maybe they did. But I just don't know. I don't know anything."

She was telling the truth. All she really knew was that she had been Roy Carter's girlfriend. Had wanted to be anyway.

"What is he doing now, Judy? Here in New York now that Jeanne-Marie's dead?"

"Trying to find out who killed her! What else would he be doing?"

"That's what I'm wondering about," I said. "Was she that important to him, Judy?"

She flushed. Shrugged. Then the tears finally broke out again, poured down her cheeks. This time she made no attempt to stop them or wipe them away. "I never thought she was, I didn't think he even liked her, but why else would he go after her, go to help her, get in all kinds of trouble like he is? He came to the city after her, he didn't call me the way he said he would. He hasn't called me at all. Nothing, you know? I don't know where he is or what he's doing or what's happening or—or anything."

It all came out as unstoppable as the tears. I let her cry, talk, think, until she finally wiped at her eyes, took deep breaths, tried to stop, even tried to smile. Then I leaned closer to her, watched her eyes.

"Jeanne-Marie was a virgin, Judy. She wasn't working in the brothel, she wasn't sleeping with Coley Evans and she wasn't sleeping with Roy. She wasn't important to Roy that way. So why was she important? Why is Roy so concerned about her? Why did he rush up here to help her? Just family? An obligation?"

She let it sink in, dabbed at her eyes with the sleeve of her baseball jacket. The brave, embarrassed smile turned into a real smile. Maybe Roy wasn't her boyfriend anymore, but he hadn't been Jeanne-Marie's.

"Jeanne-Marie?" There was the change of a whole society in her disbelief that a nineteen-year-old could be a virgin. A change for good or bad, depending on how you looked at life.

"The medical examiner says so."

Her smile turned sad. "Poor Jeanne-Marie."

"Whatever," I said, "she's dead. Roy's alive. Why did he come looking for her? What's he doing now?"

She dried her eyes, blew her nose on one of my Kleenex. "He cares about people, Mr. Fortune. He cared about his brother, and I guess he cared about Jeanne-Marie. He came to New York to help her, I know that."

"Help her how? To do what? Against what?"

"Against whoever . . . killed her, I guess," she said.

"She didn't come to New York to get killed, and she called for help before she was killed. Roy came to the city before she was killed, now he's still here after she was killed. He killed Coley Evans. Evans was involved in white slaving, stolen goods, drug peddling. When Roy killed him, it looks like he took some of Evans' heroin too."

"Heroin?"

"Smack, the Big H, hard stuff. He took maybe ten kilos. That's a lot for just a user, he didn't look like a junkie to me, and you haven't said anything about him being on drugs."

"He isn't!"

"Then why did he take it, Judy? Is it what Jeanne-Marie came to the city about? What Roy's doing now?"

She had no answer, but she didn't start crying. Something had changed for her. Jeanne-Marie had not been Roy's girlfriend. Roy was doing something else. An entirely different kind of problem she could deal with. Rational. A sad change, but she didn't know that yet. She had sensed all along that Roy was slipping away from her, had suspected it was for Jeanne-Marie and had not been able to let him go to Jeanne-Marie. But it wasn't Jeanne-Marie the woman, something else, and she could begin to let go.

"You want to make a couple of calls with me?" I said.

"Can I?" She was still shaky, nervous, but now that she knew it wasn't sex she could find out what Roy Carter was doing.

We went downstairs, then uptown along Eighth Avenue. A skinny Turk with a scimitar nose and heavy eyes fanned flies off purple steaks in a shallow box on the sidewalk. *"Best steaks in the world! Take home a* dozen. *Impress your friends. Filet mignon, buck and a half a pound!*"

The bouncer at the door of MacKay's establishment pointed at Judy Lavelle.

"No broads. The ladies, they don't like."

"How do we talk to MacKay?"

"You slides down to the executive floor. Only *Mister* MacKay he ain't there."

"Where is he?"

"I look like the CIA, brother?"

Across the street the door of the Rescue Mission was still open. It probably always was. A solitary youth with dark skin and a mustache sat in the game room reading a book with one finger. He scowled with the effort, did not look up as we passed. Anne Woollard was in her office, facing a boy with ragged blond hair and violent blue eyes.

". . . what the shit do you know? When did you sell your tight ass in cockroach beds? Tomorrow you got somewhere to go. Me, where the shit I got to go except the river?"

He heard us, whirled like a jungle animal, almost knocked Julia Lavelle down as he ran out. I caught his arm. He was so weak I held him with my lone hand. We stood face to face. His nostrils flared. His breath stank. His blue eyes had nothing behind them but an endless hate and emptiness, defied me or the world to scare him or hurt him or make him give one damn about me or it. I could hold him, the eyes said, I could kill him, but I could never reach him.

"Let him go, Mr. Fortune."

He walked away neither triumphant nor grateful. Neither a smile nor a sneer. Just walked on down the hall as if I'd never stopped him, never even been there. Into the street.

"We picked a bad time," I said.

"I don't think I was reaching him anyway," Anne Woollard said. "He's sixteen. He has syphilis, ulcers, intestinal parasites and lice. He's an alcoholic. He's been a male prostitute since he was thirteen, just to survive. His father disappeared when he was an infant. His mother and stepfather threw him out because he got in their way. He's sold himself so many times he stopped counting years ago. He doesn't like what he's learned about life from adults, and he challenges me to tell him why he shouldn't jump off the nearest and highest bridge he can find."

"What did you tell him?"

"I told him how wonderful the world is if he'd give it a chance. What a delight it is to be alive in the richest country on earth. What a future he had ahead of him if he'd straighten out, be a solid citizen. How God loved him and wanted him to live a decent, moral life. All the standard claptrap."

"If it's all claptrap, why say it?"

"Because I believe in life even if I don't know why. I want to save him if I can." She took a deep breath, looked curiously at Judy Lavelle. "Now, what can I help you with?"

"Julia Lavelle," I introduced, "Miss Woollard."

She smiled. "Just Anne. And please sit down."

"Julia knew Jeanne-Marie Johnson," I said. "She's a friend of Roy Carter's."

Anne Woollard shook her head. "I've racked my brain, but I can't think of anything more she said, or anyone she might have met. She simply didn't talk about anything specific, not even your Roy Carter, and I didn't see anyone else unusual."

"Maybe Roy came to you asking about her." Judy Lavelle said. "I mean, before or maybe after she was killed."

"I'm afraid not, Judy," Anne Woollard said.

Her voice was sympathetic, almost motherly. Maybe it was the job. Trying to mother the motherless day in and day out.

I said, "You're sure she never mentioned what she was going to do for or with Coley Evans?"

"I assumed they were romantically involved."

"They weren't."

Anne shook her head. "Then I'm totally in the dark. I wish I could help more. Do the police have any clues?"

I told her about the shooting of Coley Evans, about Eufemio Rivera who was alive and talking.

"Do the police have any idea why, Dan?"

"If they have, they haven't told me."

"What will you do now?"

"Keep looking for Carter, track down what Evans was up to."

Anne Woollard looked at Judy Lavelle. "Isn't it dangerous for Judy? I mean, going around with you? Wouldn't she be safer in Pine Dunes?"

"Not yct," Judy said. "Maybe we'll find him."

"Until dinner," I told her, "then you go home." I stood up. "You know Pine Dunes, Anne?"

"No, but I expect it's a lot like Darien where I grew up." She looked at the wall of her office as if she could see through it to the street outside. "The clean, neat, safe suburbs. On another planet."

We left her thinking about the differences between Darien and The Minnesota Strip, went out to wait for George MacKay. I sat us on the steps of the brownstone next door to MacKay's establishment, smoked. We waited on the steps as the afternoon turned into evening, and Judy Lavelle got a lesson on the other side of the private investigator trade.

"How long do you wait?"

"Until he shows."

"It sounds awful dull."

"It is. Let's get some dinner and send you home."

I found a cab and we rode down to the Village. Behind the storefront window of the Mexi-Frost restaurant on Thirteenth Street, we took a corner table. I ordered a Mexican plate. Judy had Argentinian steak with some exotic vegetables. On the street, people passed in the falling dusk. Evening comes rapidly to New York in October.

"Is it always so hard to find out anything in your work?" Judy asked.

"You don't think we found out anything?"

"You mean we did? What?"

"We found out that Anne Woollard is lying. She's talked to Roy. When, I don't know, but she's met Roy."

She watched me as if the rest of the world had gone into slow motion.

"She called you Judy," I said. "I never used that nickname in front of her. She knew you and Roy live in Pine Dunes. I didn't mention that and neither did you. Only Roy could have told her those things."

The waiter brought my enchiladas and chiles rellenos and her steak. Mine was good, for New York anyway. She didn't seem to taste her steak.

"He told her about me, Mr. Fortune."

"Sounds like it."

"Maybe he was just telling her about his past, where he used to live. Closing that part of his life."

"Why would you think that, Judy?"

"I don't know." She looked out the window to where a pair of derelicts were watching us eat. "I'm not sure I'm his girl anymore."

It had taken a lot for her to finally say it. Aloud where she could hear it herself. She didn't need any comments from me, any analysis, agreement, denial. Something she had to handle herself. We finished our dinner. She had dessert, pecan pie, and I had coffee.

"I was thinking about Roy telling Coley Evans he wanted what Jeanne-Marie had wanted," she said as she ate her pie. "There're some Vietnamese people out our way I know she talked to the week before she left. A family of fishermen down on the bay, the Dhocs."

"You know them?"

"I help some of their kids with English."

"Can you pick me up at the Bay Shore station tomorrow?"

"I guess so."

"Give me your phone number. I'll call when I'm there."

She didn't want to go home even then, but I took her up to Penn Station and she went. I waited with her in the Long Island Railroad Concourse until the gates opened, walked her down to the train and waited on the dingy platform until it pulled out. Then I went back to the Rescue Mission.

In the entrance hallway I listened, heard Anne Wollard on the telephone in her office. Back across the street I lit a cigarette in the October night. She came out in twenty minutes. I tailed her across town to the East Side and the Cheval Noir restaurant on Forty-eighth Street. She ate alone, I stood in a doorway. She had a good meal, I got cold. When she finished she walked west again to a theater showing the latest forty-five-dollars-a-ticket musical. I waited out the show in a bar across the street. I had too many beers, and when the show ended she caught a taxi before I reacted, and I lost her. I took the subway home.

In my loft there was still no word from the Chief. He was having trouble finding Roy Carter, too. There was more word from Jerry Carter. When was I going to call him? He sounded more than nervous. No news wasn't good news to him.

I opened a Beck's I didn't need and called Kay Michaels in California. Kay is the first woman I've felt really serious about since Marty. So, of course, she works in Hollywood and I work in New York. I lost Marty because our needs, besides each other, were too different, too separate. I'll probably lose Kay for the same reason. We fall in love with the same woman in different guises over and over. Those of us who fall in love. Most marry the girl next door, settle into the normal loveless marriage because that's what society wants, needs. I was never good at doing what society wanted me to do.

There was no answer in California. I thought about Judy Lavelle riding alone on a half-empty train and wondering what Roy Carter was doing in New York. I wondered what I was doing in New York. Do we invent our necessities?

11

WHEN I GOT OFF the train in Bay Shore next morning, I didn't call Judy Lavelle, I called a taxi. There was another way Anne Woollard could have learned about Judy Lavelle's name and Pine Dunes. From Jerry Carter or someone else in Pine Dunes, and a detective should report to his anxious client.

North of the old Sunrise Highway the houses become smaller and more ramshackle until in the center of the Island the process reverses and the houses grow larger up to the mansions of the North Shore. It was in the dusty center that the building boom—Levittown and its imitators—came after World War Two. Box houses on little plots that lured the returned soldiers out from Red Hook and Sunnyside, Fordham Road and Hell's Kitchen. A hundred dollars down, the rest of your life to pay. Everyone was young, so out they came to the potato fields to buy their boxes on the squares of new grass with maybe even a tree.

Pine Dunes was one of those tracts north of Southern State, elevated to villagehood but no more a village than Red Hook or Sunnyside. Number 142 Hickock Drive, thirty-five-plus years later, had been dug and planted, expanded and modified, covered and decorated. I paid the taxi driver enough to make him wait.

The woman who opened the door wore her long gray hair pulled back in the ponytail of the days when she had been a girl. Small and thin in pastel pink slacks, pink blouse, pink sandals. A downturned mouth under a fine straight nose in a face too pinched now, a grayness to the face that matched her hair.

"Is Jerry home?"

"No." She stared at my empty sleeve.

"You must be Debbie."

Her smile gave me a flash of the prom girl she must have been. "Do I know you?"

"Jerry told me what a fine-looking wife he had."

It pleased her. It was something she understood.

"Could I talk to you?" I said.

She glanced at a wall clock. A television set droned somewhere. A male voice all smile and teeth. It was 10:40.

"Fifteen minutes?"

"Well, okay. Fifteen minutes."

The front door opened directly into the living room. Stairs up to the expanded attic were straight ahead, the dining room across the living room through an arch, the kitchen to the left under the stairs. Light and sunny, it must have looked like a mansion to two kids from Bay Ridge. A mansion with everything: sun, grass, trees, children, two cars and maybe a boat, on the town every Saturday night, college for the kids, paid-up life insurance, a haven for their golden years.

She arranged herself on the couch. "What's on your mind, Mr. —?"

"Dan Fortune." I sat in an armchair. "Jeanne-Marie and Roy are on my mind. Jerry says they fought a lot. Then why would Roy have gone to New York to help her?"

"How do I know? He didn't even tell me he was going. Roy don't talk much. Just up and left like he always does. To that college Jerry was so hot on him going to, or off to New York, or wherever. Me, I'd as soon that boy got a job, supported himself for a while. We could use the money now Jerry got laid off."

"Was there anything different about him lately?"

She shrugged. "Boys are their father's problem. I got two girls not even married yet. In Brooklyn they'd of been married. Nice looking and lively too, just like me. Mel's tall like her Dad, wears clothes like a dream. Irish coloring just right for dark colors. Debbie Junior's got my coloring. Italian all over except the hair. I was blond too, the DeVastos got some Austrian in them somewhere." The coquette smile came all the way from Brooklyn, and suddenly she was somewhere else. Long ago if not that far away. "We ought never of left Brooklyn. I got all kinds of nieces and cousins, people can help girls get married. All we got out here is neighbors that work with Jerry, and with everyone getting old and laid off they're moving away. Pretty soon we ain't going to know nobody." She listened to the drone of the television in another room, looked at the couch she sat on. "We got to get new furniture. Every ten years you got to get new furniture. Paint the house every five."

"They fought," I said, "but they must have had something together for him to go to New York."

"How should I know? When Roy come home last winter she was here and he took a lot of interest. Sometimes he got awful mad at her, but maybe he liked her too. You know how it is."

"What did he get so mad about?"

"How do I know?" It seemed to be her favorite phrase. "Me and the girls never paid them much mind."

"Would Roy have talked about her to your girls?"

"I don't guess! Not the big college man." She considered the perversity of college men. "Debbie looks great in shorts, only her boyfriend don't let her wear them. He says a girl in tight shorts is as good as naked. He makes good money, Edgar. A computer company up on the North Shore. Debbie works in the typing pool. Mel's in a beauty parlor over to Bay Shore. She don't like it much, 'specially when she got to work late and maybe miss the happy hour at The Dunes."

The TV continued to talk to emptiness in the other room. The clock on the wall said almost eleven.

"Did your girls and Jeanne-Marie get along?"

"Jeanne-Marie was too crazy and too young. Eller's who should've been around to help his sisters meet the right guys."

"Why did Eller join the army?"

"How do I know? I never did know what boys think about, except you know what. I was real proud of Eller in that uniform. Women are suckers for a uniform. My girls should of had a big brother. No, Eller had to go off and marry some gook woman and get himself killed."

She lived her life in small circles around the same fixed points year in and year out. Points fixed in her by the world into which she'd been born. Like the wooden horses on carousels that fly and whirl but never leave their steel poles.

"Jerry said the boys was going to have more chance than he did. I always thought Jerry done pretty good. Sergeant in the army, got a job and bought this house soon as he got out. We lived good, raised four kids. Roy says Jerry ain't going to get his job back. Jerry gets pretty mad when Roy talks like that. He says Roy's getting crazy ideas at that college, and I think maybe Jerry's right."

The TV changed to a new voice with a lower tone but the same mechanical excitement. She stood up.

"Did Jerry and Roy fight about anything else? Maybe about Jeanne-Marie?"

She had already turned to leave for her TV show. She stopped. It was a question she had been expecting, thinking about. Her back was tense.

"They *did* fight about Jeanne-Marie?" I asked again.

"Jerry wanted her to learn English, get a job around here, become more American. Roy said she should forget English and America, go back to Vietnam."

"Yet he went up to New York to help her."

"I guess."

"Did Roy ever mention a Coley Evans? Maybe Anne Woollard?"

She shook her head.

"Did Jerry ever talk about Evans or Anne Woollard?"

"Jerry?" She frowned. "No. I mean, I don't think so."

The TV sound went louder. The first big commercial.

"What did you think Jeanne-Marie should do?"

"I told her she should go back to Vietnam, let Eller's wife take care of her. Maybe she should of listened to me."

A storm of applause announced that the Master of Ceremonies had appeared on the TV, the show was about to begin.

"Can I see Roy's room?"

"Second floor left."

She hurried to the TV room.

12

EXCEPT FOR THE ROWS of beer bottles and the photographs, Roy Carter's room looked as if no one had ever lived in it. The bottles were lined up in rows on the bare bureau, on a side table, on the empty desk. All the same: tall, old-fashioned bottles of Corona Mexican beer. The photographs were on the wall over the desk and bed.

A hundred photos of a husky young soldier and of groups of soldiers. The young soldier stood alone in German villages. In front of English pubs. Among rice paddies, mountains and the streets of a city. I'd never been to Saigon, but I knew the city was Saigon. All Americans know Saigon. It's burned into us, hawk and dove alike. A scar we won't forget.

The photos of groups of soldiers were all in Vietnam. Jungles and grass huts, quonsets and tree forts, a lot of holes in the ground. Destroyed buildings, dead water buffalo, burned fields, dead villages and dead soldiers. A lot of dead soldiers. Exhausted soldiers lying in a jungle, no more than pale faces in deep shadow, dark eyes and no smiles. Each photo was labeled: Eller on patrol, Eller in Saigon, Eller's platoon in the jungle . . .

The room itself could have been in a barrack. A narrow iron bed with an Indian blanket for a spread. A bare bed table with a reading lamp. The empty bureau and desk. A plastic armchair. A wooden desk chair and small desk lamp. In the single closet there was one suit, a sports jacket, a pair of slacks, two dress shirts, two ties and a pair of dress shoes. All hardly worn. The desk drawers held a few pencils, rubber bands and a letter stuck far at the back of a bottom drawer.

Except for the photographs, there was nothing in the room that was part of Roy Carter. Today or yesterday. Nothing from high school or his travels. No keepsakes. No emblems of Hofstra University, not even textbooks or notes. No photos of Judy Lavelle or any girl. Only Eller. If there ever had been anything personal besides the photos on the wall, Roy Carter had taken it with him when he went to New York to help Jeanne-Marie.

The letter that had slipped under the desk drawer was written in pencil on U.S. Army stationery, dated December 25, 1969.

Little Brother,
    I'm sitting here in this stinking pagoda . . .

The female voices squealed up the stairs in a clatter of high heels. I slipped the letter into my pocket. Tall and medium, two young women tripped into the room talking all the way.

"Ma says you come to find out what crazy Roy's doing in New York. You're a detective! Am I right?" She was the tall one, Melanie, wearing the dark colors that suited her. A snub nose, and freckles on her pale Irish skin.

"Is he dead? It's a spy ring! That's why he's in New York hiding out. He's in a gang!" The short blonde,

Debbie Jr., whose boyfriend didn't allow her to wear shorts. Instead she wore a pastel blue pantsuit ten years too old for her. It washed out her blue eyes, made her dark skin green.

"You think your brother's a spy?"

"Sure. Double-O-Seven! Away on missions all over."

"Or in a gang of bank robbers!"

"He was always going to New York," Melanie said.

"He had a gun in his room," Debbie said. "I saw it!"

"You never told me that," Melanie said.

"I got to tell you everything?"

I said, "I'm a private detective hired by your Dad and Judy Lavelle to locate Roy and—"

"Judy Lavelle!"

"She's got a nerve."

"How can you fight crooks with one arm?"

"I didn't know detectives could have one arm."

I said, "Why has Judy Lavelle got a nerve?"

"I mean, they're not engaged."

"She just hangs around like they was."

"He's probably hiding from her."

"I'd hide from *her*."

It was hard to keep them to a point. They jabbered and wandered around the room and touched surfaces and giggled and free-associated whatever came into their minds.

"Maybe he's not hiding," I said. "Maybe he's just doing something he doesn't want anyone to know."

"The big-deal college man and his crazy ideas."

"Out-of-his-skull crazy."

I said, "What crazy ideas?"

"Who knows?"

"Who listens?"

"Except when he yelled at Jeanne-Marie."

"Told him she'd do what she wanted, it's a free country."

"She was as crazy as he is."

They were like a two-headed cartoon monster with a single mind. Continuing each other's thoughts and words in the perfect harmony of shared certainties.

"Was she really living in a whorehouse?"

"I could never do that! Yuk!"

"I get sick just thinking about it. Ugh."

"What do they *do?* I mean, a guy they don't even *know!*"

"You think he just walks in and—"

"Maybe they get introduced first."

"At least."

They dissolved in giggles and tripped out as suddenly as they had come in. Their interest in me was as fleeting as I suspected all their interests were, including their interest in Jeanne-Marie and their brother.

Alone, I looked at the austere room. Something was missing. There were no medals. I saw a space among the photographs where a glass shadow box could have been, but there was no glass case of Eller's medals now. Judy Lavelle had been right, Roy Carter did not plan to return to Pine Dunes this time, had left behind only what he didn't want anymore, including Judy Lavelle.

Downstairs I found the two girls perched around their mother and the TV set. They watched two families try to outguess a panel on vital questions such as what does a man say to his wife when he comes home from the office at midnight. I waited for the commercial.

"None of you can give me a guess what Roy's doing?"

They looked at me, at each other and shook their heads almost in unison. A short one, a tall one and an older one, but as alike as triplets on a TV news feature. The grinning emcee returned and they concentrated on their show. It wasn't that they didn't care about Roy, or even Jeanne-Marie, but, after all, there was nothing *they* could do, so why miss their fun?

I let myself out, took the taxi back to Bay Shore and read the letter I'd found in Roy's room.

$$13$$

December 25, 1969

Little Brother,

I'm sitting here in this stinking pagoda watching skin peel off my feet and writing this letter so if anything happens to me you'll know what I'm learning over here. I know it ain't going to mean a hell of a lot to you right now, but maybe it will later.

It's raining outside and it's raining in here too. The stinking water runs off the stone ceiling just like rain. The whole platoon's in here, squatting down like monkeys in a zoo. It's been raining for a year it seems like, night and day and in between. The whole world is turning into fungus and rot. The jungle and the goddamn army and the whole world. And maybe that's good. Maybe the more it stinks, the sooner everyone starts to smell it.

I'm doing a lot of thinking, little brother. There's a Buddha in here, squatting just like us, smiling like it knows the answers to everything. I wish I knew the answers, but maybe I'm starting to see some of them out here. Maybe someone made a big mistake sending us here and giving us time to think. We go out in the rice paddies and burn villages, and we don't even know what we're burning them for. If there's no one in a village, we burn it. If there's lots of people in a village maybe they're the enemy so we burn it too. Everyone says it's all the burning makes the rain and fog.

We had this kid from west Texas, carried his guitar everywhere. When we was off a mission he tried to teach me to play it, but I don't have the fingers or the brains. The rain played hell with his strings, the last month he could hardly play. It drove him crazy, like if he couldn't play his guitar it wasn't worth living. Last week we bought a sweet ambush and Charlie shot the kid to pieces. When we broke out running for our tails, I looked back. I saw them take the guitar and smash it across his face. They laughed. They shot him and smashed the guitar on his face and laughed.

We'd have laughed too, little brother. The grunts and maybe even me'd have done the same fucking thing to one of them. Charlie's no better and no worse. He lives in holes and dies in tunnels and carries everything all the way from Hanoi on his back. When it's over he'll get shit too, win or lose. That's what I'm starting to see, little brother. None of the grunts, us or Charlie, is going to get nothing out of this war.

When I was in high school Dad wanted me to go to college, study engineering, get a big job with his company. He's so proud of his company. Him and his buddies on the block. I could see the company didn't give a shit about him or any of the guys worked there, and this here army don't give a shit about the grunts fighting for it. I've been watching this poor damn country we're ripping apart. The civvies, Viets or Yanks, all scheme to make every buck they can, the brass lives high off the hog and worries about the Commies stealing all we got back home and the grunts figure all they got to do is kill Charlie and get R & R until they can go home and pick up right where they left off.

We go out and fight and burn and lie around and it's like we're all just passing through. That ain't right, little brother, this here world, is it? All we got is a little time, a lot of real estate and each other. Like we're all walking around half asleep doing what we been told we're supposed to do and never thinking about what we really want to do.

I'm learning, little brother. I look at us lying around this stinking pagoda. Monkeys with our fingers in our ears, our fists in our eyes, our hands over our mouths. Someone wants us like that, little brother. Someone wants us here, someone's getting fat and sassy while we rot in this jungle. Someone wants us dumb and stupid, and I'm going to find out who. I'm going to figure it out, and then I'll know what I got to do for me. For me and you, little brother.

Your Big Brother,

Eller

14

JUDY LAVELLE PICKED ME up at the Bay Shore LIRR station.

"The Dhocs have been here longer than Jeanne-Marie," she said as we drove along the old Montauk Highway. "Since Vietnam ended, I guess. They were real poor for a long time, but they worked hard and they're okay now, doing fine."

She drove along a series of narrow country roads, twisted and turned toward the coast and finally stopped at a large frame house that stood among high reeds on sandy clay banks directly on a creek inlet of Great South Bay. Shutters hung loose on the big house, the porch sagged around three sides. But it had been recently painted white with colored decorations. Behind the house a catwalk led to a pier and a large modern fishing boat half as big as the house and a lot newer. It gleamed in the early afternoon sun as it bobbed on the inlet.

Judy Lavelle walked to a brass gong that hung on a double cord from the porch ceiling, hit it with a striker. The reverberations echoed up and down the creek. There was no sound or movement inside the house. She struck the gong again, louder.

Two men came around the side of the house.

"Shazzam," one said.

He was a big slob with matted blond hair and a toneless voice. The second was a scrawny black wearing a navy knit hat. They both held large Colt .45 automatics pointed at us. Blued and shiny as if never used. They spread out, watching us, the guns covering us all the way.

"Now, that there one is cute. Right, Wilmer?" the fat blond said. "You think maybe she like it?"

Judy went white. I sensed her begin to shake. I gripped her shoulder, squeezed hard, smiled at the two gunmen, backed slowly toward the front door.

"Get your stupid mind on business," the black said. "You see that guy? You see he got no arm on the left side?"

"Sure I see that. You think maybe I'm blind?"

"You know who that cripple guy is? You know that, Ernie?"

"Who is he?"

"He that private peeper—Fortune."

"The one we eliminates?"

"No, stupid, the one we only eliminates if we runs into him while we's findin' the other one."

"So we run into him."

"So we eliminates him."

"Now?"

"No, not now, dummy. He only the maybe."

"How 'bout the pussy? We eliminates her too?"

"We eliminates him, we got to eliminate her. That's logic."

"What's logic?"

"Why you got to do what you got to do."

"Besides," the fat one, Ernie, said. "She knows who we is."

All the time they talked they stood at the corners of the porch separated far enough to cover any escape. I touched the front door with my back, reached to try the knob behind me. The door was locked.

"Gong ain't rousted no one," the black, Wilmer, said. "Go check the door."

"We know ain't nobody inside," Ernie protested. "You know the door locked tight as my ass."

"Boat's in the dock, they gotta be here."

"Well, they ain't."

"I'm hungry," Wilmer said. "Let's walk 'em."

The fat one, Ernie, walked to us and took Judy's arm. His ragged pants had two buttons off the fly. Dark pubic hair tufted out with dead white flesh behind it. Judy looked away. Ernie pushed her around the house to a narrow path through the reeds along the inlet. I followed close behind. Ernie looked back at me with eyes empty of all but violence. Over his torn pants he wore a quilted jacket so filthy it had no color at all. His pants sagged low in the crotch and seat, and under the jacket he wore a sweatshirt crusted with stains.

"That way."

Wilmer followed behind me in a fake shearling jacket of imitation suede as stiff as cardboard and yellow pile worn to the cloth. His maroon rayon shirt was so dirty there was no way to tell where the shirt ended and his skin began except that the dirt ground into his skin reflected the sunlight. His pants were pink, with the shine of the cheapest rayon. Scuffed work boots half laced, the tongues loose and flapping.

"Over to the wheels."

An ancient Thunderbird stood in a small clearing among the reeds and scrub pines. Stripped of chrome, riding on almost bare blackwalls, it was parked where a dirt road ended. A wood fire burned in the clearing. Two barbecued chickens impaled on sticks heated over the fire. The black sat me down against a front wheel of the Thunderbird. The fat one, Ernie, held Judy.

"How long we waits?" Ernie said.

"For the Chinks? Or to waste these here two?"

"Whatever or both."

"Can't blast 'fore we spots the Chinks. We spook 'em."

"So how long we waits for the Chinks?"

"Hell, I don' know. We got to find out where the fuckin' kid's holed up so we gets paid off, right? That's what the boss says. Find the kid, blast him, get paid."

"Maybe a couple hours?"

"I guess."

"Then I got time to eat 'fore I splits the pussy."

"If you likes humpin' on a full gut."

"Better. Got more strength."

They considered that funny enough to laugh out loud. Fat Ernie sat Judy against the back wheel of the Thunderbird. I thought of the endless newsphotos of Vietcong squatting in their black pajamas under the guns of the ARVN and us, tied to jeep wheels, helpless and hopeless but still defiant. I tried to feel defiant, smiled toward Judy. She wasn't looking at me. She was pale as chalk, stared at Ernie. On the ground the two gunmen ate the chickens in large bites, spat out the bones and gristle. They washed the chicken down with cans of beer.

You will not move.

Their hands froze. Their mouths stopped. Only their eyes moved. The reeds waved on the sea wind that ruffled the surface of the narrow inlet. The black's hand inched toward the automatic in his belt. The shots came from three directions without any signal I saw or heard.

Into the fire, scattering embers. The fat one dropped his chicken. The black beat sparks from his rayon pants.

"One-armed man and Miss Lavelle. Walk to the inlet."

Ernie and Wilmer glared at me, but I got up, nodded to Judy. She followed me fast to the bank of the inlet. I pulled her down out of the line of any firing.

"You with weapons, why are you here?"

They sat, the two ragged gunmen, trapped, even beaten, but not yet defeated. Their eyes searched the reeds.

"Who has sent you?"

Wilmer said, "You wants talk, you come out of them weeds."

Ernie picked up his chicken, chewed. "You the Chinks we come to find?"

"Why would you find us?"

"Lookie here," Wilmer said, "we do business. We lets them two be, you tells us where Roy Carter is."

"Why do you want Roy Carter?"

"He trouble for a guy payin' us."

"You will kill him?"

"We ain't gonna kiss him," Ernie said.

"What you care what we gonna do?" Wilmer said.

"A job, right?" Ernie said. "No sweat for you guys."

"When I say, you will place your weapons on the ground. You will go to your automobile. You will drive away as you came. You will not return. Now."

Their eyes still searched for a face, a shadow, an enemy they could see. They stood. Not certain they weren't going to resist even though they were dead if they resisted. Almost ready to draw their guns in one final defiance. Life not that important to them. Other lives or their own. Their whole sense of self came from telling the world they didn't give a damn if they lived or died so get out of their way or be ready to die—because they were.

A moment, then Wilmer laid his pistol on the ground. Fat Ernie dropped his to the dirt. They walked across the clearing, got into the Thunderbird, drove off down the dirt road.

15

FIVE THIN MEN IN jeans, work shirts and baseball caps, and holding M-16 and AK-47 rifles, emerged around the clearing.

"You are well?" the oldest asked.

"We're okay, Mr. Dhoc," Judy said.

"Then come."

He turned and walked along the narrow path at the edge of the inlet. The four younger men came behind us in single file as I imagined they had walked the narrow jungle trails and rice paddy dikes of their homeland. One of the younger ones carried the two automatics. At the house another older man drove up in a new pickup truck.

"They go, do not come back."

We all went into the house. A large main room was furnished in solid American suburban and displaced Southeast Asian. Armchairs and straw mats, low tables and a couch, wall hangings and sideboards. In a big kitchen a woman and some younger children washed and chopped greens. I saw two stoves, two refrigerators, a dishwasher and a food processor. Judy introduced us.

"Dan, this is Mr. Tran Van Dhoc. This is Dan Fortune, Mr. Dhoc. He's trying to help Roy Carter and Jeanne-Marie."

Tran Van Dhoc sat on a mat. So did Judy and the other older man. The young men stood around the room. I took an armchair.

"Who can help Jeanne-Marie?" Tran Van Dhoc said.

"We can find out what happened and why," I answered.

"Who would care," the other older man said. "You?"

Tran Van Dhoc said, "He who has spoken is my brother Li. Those who stand are his sons and mine."

"Her family cares," I said. "They hired me."

It wasn't exactly true. Only Jerry Carter had hired me.

"Jeanne-Marie had no family."

"Her adopted family. The Carters."

"That is not a family," Tran Van Dhoc said, moved his arms to encompass the others. "This is a family."

"The Carters," the brother said, "worry about their son."

I said, "Jeanne-Marie went to a man named Coley Evans in New York. Did she ever mention that name to you?"

"No," Tran Van Dhoc said.

The brother said, "We do not know."

The two older men watched me the way I imagined they had watched the Vietcong commander who came to their village and demanded help, told them he was fighting to free them and they had to help him. The same way they had watched the American captain who came to save them for democracy, told them he was there to protect them and they had to help him.

"Mr. Dhoc?" Judy said. "Are you sure you —"

Tran Van Dhoc stood up from the mat.

"We know nothing of Jeanne-Marie."

The brother stood. The younger men moved to the front door. I stood. Outside, the big new fishing boat was thumping against the dock on a rising sea wind, creaking its dock lines.

"Thanks for saving our necks," I said.

"How did you know where we were, Mr. Dhoc?" Judy wondered.

"My wife is in house, she hides. She sees them take you. She call us where we work on new house for Li. We come."

"With automatic weapons?" I said.

They all looked at me with eyes that had seen gunmen come and go. In French blue and Japanese khaki, Vietcong black and American green.

"You will tell we have our guns?" Tran Van Dhoc said.

"That wouldn't be right after you saved us, would it?"

We went out through the gauntlet of younger men to Judy's car. I could feel all of them watching as we got in and drove away. We said nothing until we reached the old Montauk Highway and turned toward Bay Shore.

"They're lying, Mr. Fortune, aren't they?"

I nodded. "Those two gunmen came out here for a reason. They must be backtracking on Jeanne-Marie to find Roy. So someone in New York knows the Dhocs and Jeanne-Marie are connected."

"You mean Jeanne-Marie told someone about the Dhocs?"

"Or the Dhocs sent her to New York. To Coley Evans."

She watched the familiar countryside of the neat suburbs in the bleak October afternoon as if she'd never seen it before.

"We could go to my house," she said. "I mean, my parents aren't home, we could have a drink. It's not far."

"I should get back to the city if I'm going to help Roy."

She drove on toward Bay Shore. "Will they come back? Those two?"

"I hope not," I said. "Is there somewhere near the station to get a drink?"

"Sure. I know a nice place."

It was a nice place. A big Victorian mansion on a side street turned into a restaurant. We sat at a corner table in the bar. I had an Amstel Light, the best they had. She had a manhattan on the rocks. Her hands shook. Delayed shock. Mine weren't too steady.

"What are you going to do?"

"Find out who sent those gunmen."

She watched the old trees in the back yards out the window, leafless now.

"Someone sent them to kill Roy? The same person who killed Jeanne-Marie?"

"Maybe. Or maybe people who worked with Coley Evans and want their heroin back."

Judy shivered. "You really think that's what Jeanne-Marie was doing? Selling heroin?" She was half through her manhattan before the head quit on my Amstel. She turned the glass in her hands. "Is it what Roy's doing, too, Mr. Fortune?"

"Do you have some reason to think that, Judy? Did he ever say anything about drugs, narcotics? Something you haven't told me?"

"No. I mean, nothing I remember."

"What does he talk about when you're together?"

"Not much. I mean, the usual. You know—what's going on, the news, movies, shows, what books we're reading, what we want to do when we graduate."

"What does he want to do when he graduates?"

She stirred the almost-empty manhattan. "He used to talk about the Peace Corps and maybe the foreign service. I remember once he was going to be an engineer and build roads and water supplies in Africa. Now he's studying political science at Hofstra, says he's going into politics. Real politics he says, and laughs. I don't know why."

"Is he going to go on to grad school?"

"I don't know."

She finished her manhattan, went on stirring the ice and cherry. She seemed to hear in her own words how little she knew about Roy Carter's plans. I nodded to the waiter for another round. On top of her fears for Roy Carter, she had been badly shaken by the two gunmen.

"What are you going to do when you graduate?"

"Get a job, I guess. My parents are nice, they don't mind me living with them, but it's time I moved out. I would have before, but Roy never wanted me to. Before he went away we talked about getting married, but he never mentioned it after he got back. My folks don't like him much. My Dad's a professor at C.W. Post, he doesn't like Roy's family. I guess he's an intellectual snob, but I tell him Roy's smart enough for the whole family."

She sipped and stirred, stirred and sipped as she talked, and I drank my Amstel. I'd needed it. Those two gunmen hadn't exactly thrilled me, and maybe they wouldn't be back after Judy, but they sure as hell could come after me again.

"What kind of job do you want?" I asked.

"Anything, I guess. I'm an English major, not much call for that unless I want to teach and then I'd have to go on for my doctorate, and I'm tired of school, living at home. I want to get out, do something. I've thought of helping people with learning problems. I'd like to get into literature. You know, be an editor at some publishing company. It's hard to get that kind of job, but you meet a lot of people." She had almost finished the second manhattan. It was getting close to my train time. She stared down at her drink. "It's something criminal, isn't it?" Is it drugs?

"I hope not," I said. "The new ones running the trade now kill whole families. Life is hard and cheap in South America, they want to keep everything they've got."

Her hand shook again as she finished her manhattan and I finished my beer. I paid, and she drove me through the chill October afternoon to the Long Island Railroad station.

16

CAPTAIN PEARCE HUNG UP his phone.

"Wilmer Catlett and Ernie what-the-hell. Probably doesn't even know his last name himself. Callow over at Lower East Side made them. He'll meet us at their flop."

We rode crosstown again in the back of the captain's car. Long shadows of evening slanted down the Bowery where the El had darkened the streets when I was a boy. The El had gone, but the darkness remained. Detective Callow stood in front of a building lost in even more permanent darkness. There was no door on the tenement with its rusted fire escape in front, only a black hole like the mouth of a tunnel. Inside, the lightless corridor was as dim and silent as an ancient cliff dwelling.

"Third floor," Callow said.

No one was in the corridors or on the stairs. Only silence. Word had preceded us: *cops in the building.* On the third floor Pearce and Callow waved me back, stood on either side of a door, guns drawn.

"You never know what these gutter gauchos will do," Callow said. "They listen to voices."

I stood back. Far back. Callow knocked loudly. Again. Pearce nodded. Callow kicked the door open. They went in right and left. Nothing happened. I looked in.

Pearce and Callow stood in the center of the room. Forty enormous eyes, maybe more, watched them. The eyes of twenty or more silent children crouched all around the almost bare room. Boys and girls, a few thir-

teen or maybe fourteen, but most of them ten and younger. They squatted on the floor littered with fast-food
containers, sat rigid on a torn couch, hid in corners.

"What in hell—?" Pearce said.

They were like some zoo exhibit. An open cage of
small primates staring out at three strange creatures
watching them.

"Where's Wilmer and Ernie?" Callow asked.

They wore thin shirts and jeans, skimpy dresses,
sneakers or no shoes. They looked cold and hungry
and scared.

"Mr. Hamlish said wait," the oldest boy said.

Callow went to look in the other rooms. Pearce
crouched down to be on their level. "We're the police.
I'm Captain Pearce. Do you know Wilmer and Ernie?"

"We works for Mr. Hamlish. Candy, two-fifty a box.
We gets seventy-five cents."

"Candy?" Pearce said.

Another child spoke, "He ain't paid us nothin'."

"He don't even feed us!"

"He—!"

They all began to talk, the words pouring over each
other. They moved forward all together, closer to Pearce.
Pearce asked questions. The children answered, talked . . .

*Walter Hamlish was president of Kids Jobs, Inc., went
through the slums of small cities to recruit children from
nine to fourteen for a surefire, can't-fail-to-make-a-fortune-
for-the-families sales force guided and supplied by Kids
Jobs, Inc. "Get your kids off the streets. A once-in-a-life-
time experience and they make money too. Travel our
great land and earn money to help the family!" The kids
would be put up in clean hotels, cared for like a mother by
Mrs. Mabel Hamlish herself and earn six bits for every box
of candy sold. To the parents in the slums it was a miracle.
The kids off their hands all summer, and making money*

too. "Nobody can say no to an innocent little angel asking him to buy a box of candy for a mere two-fifty." The only miracle was for Walter and Mabel Hamlish. A free sales force too ignorant to object, too confused to run, too scared to resist. Twelve hours a day, seven days a week. Instead of hotels a series of dingy rooms loaned by "friends" of the Hamlishes. Then out into the good neighborhoods to sell the over-priced candy, with their pale faces and angelic smiles. Instead of food, candy and scraps and junk. If any-thing. Instead of cash, promises—minus the miracu-lous expenses of Mr. and Mrs. Walter Hamlish.

". . . we never gets no money . . . he gets the money . . . gets funny with the girls . . . tell them what he did to you . . . sleeps on floors . . . makes us steal food." On and on in loud voices that echoed, overlapped, reverberated.

The fat man burst into the room. Red-faced, furious, his cheap brown suit bunched over his buttocks, the stained pants stuck to his thighs in wrinkles. He raged at the chil-dren.

"What the fuck you kids doing? I'm gone a frigging hour and you little bastards start wrecking the place! Okay, no dinner, you hear? Now shut your —"

A dumpy woman in a matronly black dress with demure pearls at the throat came in behind the fat man.

"Walt," she warned.

"What the hell you want?"

Hamlish turned on her, saw us. He knew the police when he saw them. Instantly smiling, humble. If he'd been wearing a hat he would have had it in his hands.

"You guys looking for Wilmer and Ernie? They ain't here."

He didn't really hope to get away with it, but any-thing was worth a try.

"You're Hamlish?" Pearce asked.

"Yessir, Walter Hamlish. That's Mrs. Hamlish. What can—?"

"President of Kids Jobs, Incorporated?" Callow asked.

"A real service to poor families. All kosher and above-board. Even got a chaperone for the little ladies. Families signed up all the kids fair and legal. I got the papers."

"Guess we can't get them on kidnapping," Callow said.

"Fraud," Pearce said.

"Contributing to delinquency."

Hamlish tried to laugh. It came out a whimper.

"Child molesting's a bad one."

"Slavery. We ain't had a slavery charge in a long time."

Hamlish tried a feeble snarl. "You guys ain't gonna believe those rotten kids, are you? Hey, they're all fucking liars."

"Candy's got to be a health violation."

"Child abuse."

"Selling without a license."

"I got a license," Hamlish said, sullen. "I ain't stupid."

Sullen and, suddenly, almost defiant. Pearce saw the change, offered a glimmer of hope, a hint of escape.

"Tell us about Wilmer and Ernie. Where are they? Who are they working for now? Anything you know."

Hamlish's laugh was a cry of pain. "You want me to give you Wilmer and Ernie for a two-bit rap like this?"

Callow said, "The captain's all heart."

"He's as crazy as those two! They're killers!"

"This could be a lot more than a two-bit rap," Callow said.

"They're *dangerous*, for Chrissake!"

"Take him in," Pearce said. "The woman can stay with the kids until Juvenile comes."

"Why should I do you favors?" Mabel Hamlish asked.

"Because you and old Walt are going to need all the good will you can get," Pearce said.

The motherly woman swore, herded the kids into one corner of the room. Callow took Hamlish out. Pearce and I went through the other rooms for any clues to what Wilmer and Ernie were doing. The captain lit a cigarette. He was smoking more. I wondered if he was drinking more. At home alone with his color television on his days off.

"Nice little scam," I said.

"Original," Pearce said. "They've all got a scheme. Some scam, some angle, some violence to get a share of what you and I take for granted."

We found nothing, returned to the living room. If it could be called a living room. Just a room where the two gunmen could fall on mattresses and sleep their restless sleep, eat their untasted food, drink or smoke or shoot up, lie in their restless stupors.

"No reason for you to stay, Fortune," Pearce said.

When I left he was talking quietly to the children, who waited in the corner of the bare room like mice in a cage. It was time to make another try to talk to Anne Woollard about Roy Carter.

17

NIGHT NOW, THE NOISE of distant revelry coming down the dark side street from Eighth Avenue. Anne Woollard stood in the long hallway inside the open door of the Rescue Mission.

Beyond Anne Woollard, George MacKay talked into the open doorway of a larger office with more light that illuminated his angry face. The voice that filled the hall came from inside this office.

". . . couldn't possibly accept! What you do is evil."

Anne Woollard nodded to me. "Is there something new, Dan?"

"No. I still want to talk to Roy Carter."

Anger thick in George MacKay's voice, *"I run a clean house, you hear? I pay the girls fair and treat 'em good. The johns get a square deal—full time and a clean girl"*

Anne Woollard said, "I don't know what you mean."

"Yes you do."

"Take it back, Mr. MacKay, please. I thank you. We appreciate the thought, but no thanks."

"I was afraid I'd slipped," Anne Woollard said. "You never said where Roy and Judy came from, did you? Pine Dunes?"

"I didn't call her Judy, either, but you did. You just did again."

"You got no right, Mr. Priest or Reverend or whatever you calls yourself. You got no right to turn down a gift to God."

"I'm not very good at this sort of thing, am I?" she said.

"Most people aren't."

"You are. You listen. You even hear."

"Sometimes experience does teach you something. Do I talk to Roy Carter?"

"I hate what you do, Mr. MacKay. I hate what you stand for. I'll do my best to close you down. You and all like you."

"He was here, yes, and we talked, but I don't know where he is now, Dan."

She smiled, held out her hand for a cigarette.

"I don't hurt nobody, Mister. I run an honest business people wants."

I lit her cigarette. "The only reason for you to lie about having talked to Roy Carter was to protect him. From the police and from me. Help him to do whatever he thinks he's doing."

"You're the enemy, Mr. MacKay. The disease on these streets, in this country."

"If you don't know what he's doing, Dan, why not just leave him alone?"

"Because he's shot two men. One's dead, the other isn't. He left a witness, Anne. You understand?"

She smoked. "Evans would have killed him."

"I go to church, Mister. I'm a God-fearing man. I'll give the money to another church. You're a crazy man, you hear?"

I said, "Did he tell you that?"

"Yes, and I believe him. Evans was one of those who use people, destroy them."

"He took heroin from Evans, Anne."

She said nothing, smoked.

"What's he doing, Anne?"

"Trying to find out what really happened to Jeanne-Marie, everyone who was responsible."

"That's a job for the police."

"He doesn't think so."

"I'm sorry, Mr. MacKay. I have this terrible feeling you believe what you say. I'll pray with you and for you, perhaps we're both just sinners hoping in the mercy of God and his forgiveness, but I won't take your money."

"How long have you known him, Anne?"

"A week. He came to ask about Jeanne-Marie."

"That could make you an accessory."

"You ain't fair, Preacher. I got a right to live decent. I got a right to live as good as I can, good as any man in this here country. I work hard, I don't hurt no one. I like kids, I don't hold with usin' kids. That's wrong, and you're wrong when you don't let a man help God if he can."

I said, "Why, Anne?"

"I liked Jeanne-Marie, Roy needed help to help her, a place to stay where he'd be safe and could watch —"

She was right, she wasn't good at being devious. I knew where Roy Carter was. She knew I knew.

"A perfect place," I said. "Right across the street from MacKay's bordello too."

"We appreciate the children you send. We thank you, but we won't take your money."

"I can call the police," I said. "They won't just talk."

"Then you're a damn fool, Preacher, and I don't think God meant for a man to be a fool."

"I'm afraid, Dan," she said. "Not for me. He likes me. For you."

George MacKay pushed past us, his brown face angry and hurt, even mystified. A tall man in a white shirt with rolled up sleeves and a clerical collar over a black dickey came from the lighted office and stood staring after him.

"Sad," the tall man said. "Sad and terrible. He owns a brothel, yet he brings underage and sick and run-away children to us. He helps underage girls, yet he degrades other girls at a dollar a peek. Over a dozen prostitutes work for him. He's open eighteen hours a day. Yet he wants to give us money, and he says 'God Bless You' to Anne." He shook his head. "And I have this terrible feeling he means it."

I had no answer to his implicit question. I'm not sure anyone does.

"Reverend Davis," Anne Woollard introduced. "This is Mr. Dan Fortune. He's investigating the murder of Jeanne-Marie Johnson for her family."

"So many tragedies on these streets," the Reverend Davis said. "So many abandoned people our rich world has no place for, and even less time."

He walked back into his office, shaking his head and talking to himself. As if he'd forgotten Anne and I were there. Trying to help those everyone wants to forget isn't easy.

"I want to talk to him, Anne," I said, "I can hold you here and call the police."

"All right, Dan. If you must."

It told me a lot. She was more concerned with protecting Roy Carter than with protecting me.

She led the way to the stairs where I'd last seen the child hooker, Jackie, going up. We climbed to the second floor, then the third, then the fourth. All the way to the top of the old brownstone where in its glory days the servants quarters had been. A narrow hall and small rooms. Anne opened the third door on the right, took me into a room stacked with cartons. There was a canvas cot, some blankets, nothing else. A dog-eared paperback lay on the cot.

I felt the gun barrel in the small of my back.

"Roy," Anne said.

"Search him."

She did. "He doesn't have a weapon, Roy."

The gun barrel prodded my back. "Sit down."

It was the same voice I'd heard in the dark outside MacKay's brothel the first night. Someone had taught Roy Carter how to be careful, how to protect himself, how to not be caught in a blind corner by the enemy. Probably his soldier brother. I wondered what else Eller had taught him.

18

HE SAT ON THE edge of the iron cot, as tall and thin as in the dark outside the brothel. Dark brown eyes behind the horn-rimmed glasses, the squat little Ingram submachine-gun in his hands. I sat on a carton. It was hard, full of canned goods. Anne Woollard stood against the locked door.

"How much is Judy paying you?"

He still wore the baggy camouflage pants full of pockets, the scuffed jump boots, as if he were sleeping in them. The oversized nylon jacket lay on the cot, replaced by a black sweater he probably always wore under it. He needed a shave.

"Your father's paying me. He wants to know what you're doing."

"He always did, in school or anywhere. He's a good father. As much as he can be in his world."

His voice still had that young quality, but what I had thought boyish was only precise and slow, unemotional.

"That sounds like your brother."

He tensed on the iron cot, a snake alert to strike. "How do you know what my brother sounds like?"

"I found a letter in your room."

"My room?" Despite the unemotional voice, the sure movements, he was nervous, jumpy. A slow reaction. "You mean in Pine Dunes? What did you expect to find out there?"

He didn't seem all that interested in the letter. A lot more on his mind than an old letter even from his brother.

"What you're doing," I said. "Maybe what world you live in."

"The real one, Mr. Fortune." The weak light of the tiny attic room reflected from his glasses and the Ingram in his hands. "The world where they use you and throw you away. They fool you like they did Jeanne-Marie. Fooled and used and dead."

"Is that what your brother taught you?"

"My brother learned, did something."

"How not to be fooled, used, thrown away? Is that what Eller learned? Get yours, take care of yourself first?"

"Eller learned the truth! He got it all straight!"

Whatever he was doing, Eller was part of it. A big part. The emotion strong in his voice, intense. Revenge, maybe, but whatever he thought he was doing his dead brother was part of what was driving him.

"What did Evans use Jeanne-Marie for, Roy?"

"For what he needed, what he wanted. Used her and didn't give a damn what happened to her. No one ever gave a damn about Jeanne-Marie except Eller's wife and my folks. All anyone else ever did was lie to her, fool her, use her."

"Use her how?" I said. "To smuggle . . ."

He wasn't looking at me or listening to me. Wasn't looking at Anne where she stood at the door of the tiny room. He was only looking inside himself. "I was seventeen, Eller was dead, I got a job working for Birdseye out at Eastport. Frozen lima beans, Fordhooks they called them, the big ones. It was all machines, cutting vines to shipping boxes, except for getting the cut vines from a truck into the machine that shelled out the beans, and picking bad beans off the conveyor before they got packed and frozen."

His long fingers moved on the stubby little submachinegun like a spider waiting in its web. "I picked bad beans off the conveyor one whole day, then they put me out on the bean trucks. Women took the cold and boredom of the conveyor better, the foreman told me. They had more fat on them, didn't have as much imagination as men, stayed happy gossiping all day."

"Clods and idiots," Anne Woollard said behind me.

Roy Carter nodded, but his voice didn't change. "The vines were cut below the ground. Dirt, weeds, vines, beans, all kinds of gunk tangled and loaded onto the truck. You stood on top of the whole mess and pitchforked everything down into the shelling machine. It was like trying to heave a whole hedge with you standing on it, and we did it ten, twelve, fourteen hours a day when they brought in lights, and we unloaded half the night too. The beans couldn't wait, they'd spoil, so we unloaded until every truck was empty. Then we came back at seven in the morning and did it again."

His angry yet cold voice relived those long, back-breaking hours. "It was the hardest work I ever did. When the day was over all you could do was flop in bed or get drunk. The hardest work and the lowest pay. We didn't get paid enough to do anything on Saturday except get drunk, and we were all laid off after three weeks anyway. The company got a whole campful of black migrant workers from the state farm board to pitch the beans at half what they were paying us high-school kids."

"And worked them twice as hard," Anne said. "I've seen how those poor people live."

"They had to live somehow," I said. "It's better than starving."

"You think so, Mr. Fortune?" Roy asked. "I don't. No one should have to live like that."

"Is that what the heroin you took from Coley Evans was for? So you can live good? Never have to live like that? Is that why you killed him?"

He sat quietly on the iron bed. "He would have killed me."

"But you went prepared to kill him."

Anne Woollard said from the door, "If you knew someone might kill you, Dan, wouldn't you go prepared?"

"Prepared to defend myself, not to attack first."

"That's a fine point, isn't it?"

I said, "Was it the heroin Jeanne-Marie wanted? What did she have that Evans needed? Her Vietnamese connection? To Eller's wife? Is that what Eller decided to do about things? He learned to look out for himself, sell drugs from Vietnam? Is that really how he died, why he was killed?"

Roy Carter said, "Tell my father you found me, Mr. Fortune. I'm okay, I don't need any help. He won't need you anymore."

"She was going to get rich," I said. "Did Coley Evans fool both of you? She called you and you came even though she wasn't your girl. You were there that night in the alley. You knew she was dead before you ever went to the police. You knew what she was wearing, even that advertising button from the diner. You came to find her, and you found her."

He stood up in a single liquid motion, more muscle on his skinny body than I would have guessed. The Ingram in one hand like an oversized pistol.

"You found me. I'm all right. Tell my father and Judy."

"What happened to Eller over there, Roy? Did he learn to take care of himself, and someone killed him?"

He pointed at me. "I'm going to leave now, Mr. Fortune. You'll stay here until I'm out of the building."

"You might get away with self-defense on Evans. You didn't kill Rivera, and I think we could make self-defense stick if you turn yourself in now. Let the police handle Jeanne-Marie."

He shook his head. "It doesn't matter."

"Now," I said. "Before it goes any farther."

"Stay in this room, Mr. Fortune."

"Go in, Roy, tell them everything. You were there when Jeanne-Marie was killed. Tell them. Then you can go home, go back to college, get on with your life. Stop it now. You're in over your head with heroin, the people who supply it and sell it. Get out while you can. I can talk to—"

"I can take care of myself, Mr. Fortune. I know what I'm doing, and I'm going to do it."

Anne unlocked the door. Roy went out and down the stairs. I didn't go after him. He probably wouldn't shoot me, but to stop him I'd have to take the gun and then he might shoot. Anne leaned against the closed door.

"You know what you're mixed up in?" I asked.

"Helping someone who needs help."

"Should I ask why?"

"No."

"You've got time to get out. Go to the police and tell them everything you know about him. If it's narcotics, you better get out fast. Very fast."

She walked out. I followed her down the dim stairs. I still couldn't get used to the silence in a building where there were maybe fifty kids living. She went along the downstairs hall to her office under the stairs. I went out to the street, up to Eighth Avenue, and caught a taxi down to my loft. It had been a long day.

I saw the buckskin and fringe in the shadow of my vestibule, the single eagle feather, the thick braids.

"You were supposed to get back to me fast," I said.

"Roy Carter's holed up an' Evans's dead," the Chief said. "It ain't easy backtrackin' a dead man."

"I found Roy Carter myself," I said. Carter had found me, but I like to look good too. "You have something on Evans now?"

"Too many cops all over. I got Rivera. He been in the hospital since he got shot, but got sprung a couple hours ago. Shacked in his room at the Dock Hotel."

"Where's the Dock Hotel?"

"Way up on Broadway. Better take me along. He ain't gonna be so friendly."

We took the subway uptown.

19

They came up the old marble stairs, drunk and whistling. Fat Ernie was doing the whistling. Wilmer was only half drunk, swore at Ernie to keep it the fuck down for Chrissake, then giggled and began to sing.

At the top of the stairs, Wilmer peered at a piece of paper, put his finger to his lips. Ernie suppressed giggles. They tiptoed elaborately along the corridor, studying the stained porcelain numbers on the cracked and peeling doors of the old hotel until they found the number on their paper. Wilmer drew his shiny Colt automatic, listened at the door, nodded to Ernie. The fat gunman took out his own Colt, hurled his bulk against the door. It burst open with a splintering of rotten wood.

Ernie almost fell inside. Wilmer jumped in behind the fat man. The small room was empty. Ernie swayed, his drunken eyes searched for something to point his gun at. Wilmer pointed to the closed door of a second room. It was a suite. The black and Ernie flattened against the wall on each side of the door.

The door slammed open, Eufemio Rivera came out of the inner room in his pajamas, bent and weaving, the thickness of bandages on his legs. The pistol in his hand sagged toward the floor, his bloodshot eyes peered ahead. Wilmer stuck out a foot. Rivera tripped and sprawled, cursed, tried to get up. Wilmer knocked him back down with his automatic. Rivera grunted, lifted his head to see what had hit him. Ernie kicked his bandaged legs.

"Stay down, punk."

A sharp cry of pain as blood seeped through Rivera's pajama leg. Wilmer stuffed the big man's pistol into the waistband of his pink trousers. Rivera tried again to get up on his hands and knees. Wilmer pushed him flat with one foot, poked his boot into Rivera's leg.

"Where's the stupid kid?"

Rivera lay face down, too weak even to turn his head to look at the two gunmen. Wilmer again kicked his bandaged leg.

"Where's the kid? I said."

Rivera gasped for breath. "What fuckin' kid?"

Shallow breath, his face pressed against the floor. His thick neck trembled with the pain. The black hair on the back of his neck as stiff as the hackles on a chained animal. His long arms moved as if searching for something to strangle, destroy, the way he would have destroyed both gunmen three days ago. The way he would destroy them next week. But not today.

"The fucking kid wasted your boss," Wilmer said, kicked harder into the bandages on the leg under the now bloody pajamas. "What kid you think we mean? Why'd he snuff your boss?"

Rivera's barrel chest moved shallow and slow. His teeth ground against the pain. He didn't ask who they were, who had sent them. He knew what to do face down on a floor, helpless with his wounds, two gunmen over him.

"How the fuck I know?" Rivera said.

Rivera knew what to do but couldn't quite do it.

Wilmer kicked. "He fuckin' shot you, didn't he? Why he do that if you don' know why he got to snuff your boss?"

"You know what the fuck he's doin'," Ernie said. "You know where he hangs out."

Rivera's teeth ground against the pain of his opened wounds. His massive body trembled with spasms. Wilmer kicked.

"What was your boss an' the kid doin'?"

". . . don' . . . know."

Kick.

"Kid says . . . boss . . . killed . . . gook girl."

"So did he?"

" . . . don' . . . know."

Kick.

"Don' . . . know . . . kid . . . wants . . ."

Rivera bled now from both legs. The blood soaked through the sweat-stained pajamas, dripped to the carpet. Ernie bent and punched the bleeding legs. Rivera screamed.

"Talk to my man," Ernie said.

"Don' know . . . don' know kid . . . don' know where . . . don' know . . ."

"Shit," Wilmer said. "Nobody knows nothin'."

Wilmer kicked the bloody man on the floor. Rivera screamed. The bleeding man's corded muscles stood out under the blood-soaked pajamas.

"What the fuck good is he?" Wilmer said.

"Hey, Rivera," Ernie said. "What the fuck good are you?"

Rivera breathed into the bloody carpet, ". . . gonna remember . . . you . . . two . . . remember . . . you guys."

Ernie laughed. "Hey, he gonna remember us."

Wilmer didn't laugh. Wilmer stood over the bleeding man and shot him in the head three times. The massive body jerked with each bullet.

20

THE MEDICAL EXAMINER POKED around in the mouth of Eufemio Rivera.

Captain Pearce said, "The description of the killers fitted Wilmer Catlett and Ernie, so they called me." He looked at the Chief's buckskin and feathers but said nothing. "We got some of what happened from the other rooms, most from his lady friend over there."

She was a small blonde on the edge of the only easy chair. Thin, with large breasts, heavy makeup, hair ribbons and a face fifteen years too old for any of it. She watched the M.E. work over the body of Eufemio Rivera, the face resting in a sea of darkening blood.

"Her name's Magda Luk, but everyone calls her Ginger Lucky," Pearce said. "She was in the bedroom with Rivera. He heard them break down the door, grabbed his gun, told her to stay out of sight and charged out as fast as he could with two shot legs. She was in the bedroom the whole time. Listening to it. They never looked. Too stupid or too scared to check the bedroom. She heard it all."

The woman, Ginger Lucky, sat with her flimsy sling-back pumps flat on the floor, her back as stiff as if strapped into an electric chair, and glared at us.

"What the hell do I do now?" She looked at each of us in turn: Captain Pearce, me, the Chief. She settled on me, as if she knew there was no use talking to the police and wasn't sure the Chief could help himself. "What do I do? I mean, just great, you know? Femio's dead and what the hell do I do?"

Pearce said, "Did you recognize them, Miss Luk? Do you know who might have sent them? Who they're working for?"

"Them two? Hell, no." She shook her head. "So how do I live?" She looked straight at me—someone had to take the responsibility. "Tell me that? I mean, what we got in the bank ain't gonna last me six months."

"But Rivera knew them?" Pearce asked.

"Hell, Femio didn't know them. He just said he was gonna remember them, so they shot him. The black one did, anyway. He had to make them kill him. Had to be the big man. 'I'm gonna remember you two.' Shit, how dumb can you get? So now he's dead and where the hell am I?"

We watched the morgue attendants struggle to get Rivera's massive body into a body bag. The M.E. wiped his hands.

"Did they use any names? Say where they were going?"

"What I told already. All them questions about some kid and some dead girl." She pointed a finger at Pearce. "Hey, maybe the city pays when a guy gets killed like that. I mean, ain't it the city's fault nuts like them're runnin' around loose instead of being safe inside? They oughta have to pay a girl something when they murders her meal ticket."

"We shouldn't have let Rivera run around loose," Pearce said. "Why don't you think about working, Miss Luk?"

She seemed to shrink in the armchair. "What do I know how to do? I mean, all anyone ever wanted was my body. I ain't classy enough to be a call girl, I'm too old to go back on the streets. What happens to me if I don't find no other guy?"

Pearce walked away to talk to the precinct detectives. The Chief closed his eyes. He seemed to be singing to himself. Some chant with drums.

"You can get welfare," I said. "New York state aid. Give them a song and dance, look humble."

"Shit," she said. "Welfare don't keep me in beer."

Pearce returned. "Stay where we can find you," he said to Ginger Lucky. And to me and the Chief, "Let's go."

Down on the sidewalk the crowd of curious had gathered around the parked patrol cars. Pearce told the patrolmen to scatter them, leaned on his car to talk to me and the Chief.

"Whoever's paying those two," I said, "has plenty of guns. They lost two brand-new automatics out on the Island, but they had two shiny new ones for Rivera."

"They wanted to know where Roy Carter was and what he's looking for," Pearce said. "That means they don't know what Carter's doing, and neither does whoever sent them after him. So why are they after him?"

"They never asked about the heroin."

"No. It's got to be only part of what Carter's up to."

The same idea had crossed my mind too. But what else was he mixed up in, and where did the stolen heroin fit?

"Rivera didn't tell about the H," I said. "Was he that tough?"

"He was that tough, but not telling about the heroin doesn't prove anything. Rivera didn't know Carter swiped it." He leaned back against his car, looked around the dark westside street where the crowd had moved back fifty feet but was still there, silent and sullen. "Where the hell is Carter? It's not that easy to hide in the city, especially for an outsider. Somebody always tips us. This time not a whisper."

It was my cue to tell him about my talk with Roy Carter. About Anne Woollard and the room at the Rescue Mission. I should have told him, but I didn't. Telling him wouldn't look too good for me—he could take me out of action—but that wasn't the real reason. I didn't know what Roy Carter was doing or why, Coley Evans *had* been a kind of self-defense, he hadn't killed Rivera when he could have and Anne Woollard was helping him. I wanted to know more before I turned him in.

Pearce looked grim. "What I don't like is that Ingram. Where'd he get it? Evans was mixed up in white slaving, drugs, stolen goods, you name it. So far no one's come to claim the body or even identify him. A brother's flying in from Australia, but around here no one wants to know him. It sounds like a war, and where the hell does a kid from Long Island fit in?"

I wondered about Ingram too. You don't just pick up a submachinegun in a pawnshop. Or four shiny new Colts.

"Two kids from Long Island," I said. "Two kids with close connections to Vietnam."

"Yeah," Pearce said. He thought about it while I waited and the Chief sang his song under his breath. Pearce finally turned to his car door. "Want a ride downtown?"

I turned down the ride, took the Chief up to a corner tavern and bought him a beer. The police cars left and the crowd drifted away. The show was over. When the last police car had gone, we walked back to the hotel and up to the suite. The door was open, Ginger Lucky still sat in the armchair. I held out a twenty.

"Did Rivera talk about Roy Carter? Jeanne-Marie Johnson?"

She made no move toward the twenty. "He don't talk no business. We got better to do."

"What about his boss? Coley Evans?"

"Paid good. He'd of helped me out, only he got killed too." She looked at the twenty in my hand. "Everybody's dead."

"What did Rivera tell you about Evans?"

"I told you, Femio don't talk about business. All I know is there was whores and horse, Evans lived somewhere over on the Upper East. In the Eighties. Real nice place. Femio took me once, only I don't remember where it was."

"Not down around Tompkins Square? A basement?"

"East Side. The Eighties."

"Did Rivera have files? A notebook? Address book?"

I added another twenty to the first. She got up and went into the bedroom. She came back with a small address book. It had Rivera's name laboriously printed in the front, and a few scattered addresses and phone numbers. Eufemio Rivera hadn't had many friends, at least not with permanent addresses and telephones. Coley Evans was listed twice. One was the hidden office downtown, the other only a phone number.

I gave Ginger Lucky the forty dollars. She looked at the two bills as if she didn't think it was enough. Nothing would ever be enough, no matter what she got. Not that she was going to get much.

"That's all you can give us of Rivera's?" I asked.

"All he had, Mister. Some bucks in the bank, a lifetime pass to the Garden, a couple o' rings, a watch, one empty suitcase, the clothes on his back."

Don't let anyone tell you the underworld is a paradise of big money and fast living. For a few it's a high, if nervous, ride, but for most it's hard work, long hours, low pay and a short life. They go into the bleak, uncertain world on the edge of the law because they have no skills, little chance and less hope.

The Chief and I rode the subway down to my loft. I called my telephone company contact to get the address for the East Side phone number of Coley Evans.

"Five gets you fifty it's unlisted," the Chief said.

It was. My lady couldn't get the address.

"Can you get the address tonight?"

"Tomorrow," the Chief said. "Maybe early."

Alone, I listened to my answering machine. It was silent. I'd expected a frantic call from Jerry Carter after I'd missed him in Pine Dunes. Nothing. I thought about that as I showered and shaved, got a Beck's, went to bed to watch some television. Relax, maybe even sleep. If I could forget the vision of Wilmer calmly pumping three bullets into the prone, jerking body of Eufemio Rivera.

21

I HEARD THE SOUND out in the corridor under the drone of the TV. A rhythmic sound as if someone was out there breathing and shifting. Small, soft, restless movements like a small creature moving about its cage.

I got my old cannon from under my socks. It could be a salesman building his courage, preparing his pitch. A timid soul deciding whether or not to knock and ask for a friend who used to live in the building. A client or a gunman. I opened the door.

Judy Lavelle sat on the top step of the landing with her back to my door.

"I've been walking around all night. I didn't want to bother you."

I watched her back. It was a nice body, young and firm in tight jeans and white sweater, low black suede boots and loose brown hair held by a black ribbon at the nape of her neck.

"Walking around where?"

"The city. I couldn't stay out in Pine Dunes."

"You want to come inside?"

"No." She still hadn't turned. "I don't know."

"Think about it."

In my old terrycloth robe, I leaned against the door.

"I was afraid out there in Pine Dunes," she said. "After those two. That fat one with his pants . . ." She shuddered. "My folks are away. I thought about those two . . ."

"It's cold out here."

"You were in bed. I heard you go to bed."

"I'm up now."

"I was here earlier but you were gone so I walked around. I was afraid to wait for you. I went up to that place where Jeanne-Marie stayed. To that mission. I looked for Roy but I didn't find him."

"I did."

"Mr. Carter's gone too. I called, and Mrs. Carter said she didn't know where he was. She was upset, you know? He'd just gone off somewhere, sort of disappeared. That scared me. What if those two ..." She stopped, turned. "You found Roy?"

"I'll make some tea."

"Where is he?"

"I don't know." I told her what had happened at the Rescue Mission. "He won't be there now."

She came into the loft. I set the kettle boiling. She sat on the couch and watched me. As if she needed to keep her mind occupied. She watched me hot the pot, put in the tea, bring the pot to the kettle, pour in the boiling water. I was aware of her. In the tight jeans and sweater, her loose brown hair held by the black ribbon, she was both younger and older.

"He didn't say anything about me? Except for you to tell me he was all right?"

"Did you expect him to?"

I gave her a cup of tea. She refused the milk and sugar. Her face was somehow less square, her heaviness smooth and firm in the jeans.

"You're still scared for him, Judy?" I said.

"I guess I'm scared of a lot," she said, drank her tea. "Maybe he scares me."

"Since when, Judy?"

"Since he came back," she said. "Or maybe since he went away." She drank her tea. "I've known him from before junior high. Nothing special then, just a boy I liked, good in class and sports. He was always close to Eller, always talking about him. Maybe because he never had much time with Eller. I remember the way he waited for Eller's letters."

"Were there a lot of letters?"

"No, only three or four. He always kept them with him." She finished her tea. "The first two years in high school we saw a lot of each other. The last two years we weren't together so much. He stopped playing sports, started reading all the time, walking around alone. I used to think it was because he got the glasses, you know? I mean, a guy with glasses can't play sports, reads all the time, like that. But I'm not so sure now."

"He had other girls?"

"Not that I know about." She held out her cup. "If he went somewhere he took me, but he didn't go anywhere much. He started arguing about Vietnam. Then he went away for those two years."

"You know where he went?"

"No. He never talked about it. I think he went to Vietnam to find Eller's grave, but I'm not sure. Maybe South America." She drank her fresh tea. "When he came back I was going to Hofstra so he went too. He acted like I was still his girl, but started going into New York a lot. Sometimes he'd stay in the city all week, not come to school. It never hurt his grades. He's a wonderful student."

She thought about what a wonderful student Roy Carter was, listened to the night traffic of the city. "He's not the same boy I met in junior high, Mr. Fortune. He's . . . different."

"Is it recent? The change? Since Jeanne-Marie came?"

"I guess I'd like to think that, but it wouldn't be true. He was already different when he went away. He changed after Eller died. I guess I didn't notice the change so much when he was around, but after he was gone two years I saw it. In a way he was nicer after he came back. To me, I mean. But less interested, you know? Like he was nicer *because* he was less interested. We've had fun since he got back, but even then it's like he's not there. I'm the girl he goes with when he needs a girl. But he doesn't really need a girl, or even want one."

"Most men need a girl, Judy."

"I know. But I don't think he does. Not anymore."

She looked all around the loft. She looked at my unmade bed. I went to pour another cup of tea. What she said about Roy Carter fitted a boy suddenly into hard drugs, withdrawing, not even needing women. But Roy Carter wasn't a junkie, I'd swear to that. If anything he was the opposite. Half the population seemed to pop or snort or smoke something these days, but Roy Carter sounded like a choirboy. A choirboy with an Ingram submachinegun, who killed people and stole heroin. Who had maybe visited Vietnam and South America. It had all the marks of a dealer, yet he didn't act like one.

"You were in bed," Judy said.

She watched everything I did. Watched me. It had been there since I had opened the door. The way she sat there on the stairs, the way she moved, the way she looked at me. Aware of herself. Aware of me. At the stove I drank my tea. She was too young.

"Out there when . . . when that fat one was going to . . . to . . . rape me, I almost wanted him to. I felt sick when I looked at his fly . . . the hair, the white skin . . . But I almost . . . wanted it. Roy might have wanted me once. It's all on my side now. Hanging on, that's all. Playing a stupid game. When that Ernie looked at me I wanted him to do it. Someone."

She had come to the city to find Roy. To find someone. To find me. Walked the city looking for someone, anyone. To tell her she was a person. Because she wasn't Roy Carter's girlfriend anymore. Because maybe she never had been. Because fat Ernie was a horror. Because Roy was gone, and I wasn't a horror.

"I never was his girl, Mr. Fortune. I was just fooling myself. He was never in love with me. I don't know what he's in love with except maybe Eller's ghost. Maybe I don't know what love is."

She was too young, I was too old. I had my woman in California. Kay Michaels was special, I knew that and I owed her. Thirty-odd years was too much, even if I liked this girl and she had come to me for help if she didn't really know it. A certain kind of help. An antidote for the pain. So I talked, because I didn't want to think of what she really wanted.

I talked from the kitchen. "It never really gets better. The loss, the doubt about yourself. I lived with a woman a long time. She married someone else. It took me years to forget her. I'm not so sure I have forgotten her. You haven't even begun the game. You've got all the time in the world. Roy was the first, that's all. The first is always the hardest. It's never happened before, you don't know how to handle it. But it's only the first, and you'll get over it. Maybe that's the hardest part of all. To know you'll get over it. But you will, Judy."

"All the time in the world," she said. "Like Jeanne-Marie?"

I was still in the kitchen. "Judy —"

"I'm not a virgin. There were other boys beside Roy. Not that Roy ever wanted me that much." Now she looked at me. "After you left me out there I thought about Roy. I thought about that fat slob who wanted to rape me. I thought about you. I thought about how they would have killed us both. Just like that. We'd have died together."

"Judy —"

"I ... I like you. You know about the way things are. You know how people feel. You care. Even about Roy and Jeanne-Marie and Mr. Carter and me." She took off the tight jeans, the suede boots, her sweater. "I don't want to be alone tonight. I don't want to

think about that fat animal and what could have happened. I don't want to think about Roy. I don't want
to think about anything."

So young the stiff denim of the jeans left almost no
mark on her naked body, on the light and curling
wedge of brown hair. Young and scared and female.
Small enough to be picked up even by a one-armed
man. Carried to an unmade bed in silver-blue light. I'd
never turned off the television, and now it was the
only light in the loft as she came to me on the bed.

Somewhere toward morning a light rain began to
fall. I listened to the slow sounds of the small hours of
the city. She moved against me, her breasts soft on my
chest. She had needed me so she could leave Roy
Carter behind, but Roy Carter, the first for her, would
not be left so easily.

"He's not coming back to Pine Dunes, is he?"

"I don't think so. He took Eller's medals."

"I hate him."

I said, "Was there anything special about Eller's
death in Nam? Anything unusual you remember?"

"I don't know anything about Eller's death. I don't
care about Eller." She moved higher in the bed where
she could see my face. "I'm scared for him, Dan."

I was Dan now. Just a man, without age, and she
was moving away from Roy Carter. Using me to carry
her away from the pain and the loss. There are worse
ways to be used. Afraid now not for herself, but for
Roy. It had to be, but there is always a sadness . . . and
a scar.

She rolled on her side to look at my windows. The
cool rain was gone, only the dull white light of the
city morning, filled now with the full cacophony of
traffic and feet and loud voices. A woman's back is

beautiful as it flows into the curve of her hips, the rise of her buttocks.

"Want some coffee?" I said. "Eggs?"

"Some coffee'd be nice."

I got up, turned on my pot, went to the john. When the pot was steaming, I toasted a couple of English muffins, kissed her left breast, told her she was a beautiful woman and it was time to get up. She smiled and got up. I wonder if we ever get over that small tightening in the back when the other sex stands naked in front of us?

Loud knocks on the door stopped my wondering.

22

JERRY CARTER'S SMALL BLUE eyes shone like bone china in his heavy face. A pale face, white and glistening. He stood in the doorway with one hand on the door frame as if for support. He wore his real clothes this time: work pants, boots, a jacket with the company name on the back. He came into the loft and stood rigid in front of my desk.

"They—"

He saw Judy Lavelle at the breakfast table with the coffee cups and cereal bowls. She wore my old terrycloth robe. He looked at her bare feet, her rumpled hair. Disappointment all over him, as if she, both of us, had failed him. Not a matter of morals, a matter of order. The way things were supposed to be.

"Has something happened, Mr. Carter?" I said.

"Jerry." The automatic smile, man to man. He was being brave again, keeping his cool. It wasn't working. The smile vanished and he sat down in my straight-back client chair, looked up at me with those small, scared eyes.

"What's he got into, Fortune?

"Roy?"

He nodded. "They come out to Pine Dunes, two guys. Scared the shit out of Debbie an' the girls. I wasn't home. Dirty and stinkin', Debbie says, and the way the fat one looked at Melanie n' Debbie Jr. made her feel sick. They wanted to know if Roy'd called and said where he was, anywhere he'd go if they didn't know where he was. The black guy grabbed Debbie, told her she an' the girls could get hurt bad they didn't tell 'em what they knowed." He took a deep breath. "Christ, I wish I'd of been home!"

"What did they do?" I asked. "Were they armed?"

"Debbie says they didn't have no guns, but she was scared to try to close the door on 'em, scared they'd kick it down and push in. She says they would've pushed in for sure except the cop patrol we got out there showed up. When they saw the patrol, they got out of there fast in a beat-up Thunderbird. Debbie an' the girls had to lie down an hour after they was gone they was so shook up. Who the hell are those guys? What do they want?"

I told him about what had happened at the Dhocs'. "They must have gone to your house after the Dhocs chased them away."

"The cops looked all over the Island for 'em. Me an' Debbie rode with the cops, but we never saw no one looked like 'em, couldn't spot that Thunderbird. Christ, I had to calm Debbie an' the girls down all night. What the hell's Roy doin', for Chrissake?"

"Was your older son, Eller, involved in drugs in Vietnam? Smuggling? Black market?"

"Eller? I mean, I don' know. You mean dope an' all that?"

"The army never said anything to you?"

He shook his head, confused. He'd read about such things, had strong views about wiping out crooks and drug dealers, but didn't know anything about crooks and drug dealers. "Only that Eller got killed there at the end. Street battle or something. I never did know why he had to be a soldier. I don't know why he went off to the army, or why Roy's gone. I guess maybe I don't know much."

"Maybe I do." I said, and told him about my meeting with Roy, and about Coley Evans and the stolen heroin.

"A machine gun?"

He'd been in a war, he'd killed men in his time, but that was a long time ago and the men had been the enemy. Enemies of the country. It was right, even necessary, to kill them. They weren't really people, they were the enemy. You just don't go around killing people on your own, without a war or them being murderers or something.

"Roy killed a guy?"

"Maybe to steal some heroin," I said. "That could be what he's doing, dealing in drugs. It could be what Jeanne-Marie was doing, why she was killed, and why those two want to kill Roy."

"Kill Roy?" His mind seemed to lag a beat, my words out of sync with his answers. "They want to kill Roy?"

He stood up, his big hands out in front of him in a pathetic stance of readiness. I tried to keep his mind on what I wanted to know.

"Jeanne-Marie needed money. Was there anything that would make you think she was involved in drugs? Anything she said, did? Anyone she met, talked to? Letters, phone calls?"

"You mean dope? Hell, no! I mean, I don' know."

"What about Roy?"

This time he just shook his head, stared at me still in that stance of readiness to fight, knees bent, hands out and open like a wrestler about to grapple.

"When I told Roy he could turn himself in, plead self-defense for killing Coley Evans, he said it didn't matter if it was self-defense. Why—"

"Self-defense? Sure! It got to of been self-defense. Roy don't kill people." It was an answer he could handle.

"Why would he say it didn't matter?" I pressed. "As if killing Coley Evans was irrelevant. Because he'd already killed, and another killing made no difference? Because he killed Jeanne-Marie, doesn't care now what happens to him?"

"No way he killed Jeanne-Marie!"

"You're so sure?" I said. "When he left Pine Dunes this time, he knew he wasn't coming back. I think you know that. He took Eller's medals."

He sat down as suddenly as he had stood up. He nodded, shook his head, shrugged. "I knew he didn't figure on coming back. That's why I come to you. I figured maybe he was runnin' off with Jeanne-Marie, you know? Then she got killed. I figured maybe she was mixed up in something got her killed, and now maybe he was too, and that's why I come to you. Or maybe he'd been in it with her all along. All them days, nights, weekends in New York. What was he doin' all that time in the city? Maybe him and her was into something and it went bad. Something went wrong, you know?"

"And now he's after whoever made it go wrong?"

"I guess."

He looked past me at Judy Lavelle in my robe at the kitchen table, looked away out the windows over Eighth Avenue. He had more on his mind. Clearly something else he'd come to talk to me about. I waited. He'd get to it faster if I waited instead of asking.

He licked his lips, looked at Judy, at the windows, at me. "You said he had a woman with him? When you talked?"

"Anne Woollard." I said. "Works at the Rescue Mission."

"Yeah," he said. "I got this call. Yesterday, you know? A friend o' Roy's from Hofstra. The guy's got a shack down on the bay 'round Islip him an' Roy uses. He wondered how come Roy'd been out o' school, if maybe he was stayin' down at the shack."

"Why?"

"Yeah, that's what I wanted to know too. So the guy said someone seen a woman down there an' she wasn't any woman the guy sent. So I said I'd go check it out."

"Did you?" It would explain why he hadn't contacted me, if it was true.

He nodded. "Didn't find no one, the neighbor called Roy's friend said she only saw the woman, an' I didn't find nothing in the place looked like Roy been there since he come to the city." He stopped but he didn't finish. His voice rising.

"But?"

"I found stuff I never seen before." He looked up at me. "Stuff he wrote when he was away them two years. Things he brought back." There was a look of surprise in his eyes, hurt surprise. His son hadn't told him things. "He went to Vietnam, you know? He saw Eller's grave. He was in

South America, an' Europe, an' Africa, an' everywhere. Had all kinds of magazines, books, things
from them places."

"Was there anything about drugs?"

He looked at the floor. "Yeah. Notes about that,
an' about who ran them countries, an' how them
people live." He looked up at me again. "Only the
big thing was some New York phone numbers an'
one address. They was on a pad by the phone. So I
come in early an' went up there."

"Where?"

"Way up on the West Side." He shook his head
again. "It wasn't nothing. Just a empty store on a
side street. Windows is all painted, I couldn't see
inside, but no one answered and the guy next door
said the place'd been empty a long time, did I
maybe want to rent a store? So I come down here
to you."

"Give me the address."

He did.

"You have the telephone numbers too?"

He gave me those. "I tried 'em all, didn't get no
answers."

I tried them while he sat there looking at me and
at Judy, trying to understand. It was my arm and
my age—cripples and old men don't have sex with
young girls. Judy poured him a cup of coffee, held a
chair out for him at the table.

None of the phone numbers answered. I kept on
trying them while Jerry Carter and Judy sat at my
kitchen table drinking coffee and talking to each
other. Maybe he could learn.

After two hours I gave up. I'd gotten six busy sig-
nals, but none of the numbers answered. I had a
hunch why. They were the kind of phone numbers

where a special ring was needed, a signal, before anyone would answer. I nodded to Judy Lavelle.

"Get dressed." I hadn't been able to reach Roy the last two times, maybe Judy could if we found him. "You go home, Jerry. Check that shack again and stay home, he might contact you."

I got dressed. I wanted to know about telephones that never answered, and an empty store with painted windows.

23

THE EMPTY STORE WITH the black windows was on West Eighty-second Street off Amsterdam Avenue. I made sure no neighbors were watching in the noon sun, then tried the door. It was locked. I didn't knock. At the brownstone next door I pressed the bell of the ground-floor rear apartment. In a New York apartment no one would do no more than swear at a false ring—kids! There was an answering buzz.

"Let's go!"

I dragged Judy out of the vestibule, hurried to the next building, tried the ground-floor apartment there. This time there was no answer. I gave the vestibule door a hard shove and it clicked open.

The door of the rear apartment was another matter. It had three locks, one a police lock. I sent Judy back to where she could watch both the front vestibule door and the second-floor landing and went to work with my keys. It took me twenty minutes of sweat and swearing. Everything's a little harder with one arm.

We were through the apartment living room and out the back window in seconds. If anyone was asleep in the bedroom they would never know what happened. I had to lower Judy halfway with my lone arm, shoulder braced against the window frame, before she could drop to the rear yard, hang by one hand before I let go and dropped. I hit hard, took the blow bent-kneed and balanced, stayed on my feet.

"Is there anything you can't do, Dan?" Judy wondered.

"I can't button my right sleeve."

We went over to the rear yard of the empty store. It was ragged and weed-grown, empty wooden boxes stacked haphazardly against a weather-worn fence. The back door made me stare. It was metal covered, had two top-of-the-line locks that were a long way from abandoned.

"What is it, Dan?" Judy asked.

"It's not the door of an empty store. Those locks a storekeeper takes with him, and they're not unused. Keep watch."

I wasn't worried about any good citizens seeing us and reporting to the police, not in New York, but I was worried about people connected to the empty store. It took me almost an hour, I had to use my picks on the second lock.

"Jesus!"

The guns, grenades, boxes of ammunition, plastic explosives, cases of food were stacked all around the one large, dimly lit room. The only light came from the open rear door behind us, a solid partition in front between the long room and the store. M-16s, AK-47s, Uzis, automatic assault weapons I didn't even recognize, pistols and wire and fuses and timers for making bombs.

"What is it, Dan?" Judy stared around.

"Someone's arsenal," I said. "It tells us where Roy got the Ingram."

"Why? I mean, what for? Who? Why do they want all this?"

The questions came out of her mouth almost as fast as I was thinking them. It also probably explained where Roy Carter had been in the city all those days and weeks, but it didn't explain why. Smuggling? Gun dealing? Guns *and* drugs? The room wasn't only an arsenal. There were tables, chairs, cots, sleeping bags. A telephone. A police-band radio. Walkie-talkies.

The shadow blocked the light from the open doorway behind us. Judy spun completely around before I was half-turned.

"Roy!"

He wore the same camouflage fatigues. At least I thought he did. There wasn't much time to look. I knew for sure he had the Ingram.

"Side door! Quick!"

He pushed us toward a door in the right wall that was almost invisible in the gloom of the room.

"Now! Fast!"

The danger and the urgency and the fear were in his voice. We ran to the door, I pulled it open. He came through on our heels, slammed the door behind him.

"Over there!"

You sense when someone is helping you. His fear and urgency were for us, not for him. A canvas tarpaulin covered more boxes in this small second room. He held it up. There was just space between two stacks of boxes. The tarp dropped, shutting out all light. There was silence, and out in the small room the door opened, closed.

How long I was in the dark I don't know. "I," not "we." In the pitch dark, crouched and helpless while danger walks out there in the light, everyone is alone. Time stands still crouched in complete blackness waiting for the explosion of bullets, the blow of a club, the ripping away of the cover to expose you. There was no way of knowing how long it was before the door opened again and there were voices. Three voices.

"*You know who sent those gunmen after you?*" A slow, deep voice.

"*No.*" This was Roy's voice.

"*You want to crash here tonight?*"

"*I better. The other place is too hot with that Fortune and Judy trying to help me.*"

"*I don't know. I don't like those gunmen tailing him here.*" The third voice was higher, thinner.

There was a silence. I could see the two other voices staring at Roy Carter, deciding.

"*Was it those same two Laurie reported out front a while ago?*"

"*No. That was the private eye, Fortune, and Judy Lavelle. The first one this morning was my father.*"

"*That's right, Laurie reported one was a woman. What are they doing?*"

"*Trying to help me.*"

"*Get rid of them, Roy.*"

"*I will.*"

"*How you think they got this address, Roy?*"

"*I must have written it down somewhere.*"

"*It's that kind of mistake kills us.*"

"*I know. I won't make it again.*"

"Nothing written, nothing recorded, nothing left behind."

"I know now."

Silence again, and then the door closed. Judy moved beside me. I gripped her arm hard. She stopped moving. This time the wait seemed like forever, and I never heard the door open. Only the voice beyond the darkness on the other side of the tarpaulin.

"They're gone."

Even then I didn't move.

"You can come out, Fortune."

When the tarpaulin lifted, the dim room seemed almost bright. Roy Carter stood with the Ingram hanging from its black cord around his neck outside the oversized nylon windbreaker. He didn't look happy with me.

"Why the hell'd you bring Judy here?"

I came out from between the boxes. "An empty store, that's what your father said. I didn't expect an ammunition dump. I thought maybe she could talk to you. I can't."

"It's not your business, Fortune, or Judy's, or my father's! I told you once! These people aren't playing games, you understand? We can't go out the back way, we have to wait—"

"What business, Roy?" Judy asked.

She still sat on the floor between the boxes. Roy looked past me. He only shook his head.

"I never lied, Judy. I didn't promise anything."

"I know you didn't. Do you have to leave Pine Dunes?"

"Yes."

"Why, Roy?"

"It just worked out that way."

"You just happened to find friends with enough military hardware for a small army," I said. "Who are they, Roy?"

"Dangerous people you don't want to know."

"Why did you rescue us?" I asked.

He sat down on the edge of a box. "Anne says you mean well. You and my father and Judy. But you don't know anything. My father doesn't know anything. Judy doesn't belong here. There's nothing any of you can do, and I don't want or need your help. So when we leave here, just walk away and don't come back."

There was a glint to his eyes in the dimness, a gleam of something like anger, the boyish face somehow ten years older. His long fingers seemed to caress the Ingram where it hung from his thin neck, and there was a finality in his voice. There was no return now for him.

"You know there're two men after you?" I asked.

"I know."

"You have any idea why? Who sent them?"

"I have an idea, Mr. Fortune."

"What do they want? The heroin? Or are you a threat to someone? Or both?"

He shook his head, shrugged. The two gutter gunmen, Ernie and Wilmer, didn't matter.

"Who are they, Roy?" Judy asked. "They don't look like gangsters or professionals. Hired hit men. Is that the right word?"

Roy leaned forward in the gloom. "They're not hit men, not the kind you see in the movies. They're just alley killers. Two of the nine million people in this country who wake up every morning to a nothing day and a zero life. The poor, uneducated, beaten and forgotten. Dickens and Hogarth and Gin Alley, and nowhere near enough police or prisons to handle them. They're gone from the system, but they won't crawl under the nice clean streets and disappear."

Judy watched him, listened. It wasn't something most people think about in this country, certainly not at twenty or twenty-one. Not when they have almost everything they want and a fine future ahead.

"But don't they get paid a lot? I mean to—"

"Beer and rent money," Roy answered. "It beats shining shoes or running errands or mopping floors for minimum wage or less. It makes them *someone* in the gutter. They watch TV, they go the movies. They know the 'big' man gets the girl and the Nissan 300ZX, and killing makes them feel big. Their sense of being alive comes from the fear they inspire, the pain they inflict, their survival while the others are dead. Like Nazi camp guards, medieval torturers, the soldiers who serve the generals and the *el señor presidentes*. He sat back on the box in the dim light. "They're afraid every minute of their lives. Fear makes people violent, vicious. Fear makes them think only of today. Tomorrow's too frightening."

It was something he'd thought about, talked about, before the two gunmen ever appeared. He looked at his watch.

"What do we do?" Judy asked.

He listened for a moment, turned to her. "About what?"

"All those people like the two after you."

"Let them in. All of them, all over the world. Let them have their share. If you don't give it to them you'll have to control them with soldiers and police, because if they can't have some part of the pie they'll destroy the whole pie."

Judy seemed cold in the dark room. "Is that what you'd do? Destroy it all if you can't get what you want?"

He stood up. "Let's go. To the front of the big room."

He urged us out with the Ingram. In the big room with its guns, grenades and explosives, we hurried to the front partition and an almost invisible panel barred by a steel rod. It took both Roy and me to lift it, slide back the panel and squeeze out into the narrow storefront area behind the painted windows. Roy quickly unlocked the front door and we were on the street.

"In the car!"

He pushed us into the rear of a new gray Honda Accord, motor running, jumped into the passenger seat, and the car pulled away before I had my door closed. It took the corner into Broadway and headed uptown. Anne Woollard was driving, I didn't have to guess whose car it was.

"Is she why?" Judy said.

"Go home, Jude," Roy said. "Find someone who wants what you want. Be happy while it lasts."

Anne said, "I only met him two days before Jeanne-Marie was killed, Judy."

"Love at first sight," Judy said.

"Go home, Jude," Roy said.

"No," Anne said. "Only after we talked a lot."

"I never knew he was such a brilliant talker."

"Perhaps you didn't listen."

We were past Columbia Presbyterian Hospital as rain clouds drifted across the late afternoon sun. Roy and Anne hadn't spoken to each other as if they had no need of words. I've seen it in couples who've been together a long time and are so well suited they seem to be a single person. Whatever they had going had to be strong to have happened in only a week. If Anne Woollard was telling the truth. If both of them were. We turned where St. Nicholas crosses Broadway and drove on uptown.

"I'll tell the people at that store those two slobs after me found the place," Roy said. "It'll be empty ten minutes later, don't waste your time telling the police."

"Where do I tell the police you'll be?"

He almost smiled. It was the first time I'd seen even the hint of a smile since the dark night on the steps next to MacKay's brothel. "Tell my father you talked to me, I'm okay. Tell him I'll try to talk to him before I go away."

"What about your mother and sisters?"

"They'll never know I'm gone. They never really knew I was there. Not me and not Eller."

The Honda stopped. We were in Fort Tryon Park. Trees and grass, and couples on the paths. Roy Carter looked back.

"Give me your money," he said. "Bills and change."

"Roy—" Judy said.

"Tell my father," Roy said.

We gave him our money. He made us turn out our pockets.

"I'll leave it in your mailbox."

He got out, opened the rear door. We got out.

"Stay away from me, Fortune. Next time I won't save you."

He got back into the Honda, it drove off. We stood there for some time in the brisk October wind. Judy looked like she wanted to cry. Just once more for what she had daydreamed so many years, even if she had already begun the trip away from that daydream in my bed last night. I wanted to swear. He'd done a good job of stranding us without even telephone money. Protecting his friends and himself. Judy didn't cry, turned to me.

"What do we do?"

"Walk," I said. "As far as the first bank machine that'll take my fast-teller card."

24

AFTER I FOUND A machine near Columbia Presbyterian that took my card, I called Pearce from a drugstore phone. I told him about the store, but we both knew that by the time he got there it would be empty, just as Roy said.

Judy and I went down into the subway. She stood silent beside me as we waited for the downtown express. When it came we had to stand in a packed car of sullen people heading home for those few hours until it was time to head back to work. I thought about Anne Woollard. She had known Jeanne-Marie before she was killed, and now she was involved with Roy Carter.

"What are we going to do?"

"You're going home."

"No."

"He's right about that much, Judy. I shouldn't have brought you up here. Go home. Walk around Pine Dunes. Go fishing. Be alone a while."

We swayed among the silent people. She said nothing more until we walked down the steps and through the exits and across the wide Long Island Railroad concourse of Penn Station to the gate for the Bay Shore train.

"I want to stay with you."

"No, you just don't want to stay with Roy, the past. I made it easier last night, but you have to do it alone in the end."

"I want you."

"No, you don't."

"I want someone like you."

"A lot younger, and with two arms."

"I don't think anyone younger could be like you."

"Not many," I said, "but take a chance."

I kissed her and let her go down to the train by herself. She needed to work it out alone.

I walked on up Eighth and across to the Rescue Mission. The door was open as always. The Reverend Davis was in his office.

"Does Anne Wollard live here in the mission?"

"Just up the block, Mr. —?"

"Dan Fortune. What's the address?"

"I was just going to go up there myself. She hasn't come in today." He was puzzled. "I've called, but she doesn't answer."

"I'll go."

He gave me the address and I walked up the street to another brownstone now turned into a rooming house. Anne Woollard's room was at the rear of the second floor. I got no response to my knocks, used my keys. This lock was simple. There wasn't much point to a good lock in this neighborhood. As soon as the roomer was out, there were fifty ways to break in.

The single room was neat and clean and almost bare. Anne Woollard's life was lived at the mission, or somewhere in Darien with her parents. Or it had been up until now. If she was telling the truth about Roy Carter and her. It took less than half an hour to search. I found nothing about Roy Carter or what he was doing, nothing to show he was even in her life. I found nothing much about Anne Woollard either. Whatever letters or papers she had were probably in her office.

As I got back to the mission, Reverend Davis came out and walked fast across the street toward MacKay's brothel. I followed. Davis went around the steps to the barred gate that led to the pantry floor and the office where I'd talked with Coley Evans. He rang the bell. George MacKay himself appeared inside the iron gate.

"You wants something, Preacher?"

"The girl's gone. Jackie. The one you brought over."

MacKay unlocked the gate. We followed him along the shadowy corridor to his office. He sat behind his desk. A gray computer screen blinked at him.

"How long?"

"She didn't come to lunch."

"Okay," MacKay said.

Reverend Davis went closer to the desk. "We try so hard to convince them that their pimps don't own them, but it's all they know. All they have to hold on to out on the streets are their pimps, their madams, their porno bosses. Father and mother and teacher. For a homeless child, anywhere is better than nowhere, any protector is better than none. So they go back. To men like you, Mr. MacKay. And you wonder why we won't take your money."

MacKay's face was stone. "I don't sell kids. I don't sell porn. I don't beat up on my girls. I don't strong-arm their cut. I don't play the fancy man. I'm a married man, a God-fearing man. My girls're grown women, they knows what they're doin'."

"She was terrified the whole time. Terrified to stay, terrified to go. She never stopped shaking."

"I'll get her back."

"Can you get back her childhood, Mr. MacKay?"

Davis turned and walked out. I listened to the door close along the hall, the clang of the barred gate. MacKay stared at the open doorway for some time.

"You know a Wilmer and an Ernie?" I asked.

"Wilmer Catlett, Ernie whatever?"

"No."

I described the gutter gunmen.

"Hell, how'd I know two losers like that? They couldn't buy two minutes with one of my girls."

"Just a businessman, right?"

The muscles in his brown face were taut, rigid. Anger in his eyes. I smelled some expensive cologne. A rich odor, as smooth as the dark blue pinstripe suit he wore now.

"I got born in the white man's shit, Fortune. My old man never had a steady job his whole miserable life, he died 'fore he was fifty. I ain't livin' like that, an' I ain't dyin' like that. My family got a good house, wears good clothes, goes to a white school an' a white church. I got 'em out of the sewer, I'm keeping 'em out." The anger was like a flame in his eyes. "How many businesses I could of got into was gonna do that for me?"

In the gloom of his office I had no argument. I'm not sure anyone would, not down here. Not one that would have meant anything to him.

"Evans supplied Oriental girls?" I asked. "That's all?"

"That's all, Fortune."

"Why did he stash Jeanne-Marie Johnson at your place?"

"How the hell do I know? He asked, I said okay. No questions."

"How did he 'use' Jeanne-Marie? Get her killed?"

"Who says he did?"

"Roy Carter."

"What the shit does he know?"

"She called him."

He thought about that, said nothing.

"What did she want from Evans?"

"I don't go pokin' around askin' questions, Fortune."

"What did Evans want with her?"

It was a try. He didn't even smile.

"Evans worked on his own?"

"Far as I knows."

"Got the girls, shipped 'em over, did it all?"

He just shook his head.

"What kind of Orientals?"

"They all looks the same to me."

I sat down now. He hadn't invited me, but he didn't object. He took a long, thin cigar from an inner pocket. There was no cellophane wrapper. An expensive cigar, probably smuggled in from Cuba. He lit it carefully.

I said, "Jeanne-Marie Johnson had big plans, was going to get rich. She came up here and met Evans. Evans used her for something. She got killed. Roy Carter came up looking for her, located her, was there when she was shot or right after. Then he shot Evans, disappeared with enough smack to supply Detroit. He told Evans he wanted what Jeanne-Marie Johnson had wanted. It looks like the H, maybe revenge, but something else too."

He let the blue smoke of his cigar rise slowly. "Maybe he killed the girl hisself. The gig with Evans got busted." He gently fanned the cigar smoke toward his nose. "Or Coley screwed the deal, got her killed, the kid's mad."

"What deal?"

MacKay studied the ash at the tip of the cigar, admired the symmetry of the tube of pale ash, the solid yet delicate texture that blows into nothing on the lightest wind.

"I liked that girl, you know? Kept her nose clean, didn't make no waves." He thought about it. "How the cops know this Carter kid was there?"

"When they asked what she was wearing the last time he saw her, he was surprised. They're sure he knew she was found stripped, forgot he wasn't supposed to know. He covered by describing what she'd been wearing."

"Yeah," MacKay nodded, "they checked with me. He had it right, too: blue Chink dress Evans give her, black pumps, three-hundred-dollar watch, rings, even that button from over to Aldo's Diner." He smoked the slender cigar. "You know where the Carter kid's at?"

"Not now," I said.

He drew deeply on the cigar, closed his eyes like a cat being stroked. "I figure Evans had a big man back of him. Got him the broads, maybe the H. I ain't sure, you understand, but I got the feelin'. Big operator. The connections an' money."

He was giving me something for nothing again. Because he'd like Jeanne-Marie Johnson. He was telling me that Coley Evans was only a hired hand, that someone else really ran the white slaving and narcotics operation, and maybe that was who Roy was looking for.

"Thanks," I said.

I left him in the shadows of his office. The rich aroma of the cigar followed me out. It turned into the smell of rain in the night air. As I turned east toward the much less pleasant odor of Eighth Avenue, the Chief stepped from a dark doorway.

"That girl kid you got too young for you, dad."

He had his war paint on, three red bars under each eye, yellow and blue slashes on each cheek. He looked almost like a real Indian.

"Advice I can get free," I said. "You make Evans' place?"

"Bonus, too. The joypeddler had a joy-tootsie hisself."

25

COLEY EVANS HAD LOST more than I'd suspected.

The Chief and I stood on the tree-lined sidewalk of East Eighty-third Street in the night and looked at the lighted building. Another brownstone. Only this one was still a single-owner townhouse with scrubbed front steps and polished brass on the elegant, dark-wood front door.

A woman answered our rings.

"Yes?"

She saw my missing arm, the Chief's warpaint and feather, and maintained a polite expression. Class.

"Mrs. Evans?" I said.

She wore no ring, gave me a faint smile.

"Not quite."

"Sorry," I said.

"Under the circumstances, I'm not really."

She wore heeled black boots, a tan suede full skirt and a wool top in large tan and black checks with a high cowl neck and raglan butterfly sleeves that ended in tight cuffs at her wrists. Each designer part had cost a bundle, had been put together to give the exact effect she wanted.

"Could we ask some questions? About Evans?"

She had a face more square than long, with the high cheekbones and dark eyes of a Russian princess. A perfect nose, slim neck, firm chin and short black hair cut to her shoulders and swept boyishly back. The deep-set eyes were polite but vague, as if not quite there.

"Questions? You're the police?"

"Private," I said.

The dark eyes were surprised. She had expected the police, but not me.

"Come in."

The broad entry hall was bright, even with the rain clouds gathering outside. Stairs curved upward to an off-center second-floor landing. The living room was to the right, the kitchen somewhere straight ahead at the rear. Antique furniture of no clear period, or even country, filled the living room, yet the whole effect was clean and harmonious. In it sat an older woman who had the same high-cheekboned face and dark eyes as the younger. Only her eyes were less confident, her hands bonier, her hair gray.

"Mother, these men are here to ask us some questions about Coley."

The older woman was dressed like a twin of her daughter, but the boots were plastic, the skirt imitation suede. The top didn't have the cowl neck or designer sleeves, the checks were smaller and the fabric synthetic. As if Coley Evans had come across with the money for only one to shine.

The mother stared at my empty sleeve and the Chief's feather and warpaint. "We have no idea what happened to poor Mr. Evans."

"I'm sure they have other questions, Mother. Isn't that so, Mr.—?"

"Dan Fortune," I said. "That's the Chief."

"Hally Balada," she said. "My mother, Antonia Balada. What do you want to ask, Mr. Fortune?"

She took a cigarette from an ebony box, offered the box to us. The cigarettes were long and gold-tipped. I hadn't seen that in a lot of years. I declined. The Chief took three: lit one, tucked the other two behind his ears, lit her cigarette and grinned. Hally Balada smiled.

"The police haven't talked to you?" I asked.

"No."

"That's unusual."

"Coley kept me separate from his work. I only learned of his murder from the newspaper, I expect the police don't know about me. I'm surprised you do."

"We asked in the right place," I said. "You didn't feel you should go to the police? Claim his body, at least?"

The mother made a noise.

Hally Balada shook her head.

"I loved a live man, Mr. Fortune. There was nothing I could do. He has family in Australia, I would only embarrass them. I know nothing about his work or why he was killed, have nothing to tell the police that would help anything."

"So you can't tell us about his business, his associates or maybe a girl named Jeanne-Marie Johnson?"

"I'm afraid not."

"Roy Carter? The boy who killed him?"

"No." Her lips tightened. She wasn't quite as cool as she pretended.

"You believe any of that, Chief?" I asked.

"No way." He smiled at Hally Balada.

She smiled at him. "You'll just have to take my word."

I said, "No matter how much a man wants to keep a woman from his work, if she wants to know bad enough she usually finds out. You don't seem like a docile woman, Miss Balada. I think you'd want to know where the money came from, what your future was."

She stubbed out her cigarette, smiled at the Chief. He smiled back. Her mother watched both of them.

"For instance, you know Eufemio Rivera. He wouldn't know you, but you'd know him."

She offered the Chief another gold-tipped cigarette, lit it for him. Some people are attracted to the schemers, the freebooters who see the world as a battle of wits.

"Rivera's dead too, Miss Balada. Roy Carter didn't kill him, but someone else did."

She looked at me now. I told her about Wilmer and Ernie, saw the slight hesitation as she lit her own cigarette. She glanced at her mother. The older woman sat with more than a little fear.

"They're looking for the man who murdered Coley," Hally Balada said. "They killed Rivera?"

"We don't know if they had a reason, or killed him because he knew who they were, or maybe just for fun. They're talking to anyone they think might know where Roy Carter could be. That seems to include anyone who knew Evans."

Her mother made the noise again.

Hally Balada didn't look at her mother. "There is no way they can get to me. The house is in my name only. So is the safe deposit box, the bank accounts and the Mercedes. No one can connect me to Coley. That was how I wanted it."

"Nice," the Chief said, positively dazzled by such deviousness from someone with her looks and clothes and manners. "Real nice."

"Then you did know his work was at least illegal."

"It doesn't matter what I knew. No one can find my connection to Coley."

"We did," I said.

She continued to smile. With her eyes anyway. Her mother wasn't smiling.

"In this city," I said, "there are no secrets if you have enough money, know enough people. If they want to, they'll find you. Help us stop them, find out what happened to Jeanne-Marie Johnson, end the whole thing before it's too late."

Hally Balada looked at her mother. The mother tried to smile but couldn't. Then Hally Balada looked at the Chief. At me.

"You'll keep me out of it? Even with the police?"

"As much and as long as I can."

"That's all anyone can do." She nodded, put out her cigarette in the ashtray again. "All right, yes, I knew more or less what Coley did. Not the details, you understand, but he got drunk a lot and I pieced together most of it."

"What do you think, Chief?"

"She still lyin'," the Chief said cheerfully. "Only I figure she tell it straight long as we let her play like she clean."

Hally Balada smiled at him again. "What do you want me to tell?"

"How did Evans *use* Jeanne-Marie Johnson?"

She lit another of her gold-tipped cigarettes. "One night about three weeks ago he came home and said he had met a girl named Jeanne-Marie Johnson, asked me to guess what nationality she was. We were having cocktails, he laughed and said I'd never guess. He liked to play games like that, didn't really like it if you knew the answer, so I gave up on Jeanne-Marie Johnson's nationality. Vietnamese! How about that! Half-American, half-Vietnamese and a French name. A Saigon street kid with big ideas.

One hundred percent free enterprise, and she was going to be a big help to him."

"How?"

"I had the impression it was some plan to get the better of a business competitor, but he never said anything specific."

"What about Roy Carter?"

"I never heard Coley mention his name." She inhaled deeply on the cigarette. "Strange, isn't it? Someone I don't think he even knew. A boy."

She hadn't missed the irony. A man who lived with pimps, thieves and killers, dead at the hands of some unknown youth.

"You know anything about a George MacKay?"

"One of Coley's customers."

"Nothing more?"

"I don't think so."

"Customer for the girls and the hard stuff?"

"Only the Oriental ladies. I remember Coley laughed because MacKay wouldn't touch anything except his bordello, went home to Great Neck every night. His status at home and his family were all he cared about. Coley thought it was funny."

"Who did Evans work for, Miss Balada?"

"Himself, didn't he?"

"An informed source tells me he didn't."

She smoked. "He got the girls and the horse from someone in California. And that's all I know."

It wasn't, but we weren't going to get anymore about who might have been behind Coley Evans without boiling oil.

"What do you plan to do now?" I asked.

"I work, Mr. Fortune, strange as that may seem to you."

"It doesn't seem strange to me, my lady works too. What do you do?"

"I'm a fashion editor, and I'm rather good. Mother and I should be comfortable with what's in the bank and this house."

She and Ginger Lucky were about the same age, had probably both been striking young women. The kind of girls mothers worry about and fathers watch with a certain confusion. Both had lost their men, their livelihood. There was no difference between Hally Balada's relationship with Coley Evans and Ginger Lucky's with Eufemio Rivera except financial and social. No difference between Hally Balada and Ginger Lucky except the help Hally had gotten all the way and Ginger hadn't. Now Hally would be fine and Ginger would be on the streets.

"Keep the door locked."

"The police watch this neighborhood well."

I believed her. The job of all police forces is to protect the security, privileges and property of those who both hire them and pay their wages.

"If those two show up, call the police."

"I will, Mr. Fortune."

We left her standing in the tasteful living room, smoking one more gold-tipped cigarette. On the well-lit, tree-lined street a hard October rain had started. We walked up toward the Lexington Avenue subway.

"She knows who was behind Evans," I said. "Or at least how to reach him out in California."

"Yeah," the Chief said, admiration in his voice. "She got big ideas. One real sneaky broad. Class."

"You think she wants to take Evans' place?"

"She thinkin' 'bout it for sure."

It was my conclusion, too. Hally Balada wanted more than an editor's job, a bank account, a town-house and a Mercedes. The more you have in this world, the more you want.

We rode the subway down to Forty-second, took the shuttle to Times Square. The Chief had to go uptown, would get his money later. I caught the Seventh Avenue down to Twenty-third, ran for my loft through the now heavy rain. The money Roy Carter had taken from me was in the mailbox, but there was nothing on my answering machine. I put on a pot of coffee, called California, got Kay's answering machine. I drank my coffee, watched some dull television. There was nothing better to do after the coffee had warmed me up, so I went to bed.

26

DID YOU EVER WISH you hadn't been so damned noble? I lay in bed in the morning light, smoked a cigarette with my solitary hand, listened to the rain and wished Judy Lavelle were still in the bed. Yesterday morning had been nice.

I drowned my needs in two more cups of coffee, went down into the rain. Anne Woollard was my only real lead, and my hunch told me she'd have to show up at the mission, or her room, sometime. It wasn't the best weather for a stakeout, but that's show business. As I watched hopelessly for a cab on my way to the subway, one stopped near my corner and a gaudy bird got out.

He was a skinny black, stoop-shouldered and hollow-chested, in a green felt hat, green nylon shirt, orange sport coat, brown slacks and green suede shoes. He hurried from the cab into the first doorway, looked around quickly, carefully, his eyes white in the gray day. Then he slipped around the corner close to the buildings and into my doorway.

I went back. He was hunched in a corner of the vestibule where he couldn't be seen from the street. He coughed with a force that shook his whole emaciated body. Shivered and coughed, the gaudy indoor clothes too light for an October rain.

"Looking for a detective?"

"You Fortune?"

"Why?"

"Cause if you's Fortune I got what you wants."

"I'm listening."

"You got a office up there."

"Not without a name."

He glanced around, nervous. "They calls me Rags."

Rags. The pimp of the twelve-year-old prostitute George MacKay had taken to the Rescue Mission. The child, Jackie, who had gone up the safe stairs so reluctantly, then had disappeared again.

"Second floor."

He scanned the stairs all the way up. A reflex. The search for danger and opportunity. His clothes were soaked, and he shook himself like a soggy macaw. A jacket in an open field. Fear and bravado.

"Want some coffee?"

Rags assessed the loft.

"You ain't got nothin' better'n coffee?"

"Beer."

"Coffee's okay."

He sat on my straight chair, crossed his skinny legs, leaned back cool and casual, a fixed sneer on his thin lips. His face was immobile, but everything else about him moved, twitched, tapped, swung. A jackal in an open field. Fear and bravado.

"What do you have that I want?"

"You wants how come the gook kid got wasted."

"You know?"

"He let 'em use the kid for the sweep on the Big Bag Lady. The kid was the candy."

He sat back as if he'd just revealed a bombshell, laid it all out for me clear and straight.

"The candy for what?"

"Like I just tol' you, man, for the Spic Queen."

"Who's the Spic Queen?"

"La Reina, man." I was being dense. "The Chicken Lady, the big supplier."

I poured the coffee. Rags sucked at it. I sat behind my desk, watched him.

"Supplier of what?"

"Latin meat. Big C. Doojee. You puttin' me on, man?"

"What happened to her?"

"Christ, she got wasted." Didn't I know anything?

"She's dead?"

"Like Moses."

"Lured into a trap?"

"Slick as a greased asshole."

"By Coley Evans?"

"That the word."

"You're sure?"

"Ever'one knows, an' nobody knows."

The street telegraph. Everyone knew but no one would talk about it. The less anyone said, the more everyone knew.

"This La Reina was lured into a trap and killed by Coley Evans using Jeanne-Marie Johnson as the bait? That's the word? George MacKay knew about it, let Evans use the girl?"

He hunched in the chair like the sharp-beaked gargoyles poised high on the arches and buttresses of Gothic cathedrals. He leaned toward me, his sneer thinner. "No way that MacKay motherfucker gonna do shit to Rags. Ain't nobody messes with my stuff. He done let the kangaroo use his pig, he on the street that there night. You find out 'bout *Mister* MacKay."

George MacKay had taken Jackie to the Rescue Mission. There was no way Rags could turn away from that. He had to strike back or lose face in a world where face was everything. Where power was in fear and reputation.

"You're telling me MacKay and Evans worked together?"

"How he let the kangaroo use his pig for the candy if they ain't tight in it?"

The logic of the streets. Only this time there was a flaw. Rags didn't know enough about Jeanne-Marie Johnson. The pimp didn't know that she hadn't been one of MacKay's girls. He didn't know that Evans had brought her to the brothel.

"That's all you've got?" I asked.

Rags stood. "Tell the cops. Ain't nobody fucks Rags."

Then he was gone.

I pulled on my duffel coat and beret, went back out into the rain, took the subway downtown. To talk to Captain Pearce about La Reina—the Spic Queen, the Big Bag Lady.

27

The gray Lincoln Continental slipped through the darkness and silence under the abandoned West Side Highway, headlights reflecting from the tongues of river between the empty piers. It parked in the shadows of the rusted steel supports, the headlight beams shining up the empty street. Nothing moved for some time on the side street or under the elevated roadway.

Then the Lincoln drove out of the shadows and up the side street away from the river. It drove slowly to the next corner and parked again, its lights out this time. It sat there some ten minutes. No one got out. After the ten minutes, the big gray car started once more, turned the corner into Eleventh Avenue, turned again toward the river and completed the circle of the block, back under the legs of the silent elevated highway.

The driver, a big man with a thick black mustache and a pockmarked face, sat behind the wheel without moving or talking. He held an ugly little Uzi submachinegun hidden on his lap. The man beside him in the front seat of the car held a 9-mm Luger. The second man's eyes never stopped moving, searched the shadows all around the car.

The silent men in the car waited in the darkness for half an hour.

Until two quick figures appeared out of the night, one on each side of the car. The newcomer on the driver's side leaned against the car without speaking. The second tapped lightly on the rear window of the Lincoln. The window rolled down with a faint whir.

"Well?"

It was a woman's voice from somewhere in the blackness of the rear seat. A low voice, husky and hard, coming from the blackness without movement or location.

The small man peered in the open window, spoke to the direction of the voice the way a blind man speaks to where he imagines a voice to be.

"She there. She come alone."

"You checked out the store?"

"Up, down and sideways."

"Anything happen when we passed, parked?"

"Nada."

The man beside the driver spoke from the front seat, "Anyone see you or Escudo?"

The little man at the window bristled. "La Reina don' hire men who are seen by those they watch."

"La Reina pays me to watch those she hires," the man beside the driver said coldly. "You and Escudo examined the walls, the floors, the ceilings, the roof? One of you watched always to be sure no one entered the store all day?"

"We know our job, Esteban. La Reina is impressed with your questioning."

"Enough," the husky unseen voice said from the back seat. "Jaime, tell me about the girl."

"Nineteen, twenty. Tall. Black hair, kind of pale skin, Chinese eyes and 'an Anglo nose. Real half-breed. Hot-stuff chick, you know? Johns pay plenty. Got a blue dress with a real high neck and a tight skirt slit almos' up to her pussy."

"Chinese dress," the voice from the back seat said. "That fits. What else is she wearing?"

"High heels, no stockings, plenty of jewelry, a watch."

"How is she acting?"

"Kind of eager like. Don' act nervous or nothing. Smokin' some an reading a book! I swear."

The man beside the driver, Esteban, said, "Sounds pretty good, Reina."

The dark of the rear seat was heavy, brooding, as if the unseen woman were thinking long and carefully. The small man at the window lit a cigarette, cupped the lighter and the cigarette itself so that no

light showed at all. The driver and the second
small man outside the car said nothing, only
waited. The rear darkness spoke at last.

"Maybe I really get the no-good gook this time.
All right, Zero, go."

The two small men disappeared again into the
night. The big Lincoln drove once more out of the
shadows of the old elevated highway and slowly up
the same side street. This time it parked in front of
an empty storefront with boarded windows that
stood between two darkened brownstones with broken windows and crumbling outside steps. Esteban
got out and scanned the night street like a guerrilla
scout entering a strange village. The two small men
came up on foot. The mustachioed driver remained
behind the wheel. Esteban opened the rear door.

The dark-skinned woman who stepped out was
tiny, no more than five feet tall, less than a hundred pounds. Slender, with sun-wrinkled eyes and a
hard, narrow mouth. The faint light of the dark
street reflected from the rings on every finger, the
bracelets heavy on her thin wrists, the jeweled
comb in her dark hair. Dressed all in red, she had
extreme high heels and walked straight to the
boarded-up store. The man from the front seat, Esteban, accompanied her, his Luger in his hand. Here,
a block from the river, the distant heavy traffic of
Ninth Avenue and farther east seemed in another
world remote from the dark buildings of the river
block, the garages and warehouses near where the
great liners had once docked but where only rats
now lived on the cavernous piers.

La Reina and Esteban entered the boarded-up store.

On the street, the small man who had talked into
the rear window of the Lincoln, Jaime, walked to

the crumbling brownstone steps to the left of the store. He leaned against the steps with his back to the dark building and watched the street in the direction of the river. The second man on foot took up his position to the right of the store against the second set of brownstone steps, watched the street away from the river. They both held pistols. The driver, Zero, remained behind the wheel with the car door open on the passenger side facing the store, the Uzi submachinegun on his lap.

Five minutes passed.

A woman in a Chinese dress came out of the store. She stood for a moment in front of the empty store as if expecting someone to appear in the night. Then she hurried toward Eleventh Avenue.

Four more minutes passed. Perhaps five.

The bodyguard, Esteban, came out of the store, took a few steps toward the street, looked at the two shadowy guards who leaned against the brownstone steps. He looked at the driver, still in the car with the Uzi still on his lap. Then he turned and nodded. La Reina hurried out of the store, headed straight toward the Lincoln.

The limousine driver opened fire with his Uzi.

The shadow against the steps toward the river opened fire.

The man toward Eleventh Avenue shot.

La Reina was dead before she hit the sidewalk. The bodyguard never fired a shot, lay in his spreading blood.

One of the three gunmen tore a large manila envelope from La Reina's hand. Then they separated and vanished into the night.

Somewhere nearby a car started and faded away.

Up at the corner of Eleventh Avenue a woman screamed.

The big gray Lincoln and the two dead bodies on the sidewalk lay undisturbed. Until distant sirens began to wail.

28

CAPTAIN PEARCE HAD TAKEN to drawing the shades on his windows even in the morning, just as old Captain Gazzo had. His voice had Gazzo's same flat tone that came from knowing that something had to change but never would.

"She was a sweet lady who made a good living off anyone she could con, hustle or cheat," Pearce said. "From somewhere down in Central America. Nicaragua, Guatemala, El Salvador, maybe all of them. She was a kitchen maid for one of Somoza's colonels, got caught stealing the family silver or something, got away with her skin somehow and joined the Sandinistas for a while. A 'cause' wasn't going to hold her long, so the next thing you know she showed up in El Salvador working with the right-wingers, maybe even with the death squads. About five years ago she turned up in southern Mexico with her own gang, and then up here in East Harlem, 'helping' people who wanted to come to the land of opportunity or just plain get the hell out of down there and stay alive."

Pearce stared at his wall, lost in his own thoughts of the vagaries of human nature. "La Reina, the Chicken Lady, the Spic Queen, the Big Bag Lady. They called her all those and more on the streets. That's respect. The more names they give you, the more respect you have. Only I guess someone didn't respect her enough."

"Or too much," I said.

He only nodded. "When we got there the Lincoln was at the curb, doors open, not a bullet hole in it. The driver, an old smuggler named Zero, was in the back seat knifed dead center. Looked like someone used his hat and coat, took his place. Another of her men, Jaime Huerta, was dead behind the steps of the next building on the river side. She was in the middle of the sidewalk with her bodyguard, a hooligan named Esteban. We knew she always operated with a bodyguard, a driver and two point men, probably picked it up from that Somoza colonel she worked for. One point man was missing, Escudo Madero. We found his gun near the building on the other side of the store, went hunting and picked him up, he told us what'd happened."

"Did he tell you who and why?"

"All he remembers is that La Reina got excited about a break in her running battle with Coley Evans and the 'Lotus Blossom' trade a week or so before. Keyed up, but suspicious too. You don't survive and stay in business in her kind of operation if you're not suspicious and wary of just about everyone and everything."

"What break?"

"She never said, wouldn't even trust her own people more than she had to. She told Jaime and Escudo to search that store inside out, watch it all that day, watch the woman who would arrive to be sure she was alone, watch that night while Reina drove around the block a couple of times and observed. They watched, reported, took up posts outside the store while Reina went in with her bodyguard. After that, Escudo says he doesn't know what the hell happened.

"He was in position at those steps, watching the street up toward Eleventh Avenue, when he heard a small noise behind him. He turned in time to take a knife on the arm. He knocked the guy down but lost his gun and didn't hang around to make the guy or ask any questions. He knows the block, so he made it down through a basement and away up the next street."

"Then how did he know about the shooting?"

"You worked for La Reina, you ran far enough to keep from getting killed, then you went back—carefully. On the river side. He heard the shooting, saw La Reina and the others on the concrete and really took off. He was scared out of his mind and lying low when we picked him up. He's still scared now."

"Where?" I asked.

"We've got him in a precinct in Brooklyn."

"How did she and Coley Evans compete? Was Evans into smuggling illegals too?"

"Not that we know," Pearce said. "Reina's basic pitch was conning other Latino refugees. The desperate will believe almost anything. She told them she could get anti-Communists out of Nicaragua, pro-Communists out of Guatemala and both out of El Salvador. She told them she had an army of coyotes to take them through Mexico and across our border. She even got some through for real to make it look legitimate."

"You couldn't stop her?"

"There were always delays, people got 'caught' crossing the borders. Even those who finally made it up here after a couple of tries couldn't prove she'd played any tricks. Most of the families she worked with would never talk. Afraid of us, afraid of her, afraid they would spoil what little chance their relatives back home had. She charged up to ten thousand dollars per person, at least half up front to 'bribe' officials, and no refund for failure. And she branched out into some juicy side enterprises like drug smuggling and white slaving. A hell of a good living for a lot of people."

"White slaving?" I asked.

Pearce nodded. "When a client didn't have enough money, she'd tell them she could get their girls jobs to make the money to pay her, maybe they wouldn't even have to pay her fee at all. A lot of the families wouldn't play, but enough did to make her a big supplier of girls to bordellos all over the East."

How can parents sell their children? It's impossible, but sometimes the impossible is the only choice they have. Because it's life and death for them, for the rest of their children. Because they're afraid in a new country where they see no other way out.

I said, "So she was competition for Coley Evans. He set her up by using Jeanne-Marie Johnson as a decoy, bait. Who did La Reina think she was meeting?"

"A Eurasian prostitute who had information against Evans and his supplier, whoever that is. We found an empty bag inside the store, and a corner of a manilla envelope in Reina's hand. Looks like she got her information, the killers grabbed it back."

"So that's why they used MacKay's house. Jeanne-Marie was Eurasian, her English was bad. Dressed up, she made a believable 'Lotus Blossom' supplied to MacKay by Evans. The perfect bait: she could look the part, had no real connection to Evans, had some reason to go along with it, whatever that was. Stashed at MacKay's, she'd look legitimate to La Reina."

"Evans probably had the plan all set up, but no really good decoy to fool La Reina. Then your Jeanne-Marie walked in."

"When was La Reina shot up?"

"Around ten o'clock that night."

"Within an hour or so of Jeanne-Marie's murder, and no more than five blocks away. You never made the connection?"

Pearce shrugged. "We had seven homicides that night on the Minnesota Strip alone. None of the victims had any connection to each other we could see then." He got up. "Let's go have a little talk with Escudo Madero. Maybe he'll 'remember' more now we know how and who on the setup."

The precinct where Madero was stashed for his protection was way out in the Jamaica Bay area. We drove in the steady rain through the Battery Tunnel, around the Belt Parkway past Coney Island and Sheepshead Bay. The night sergeant took us back to the lockup. We got to the outer barred door just in time to see three uniformed patrolmen cutting Madero's body down from the bars of his cell.

29

THE PRECINCT CAPTAIN WAS scared and angry at the same time. "You know the conditions we have, Pearce. Not enough men to patrol the streets or handle the investigation load much less mind the lockup. Nobody told us he was anything special. I'm not accepting any blame for this. You got a 'danger-to-himself,' you file a report in my office. No way I'm taking the rap. You interrogate those goddamn jailhouse lawyers yourself!"

"Yessir, Cap'n, I was in the cell right enough, on'y I was sleepin'. I hears this bump like. You know, kind of a

thump, a bang on the floor. Didn' think nothin' of it. Figured the spic just fell off the bunk, right?"

The turnkey guard was a small, dapper man in rimless glasses. "I was sitting at my desk when I heard the yelling inside the lockup. I went in and saw him hanging from the bars. There are six assigned to that cell, none of the other five called out. Some prisoners in the other cells were the ones who yelled. It took me maybe three minutes to get to him after I became aware of the commotion inside the lockup. Maybe another couple of minutes for help to arrive. While I waited for assistance I held him up by his legs taking the weight off his neck. We gave him CPR the moment we had him down, but it didn't help."

"You bet your fuckin' ass I heard the bump. Heard both damn bumps, both damn times. Heard him bang the wall or the floor both times. What the hell, right? Guys're fallin' down all the fuckin' time around here. If they ain't drunk and fallin', they're stoned and flyin', and whichever they's slammin' the floor. You could hear him cussin' an' banging around. I go right on sleepin'. None of my fuckin' business."

The red-faced patrolman on lockup was nervous. "I don't know where he could have gotten the rope. Some of the inmates saw him hanging and started yelling. We have no explanation for how he got the rope. It was three minutes, maybe more, before anyone got to him, and another couple of minutes before they cut him down. None of the five in his cell did anything. They never moved, never tried to stop him or help him or even see what might have been happening at all. They just stayed on their bunks and looked the other way, looked at the walls."

"Heard him swear up shit and climb back up the bunk over me and sit up there sort of mumblin' to hisself. Ten minutes later damn all if he don't fall

off the bunk again. Saw him hit the floor this time, got that 'ere rope 'round his neck. That's when I sees some guys 'round the cell I didn't rightly know. I could see 'em some from my bunk, sure didn't think nothin' about it, most asleep an' all like I was. Just figured he'd sure fallen off the bunk an' they was a helpin' him up, right, Cap'n? I got no call doin' nothin' 'cept gettin' my rest."

The duty sergeant stood his ground. "I questioned them all myself, they all say the same damn thing—they thought he was drunk or drugged or sick. The one on the bunk under him admits he saw the rope around Madero's neck but thought he was simply 'clowning' with some other prisoners. We don't know if he's lying, dreaming or if there were some other men around Madero. No one was out of his cell, all the cell doors were still locked. We've searched for any picklocks or keys, found nothing, but there are windows, a key or a picklock could have been thrown out to a confederate."

"Sure I could see him hangin' on the bars, what the fuck you think? Damn, I ain't never seen no fuckin' dead guy up close like that, jus' hangin' like a goddamn skinned pig. Scared? I tell you! I just stepped back up 'gainst the wall, an' kept my mind on sweet damn thoughts an' pure fuckin' ideas."

The precinct captain raged as he paced his office, the wind and rain driving against the windows. "Murder? Of course it could be murder, Pearce! You think we can stop murder in here? Murder or suicide, we can't stop either. If someone wants someone else dead in this country, almost any prison or jail in any state is the easiest place to get it done. Any one of those roses back there could have gotten himself sent here just to kill Madero. How the devil would we know, if someone didn't tell us, Pearce?"

"*I tell you true, Cap'n, it scared hell an' the Pope out of me seein' him hangin' there on them bars. I mean, I never seen no one die before, even my poor Daddy was killed 'fore I was born. I sure as shit never seen no guy hang hisself. I pulled my blanket up over my head and stayed real quiet on the bunk. I mean, I wasn't hardly here 'tall. You believe it.*"

The precinct captain was warmed up now, even if he could see a reprimand down the road. "Suicide or murder, Pearce, take your pick. They all watched and didn't do a damn thing to stop him if it was suicide or help him if it was murder. If any of them saw or even suspected murder, you and I won't ever know about it. Hell, he could have been stoned, tangled the rope around his neck by accident and really fallen off the fucking top bunk."

"*I don't go near no guy hangin' from no cell bars, Cap'n. Not this sucker. I got six foot one way and three t'other of nice, quiet bunk an' I stays in it. A guy wants to hang hisself, he don't got to worry about this old boy doin' nothin'.*"

30

WE SAT AGAIN IN Pearce's office. The shades were still drawn. With the rain it didn't really matter.

"None of them tried to do anything?" the assistant D.A. asked. His name was Albondo, and he was young.

"None of them," Pearce said. "No matter how dangerous they sound, they're scared every minute. In a cage, helpless."

I said, "He could have been killed to shut him up."

"He could have been. He also could have killed himself, terrified that whoever got La Reina would come after him."

"Suicide to escape being killed?" Albondo asked. "That's crazy, Captain."

"Escape the fear," Pearce said. "Maybe not so crazy. Panic, like a frantic bird in a closed room."

We listened to the rain. It fell heavily outside the captain's darkened office, hammered against something that echoed, hissed under the tires of passing vehicles.

"We're not birds," Albondo said. "No one would kill himself like that without a real reason."

Life was too important. No one would commit suicide unless facing something so terrible it was worse than death. Albondo was young, safe, secure. He didn't know that life could be worse than death.

"You could be right, Counselor," Pearce said.

I said, "Someone could have been sent in to kill him."

"We checked for Wilmer and Ernie," Pearce said. "No one answering their descriptions was in there. Escudo'd been held five days, we're backtracking everyone we put in these last five days."

The sound of the rain outside was lighter, the drone of voices beyond the captain's door rising and falling like the voices in a late-night hospital.

Albondo stood up. "I've got work. Keep in close touch, Captain. The D.A. doesn't like a death in custody."

"Who does?" Pearce said.

We both sat and watched the young assistant D.A. leave. The captain closed his eyes.

I said, "The pimp, Rags, said MacKay was with Evans that night. There had to be at least three men in the ambush, at least one driver in one car. Four in all. Evans, Rivera and Evans' Latino driver would make three. Mackay would make four."

"Don't I wish." Pearce opened his eyes. They filled with hope as he enjoyed the thought of nailing George MacKay. "He was at his place the night La Reina bought it. Didn't leave until ten-thirty as usual, took his regular eleven-fourteen train out to Great Neck. He couldn't have been at the Reina setup."

"So Rags was lying."

"Hoping, like me," Pearce said. "And Evans wasn't there, probably not Rivera or the Latino. Evans' alibi for the night was solid as steel. The men who carried out the operation were trained and experienced. Hired for sure. In town and out before we could smell them."

Outside, the rain was down to a low hiss under passing tires. Voices and footsteps went on and on beyond his door. The perpetual flow of trouble and anguish in the city, the struggle for order, even, sometimes, for justice.

"Over an hour later, five blocks south, Jeanne-Marie was running scared," I said. "From who and why?"

"Maybe she was that scream Madero heard up at the corner. She came back to watch whatever Evans told her was going to happen, saw what was really happening, screamed and ran."

"Okay," I said. "So what? If she talked she accused herself, and Evans was alibied from here to Hong Kong."

Pearce nodded. "She couldn't have incriminated Evans enough for a warrant, much less a grand jury. Evans shouldn't have been worried about her talking."

"Then who could she have hurt? Tied to La Reina's killing?"

"Maybe she wasn't killed because of La Reina."

"Evans could have been super cautious, took no chances."

I said it, but I didn't believe it. Not the way Coley Evans had acted with me and Roy Carter. He had been a man who talked first, calculated the risks, did nothing precipitous, and he'd been worried only about what I knew about Jeanne-Marie, not about her killing. He'd known he was clear on the killing.

"At least now I can close MacKay down," Pearce said with some satisfaction. "The brass won't take a whisper of trouble around an illegal operation we're winking at."

I got up. "Let me know about Madero, okay, Captain?"

He nodded.

Down on Pearl Street the rain had stopped. I walked through the dark Police Plaza and along Chambers to the Independent subway. The night was colder after the rain. If Evans hadn't chased Jeanne-Marie and killed her, who else could have, and why?

I rode uptown to Forty-second Street, walked over to the Rescue Mission. The Reverend Davis said that Anne Woollard had been there but had left again at once. He seemed confused.

"She's been away so much lately," he said. "That's not like her. The children seemed to be her only interest."

I didn't have the heart to tell him Anne Woollard had found another interest. I went up the block to her room. There was no answer to my knocks. I hadn't expected there would be. I had a hunch Anne Woollard wasn't coming back either.

I tried the brothel for MacKay, but the janissary at the door informed me that Mr. MacKay was once again not there. For someone who tended to business every day until his regular eleven-fourteen train home to Great Neck, MacKay too had been out a lot the last few days.

I staked out and watched both buildings. A hard-edged wind from the river blew a strong hint of November. Snow wasn't far away. Neither George MacKay nor Anne Woollard showed up. At midnight I gave up and on Eighth Avenue picked up a cab for my loft. There were no messages on my answering machine, both the Chief and Jerry Carter strangely silent.

31

AFTER MY RITUAL TWO cups of morning coffee, I called Pine Dunes. One of the girls, a sullen Melanie, told me her father had gone out early, she didn't know where. There was still no word from the Chief on anything.

I went down into the October wind. Gray clouds blowing low over the city. A day for codfishing, for reeling fat yellow ling up from deep in the massive gray-green sea off Ambrose Light. I bent against the wind at each cross street, duffel coat blowing but hat secure. A day for a beret.

At the Rescue Mission the always-open door admitted me to a silent downstairs hallway, where both offices were closed and locked. I went along the windy block to Anne Woollard's rooming house. There was no answer at her room, so I staked out again across the block. It was getting to be that time of year when a sensible New York detective looks for cases that will send him to Florida after a runaway wife or two. I warmed my hands in my pockets, shifted from foot to foot and watched the residents and transients blow past on the wind.

She wore a dark green trenchcoat, almost invisible when she moved close to the buildings. High heels that ruined the invisibility, hatless, her auburn hair soft on her shoulders. Her eyes searched the windy street as she reached her rooming house and hurried up the steps. I waited until she was inside, caught up with her just as she was opening her door.

"Where is he, Anne?"

She tried a smile. "Is that all you want from me, Dan? How sad." She went inside, left the door for me to close. "I don't know where he is, Dan."

"Yes you do. I can hold you, call the police."

"We knew you'd be back, and if I didn't know where he was I couldn't tell you even by accident or under duress."

"You expect to be tortured?"

"Persuaded, perhaps."

In the kitchen area of the room she took a can of cat food out of a small refrigerator, put half of it into a plastic bowl. Almost instantly a black-and-white cat with sorrowful eyes and the look of a fat rabbit came in the open window from the fire escape and waddled swiftly to the food. She put down a second bowl of water, petted the cat.

"Not my Persian, but a friend," she said.

"What's he really doing, Anne? Why are you helping? How long have you really known him?"

She began to tidy the small room.

"So many questions. Which do I answer first?"

"Take your pick."

She watched the cat eat, folded her arms tight over her breasts. "He's trying to do what you and the police don't seem able to do, find Jeanne-Marie's real killer."

"I thought Coley Evans killed her."

"Not alone."

"More killing, Anne?"

"Evans was self-defense. You said so yourself."

"I said he could probably get away with self-defense if he went to the police and cooperated, told them everything he knew. Evans was a drug dealer, a white slaver, and the police are human. But if he kills again, that finishes him, and if you help him you're an accessory. Where is he, Anne?"

"I told you I don't know."

"He said he doesn't care about self-defense anyway, it doesn't matter. That means he expects to kill again, or maybe he killed before Evans. You know who shot Jeanne-Marie, Anne?"

"It wasn't Roy!"

"A week," I said. "That's how long you've known Roy Carter?"

"Yes."

"And Jeanne-Marie?"

"A few days." She looked at me. "Then she died."

"How close did you get?"

"We talked! I liked her! She was killed for no reason!"

Her voice startled the feeding cat. It looked up at her, wary and watchful, to be sure the rage was not directed at itself. Anne spoke reassuringly to the cat, squatted down beside it. The cat let Anne pet it, even purred as it drank with tiny licks of its tongue. When it finished drinking it began to lick its paws and groom itself, oblivious to both of us.

Anne Woollard stood up. "You want to know why I'm trying to help Roy? Do you remember that girl you saw at the mission the first time you came? The one MacKay brought over? Twelve years old, working the streets for a pimp she'd run away from?"

"Jackie," I said.

"Yes," she said, "Jackie." She crossed the room to the window open onto the fire escape. She stared out over the littered back yards, the grimy backs of buildings on the next street, the distant towers of midtown. "She went to MacKay for help, he brought her to us to send her home. I suppose no one is all bad if you go down deep enough."

It wasn't a point I felt like arguing about. Too much depended on your definitions of *all* and *bad*.

She watched the clouds low above the gray-brown backs of the old buildings, seagulls flying inland in the gray day. "Jackie stayed at the mission two days. She never told us who her parents were. She never said where she came from, where she'd lived before the Strip and the streets. She never said much of anything, talked to anyone. I don't think she ever really learned how to talk. She just sat in the room with two other girls and smoked and looked out the windows. You can see the Empire State Building clearly from that room. I think that was what she watched all day. The top of the Empire State. But perhaps not. Perhaps she was watching the boy on the roof directly across from us with his pigeons. I like to watch his pigeons too. Sometimes we feed them from the kitchen."

She came away from the window. The small black-and-white cat jumped onto the sill and sat hunched in a ball half in and half out of the room. She sat down on her daybed. "They found pieces of her in garbage cans along Tenth Avenue last night. Cut up, wrapped in Halloween paper and dropped into garbage cans along four blocks of Tenth Avenue. It took them until this morning to identify her, and they only did that because she'd been arrested so many times the police knew her face when they finally found her head, had her fingerprints on file when they found her hands. She still had one of our tags pinned to her blouse so they came to the mission to talk to Reverend Davis."

"Rags?" I said.

"Who else cared about her enough to kill her? She betrayed Rags by running away and taking some of her money with her, and no one betrays Rags. Now he can walk tall on the streets. He took care of a problem and everyone will respect him. He handled a potentially dangerous threat to his 'business.' He'll go around boasting about it and no one will touch him!"

"They will someday, Anne. Rags won't last long one way or another."

"Will they? After how many more Jackies? How many more will he cut up, push off a roof, shoot, strangle, hotshot or overdose?"

Nothing I could say would change her rage. She didn't want advice, only an outlet. All I could do was listen.

"No one cares. A thousand like her are dead and no one cares. Ten thousand and no one cares!" She was up, pacing the spartan room. "Only someone does care. About one of them anyway. Roy cares. Roy *cares!*" She breathed hard with her anger. She went to the window and stroked the black-and-white cat. She looked out the window. The seagulls were still circling low over the roofs. "Even if they get Rags, it won't help the Jackies. They'll keep on coming to the city, and they'll keep on being found by one Rags or another, and they'll keep on working the streets and they'll keep on dying. Because they have nowhere else to go and nothing else to do. Neither them nor Rags." She stroked the cat's soft fur. "Can't all of you let him do what he has to, Dan? Let him care? Can't you stop the monsters, not him?"

"Are you so sure he's not one of the monsters?"

She just stood there, face to the window, stroked the cat that still sat purring on the window sill. Her anger had created a barrier, a line of resistance that stopped all discussion, all argument, all reason at a wall of commitment. She set the cat down, faced me.

"I'm sure, but you probably wouldn't be. A few years ago I wouldn't have been sure, wouldn't have known the real monsters, but now I do." She turned back to the window. "I don't know where he is. I don't know anything."

I left her watching the city and the seagulls, petting the black-and-white cat. She knew where Roy Carter was, or knew how to find him, but she wasn't going to tell me. I could take her in to Captain Pearce, the police would get her to talk, but Roy Carter would have some safeguard for that. Check-in calls, passwords, fixed meeting times, something. My best chance was her inexperience.

I found a different doorway, staked out again. The wind was still cold. She came out after almost an hour, walked straight up to the Rescue Mission. Maybe I was wrong on all points. Maybe she didn't know where Roy Carter was, wasn't leaving the mission behind.

I waited two more hours. Then I walked across to the mission. Either she was back at work and I could get some lunch, or she was learning fast and had suckered me.

Her office was locked and dark. A lady in the kitchen said Anne Woollard had gone out the back way two hours ago.

32

GUARDING THE DOOR OF a brothel is a lonely job. All the fun goes on behind you. Today at Mac-Kay's door it was more lonely than usual. The black doorman had just turned away two annoyed johns who grumbled out loud as they walked up the block.

"What the hell I'm gonna do before five o'clock?"

"MacKay runs a nice place. Damn cops close him down and leave all the bums on the streets."

The doorman gave me a grin. We were friends now.

"You here so much you oughta turn tricks."

"I'm not pretty enough," I said.

"You ain't seen some o' the stuff we peddles."

We're a nation of standup comics looking for an audience. One-liners, quick repartee, the zinger. A joke for every problem, a quip for every question. Maybe because we don't want to answer the questions, or even hear them.

"I'll think about it," I said. "He here?"

He shook his head. "For a guy puts so much time in a cathouse you ain't havin' much fun. Take a trick. Any girl you want, now we's shut down."

"How about Georgia?"

He was disgusted with me. "More talk? You sure you missin' on'y the arm?"

"I'll look later," I said.

Upstairs, Georgia lay on the iron bed, smoking. She saw me without looking at me, blew smoke at the ceiling.

"Who you chasing now? I know it ain't me." She turned her head on the pillow to look at me. "After you sell it, it's hard to give it away."

"Friends don't buy each other, Stell."

"Like Australia," she said. "Everyone knows where it is, but no one wants to go there. What do you want, Dan?"

"Anything about Jeanne-Marie Johnson you didn't know the first time. She was running from someone that night. Did she talk about being scared of anyone? Having trouble with anyone?"

"Maybe she was just runnin' from her private man."

"Evans?"

"Looked like the Aussie's private stuff."

"She wasn't anyone's stuff." I told her about the M.E.'s report that Jeanne-Marie had been a virgin.

"What the shit was she doin' here then?"

I told her about La Reina and the ambush. "Did she ever mention La Reina? Say anything about talking to her?"

"The Spic Queen? Hell, no, she never said nothing I heard. No one said nothin' around here about those killings."

"Anything you can remember about her, Stell?"

She shook her head. "She sat up in that room on the top floor readin', eatin' candy, watchin' TV. Talked to the Aussie some, never even went out 'til the night she got shot."

"Never? She—"

"Never. I remember Sam sayin', 'That new kid on the fourth floor never goes out.'"

"Not even to make a telephone call?"

"You ask Sam."

"Guy on the door?"

She nodded.

"She must have talked to someone, Stell."

"She talked to that broad from the mission who comes over here to save us. Jabbered about how rich she was gonna get, what a big shot she was gonna be. Who listened? We turn a lot o' tricks here. When we ain't busy, who wants to yak with some dumb kid thinks she's gonna be a tycoon and movie star rolled in one?"

"No word going around on who killed her? Why?"

She pinched the cigarette, dropped it to the floor. "Someone didn't want her around. Big deal. You know how many die every year around the Strip? Another dead cunt. What the hell."

She lay on the bed with her hands folded on her breasts. As still as a corpse, laid out and motionless on the iron bed where she did her work. She stared at the ceiling.

"Why don't you get out of it, Stell?"

"Don't be a jerk, Dan." She watched the ceiling. "I never got out of grade school, you know that. We needed money, and I was in too much hurry to grow up to be playin' schoolgirl. Poor and stupid, it's a hell of a combination. I got a yellow sheet longer'n a supermarket bill. What else pays for what I need every day? I got nothin' but habits. That's all there is between me an' the river, a lot of habits that cost money. Maybe we all got nothin' but habits."

She looked around, maybe wondering how she'd gotten there. Not bitter, not with any particular regret in her dark eyes, just curious, trying to remember the details. I went down to the door and asked Sam the guard how he knew Jeanne-Marie had never gone out the week or so she was there.

"This the on'y way out you ain't got a key, an' that Evans paid me I tell him if she goes out. He paid good."

"She didn't go out at least once?"

"Didn't even try."

There were no phones in the bedrooms. It distracted from good work.

"Where are the phones in the building?"

"On'y phones is in Mr. MacKay's office."

"He back yet?"

"Go on down."

Down in his office on the ground floor George MacKay was working the keys of his computer, checking figures on the screen. There were two telephones on the desk. He heard me, looked up and looked back at his work.

"Get the fuck out of here."

"Pearce was here?"

Immaculate in his gray silk again. His tie neat, his collar clean. "I'm closed down, ain't I?"

"You should have been more careful who you did favors for."

He checked figures on the screen. "I'll start with you."

"Maybe I can help you open up again."

He manipulated the keyboard. "Shit."

"How much did you know about the La Reina setup?"

"Zero! I knew diddley-shit, and now maybe they close me down permanent! What do I do? How do I make a living?"

"Rags says you were with Evans that night."

He studied his screen. "Rags went to the cops?"

"To me."

"And you went to the cops?"

"Yes."

He touched some keys. The screen went dark. He removed two floppy disks, returned them to a file box, sat back in his desk chair and looked at me.

"I guess I should of laid off doin' Jackie favors too. All I got for it was shit from that preacher, a pain in the ass from you, the Judas from Rags and the shaft from the cops."

"It didn't do Jackie much good either."

"She was never gonna make it. All downhill for her, hurtin' all the way. She's out of it. I'm still in it."

"Help me find out who killed Jeanne-Marie Johnson and I'll talk to Captain Pearce."

"You ain't got that kind of muscle."

"A voice on your side never hurts."

"They already shut me down. On the Big Bag Lady I'm clean. What can you do for me?"

"You weren't involved with Evans?"

"I ain't in jail."

"You were here all night the night Jeanne-Marie was killed?"

"That's what I told the cops."

"Did she say anything when she went out?"

He shook his head.

"She left at eight P.M., and that was the last you saw her?"

"You got it."

"How did Evans meet Jeanne-Marie?"

He turned in his chair, back to the desk and his work. "So long, Fortune, I got work to do. I'm closed down, it's cut an' scramble time." He picked up his pen, switched on the computer, bent over the papers on his desk.

"There's a kid out there," I said, "who's killed once, maybe twice, and is going to kill again. I'm not sure who or why. But he's looking for someone.

Maybe anyone who was around Jeanne-Marie. Maybe you. I've found him once, I'll find him again, but I've got to know what happened that night."

The screen ran figures like a river of light as Mac-Kay manipulated the keys with slow, thick fingers. He must have plodded the same way around a boxing ring. His fingers were slow, but I had a hunch his mind was fast enough, and he was thinking. He decided in my favor.

"She got sent up to Evans by somebody out aroun' her home town. Lookin' for a favor."

"Who sent her to him?"

"Evans don't name no names, Fortune."

"Who did Evans work for?"

He continued to manipulate the computer keys. "Big operator out in California. Never did hear a name there neither."

"Where in California?"

He shook his head. The lines of light moved around the small amber screen.

I walked to the door.

Behind me he said, "I'd of knowed what the son-of-a-bitch was gonna do, I'd of thrown 'em both out. You believe that, Fortune."

"I believe it."

As I headed downtown for my office, a clearing sky had brought out the crowds to hunt for action, for fun, for each other. For their share of the good times. Crowds watched by the quick and silent ready to sell them the illusion of whatever they wanted. For a price that would always be more than the illusion would be worth, more than even the reality could be worth. If the reality existed. But the only reality here was for the suppliers. Here buyer and seller were equally victims, and only the middlemen wore diamonds and silks.

There was no message from the Chief on my machine, not even to ask for his money. There were no messages at all. I sat and thought. Coley Evans might have told one other person who had sent Jeanne-Marie to him

33

THE TOWNHOUSE ON EAST Eighty-third was shuttered, the scrubbed front steps swept and clean. Elegant in the now sunny noontime. I could have used the bell, but it seemed somehow more fitting to raise the polished brass knocker on the massive wooden door and let the knocks echo inside.

They echoed, but nothing happened. So much for romanticism. I used the more efficient electric door-bell. I didn't get any more result, but at least I was sure the bell would have been heard. The mail in the polished brass mailbox told me Hally Balada and her mother had gone out early, what I saw on the marble doorstep told me something else.

A semicircle of narrow, zigzag lines on the scrubbed white stone that looked black but were really a very dark red. Traces of a dirty white powder. Traces of white powder showed more clearly on the top brownstone step. Not much, a thin trail of spilled white. I tasted it and looked at the silent door.

A bitter powder. Heroin?

Traces of blood on a shoe that left the mark on the white marble doorstep?

I didn't want to be caught picking a lock on this street. I could wait half a day in precinct lockup before Pearce would hear and get me out. So every minute I checked the street as I tried my keys, and it took longer. That, and the shaking of my hand.

The fifth key did it.

Inside, the broad entry hall was sunny and silent. I stood and listened. The house listened with me. The stairs that curved up to the second floor landing seemed to beckon me to go up. I resisted, checked the living room with its clean, harmonious furniture, the formal dining room across the entry hall, the high-backed oak chairs around a long oak table set with white linen, silver and cut crystal as if ready for a state dinner.

The library was untouched, the kitchen and breakfast room littered with the cold remains of breakfast. A breakfast for two, the pans and dishes piled haphazardly around the kitchen. Cold dishwater in the sink. A book open on the breakfast table. The glass carafe from the coffee maker still half full of cold coffee.

In the front hall I looked up to the second-floor landing. I saw dark red stains and a dusting of white powder that seemed to echo like a loud noise in the silent house. I followed the stains and white grains upward.

The mother lay in the carpeted hall, her body facing an open doorway, hands out in front as if reaching to something, a fingernail torn off one wrinkled hand, blood under the other nails. She had scratched someone as she clawed toward the room beyond the open door, and someone had cut her throat. Almost cut her head off, the head propped up on its chin with the dead body behind like a bear rug.

Hally Balada was inside the room. They had not killed her in a hurry.

She had been shot twice in the head, but her dark gray slacks had been ripped and her firm thighs slashed like meat. Her white blouse was ripped half off and her breasts cut. One finger had been sliced from her left hand. That must have been when she gave them whatever it was they had come for.

Shot once standing up, the bullet shattering the antique mirror behind her body after it had blown the back of her head off. The second time while on the floor, the bullet in the wood. Once had done the job, but someone had wanted to be sure. The holes were in her forehead, leaving the perfect nose, firm chin, high cheekbones as beautiful as ever, but the dark eyes stared empty and the short dark hair was a mat of blood.

I sat down on an antique green-brocade occasional chair. I sat there for some time. I had known, really, since the silence of the downstairs hall, maybe even when I saw the small stain and the white powder on the doorstep, and it helped. You never get used to it, but there is a numbness that comes with the years. An insulation. Like a soldier's, violent death is a policeman's stock in trade, and even a private detective has to learn to deal with it.

Five minutes, without looking again at Hally Balada or the blood soaked into the white rug, then I went out and looked in the other rooms. I didn't look again at the dead mother. None of the other rooms on any of the floors had been touched. I went back down to the blood-soaked bedroom.

The heroin had been in her bottom bureau drawer. The torn package had leaked, the killers had simply unwrapped the packages and lifted them out, leaving the nest intact where they had been. From the empty space, at least four or five kilos. A green paper band with Spanish printing and an outer plastic bag were still in the empty space. I had little doubt where the smack had come from anyway, or who had wanted it back.

I called Pearce, went down and opened the outside door and sat in the entry hall to wait. I smoked. I tried not to think of Hally Balada a day ago in her full skirt and checked tan and black high cowl top with the voluminous raglan sleeves, her high-heeled black boots. The high cheekbones and dark eyes of a Russian princess, the black hair swept boyishly back, the slim neck. Beautiful and confident and so sure of what she could do.

The precinct police arrived first. They were not friendly. Pearce had told them about me, and no one likes his power limited. Pearce came next and motioned me upstairs. The captain had brought Callow from Lower East Side with him. While the precinct squad and the M.E. worked on the bodies, the rooms, the furniture, Pearce and Callow listened to my story, checked the drawer where the heroin had been, examined the paper wrapper and the plastic sack.

"Yeah, it's the same as the H we found in Evans' cellar," Callow agreed. "Same wrapper and bag."

"How much?" Pearce asked.

"Looks like about five kilos," Callow estimated. "Maybe half what that kid lifted from Evans."

Pearce looked at me. "Roy Carter gave her half his haul, those two gutter killers, 'Ernie and Wilmer, took it back?"

"This isn't their work, Captain," I said. "There had to be three men in this, probably more. One to hold the mother out in the hall, more likely two. At least two in the bedroom to work on Hally Balada, but I'd bet on two to hold and one to use the knife and gun and ask the questions. Three minimum, five more likely, six or seven probable."

"Evans' people getting their smack back?" Pearce said.

"That's how I read it." I looked to where the M.E.'s men were lifting Hally Balada's bloody body into a body bag. I felt scared, empty. I wanted to say goodbye. Not just to her, to all of us. I took a breath and it passed. It has to.

"How do you think she got the H?" Pearce said. He watched me, had more experience with body bags and corpses than I did.

I breathed slowly. "Roy Carter must have traded for something. She tried to sell it, or more likely tried to make a deal to take Evans' place, used the heroin to show how smart and tough she was."

Pearce nodded. "Over her head. These people kill babies to make a point. What do you think Carter traded for?"

"The name and address of the big man behind Evans," I said. "It's what Roy's been after all along. We've been wrong, it's not drug dealing, it's a vendetta. Justice. Roy wants everyone who got Jeanne-Marie killed, especially the man who ordered it."

Pearce shook his head. "Only half the junk was here, Carter could have wanted her contacts to move in on Evans' and La Reina's territories. We've got a dealer war going on, that's for sure. The only question is, is Roy Carter part of it or not? The guns, the hideout, don't sound like any private vendetta."

"They could be Vietnam friends of Eller Carter's," I said, "helping Roy out while he chases everyone he thinks killed Jeanne-Marie."

"They could be," Pearce agreed, "but I doubt it. These killers wanted more from Balada than the H."

"I think they wanted Roy Carter."

"You think she gave him to them?"

"No," I said. "She wouldn't have had him to give. He's too smart for that."

Pearce watched the M.E.'s men carry the bodies out, watched his men working around the rooms. "Smart, and not working alone, and half the H is still missing. It's not just a private chase, Dan."

"Maybe you're right, Captain. You need me anymore?"

"No. But keep in touch. Anything you know, right?"

"Sure, Captain." I nodded to Detective Callow and left.

I wasn't ready to give him Anne Woollard. Not until I knew more of what they were doing, or thought they were doing.

34

AT THE TOP OF my stairs I saw my broken office door. The lock had been torn out of the wood.

There are times when I wish I carried my old cannon. Leap into danger, gun blazing. Part of the American character formed by the freebooting loners who came to a raw land to grab their fortunes. I resist the urge. It got most of them killed.

"Come in, Mr. Fortune."

The man behind my desk tossed a hundred-dollar bill on it.

"Fix the door. I don't like waiting out in a hall."

He wasn't alone. A short man in a corner held an instrument I knew well. The office had been swept for electronics, anything that recorded. They hadn't even missed pulling the tape out of the answering machine.

I picked up the hundred. "Now that you're rested, what can I do for you?"

He was a thick man with fine silver-gray hair and wearing a navy-blue cashmere topcoat. Under the cashmere was a gray flannel suit of a modish cut that had probably cost more than the cashmere. His round face had that pink, powdered texture that comes from hot towels after a barber shave. The fierce mustache of a Cossack raider. A modern Hun.

"Are all private detectives comedians?"

"We're alone a lot. You going to tell me what you want? Maybe even who you are?"

He reached into an inner pocket, produced a wallet, took out two more crisp bills. These were five hundreds.

"These say I ask the questions and you give the answers." He laid the bills on the desk. "Who is the young man who shot Coley Evans?"

"Who wants to know?"

"All right, protect your client's interests. I understand that. Can you tell me exactly what he wants?"

"I don't know."

"He stole a valuable item. What does he plan to do with it? Does he wish to sell it?"

"Who wants to know?"

He smoothed the bills on my desk in front of him with his long, manicured hands. There was something familiar about him. He rolled the five hundreds, looked thoughtfully over them like a fortune-teller over a crystal ball, a doctor trying to decide how to best explain his patient's illness too him.

"I have a friend, Mr. Fortune. A rich and influential friend. Your young man has caused him discomfort and annoyance. My friend is a busy man with important affairs on his mind. He is willing to overlook certain actions in exchange for the stolen item and your young man's promise to return to his own business."

"He's not my young man. I work for his father."

The eyes that watched me over the tube of five hundreds got that look you see on politicians when they have been asked a question by someone they know is an enemy. There are, in the end, only two kinds of active people in this world, those who have principles and convictions, and those who only have friends and enemies. This man knew an enemy when he saw one, and I knew a politician. A face I'd seen solemn in newspapers, smiling out of television sets. A Congressman. Or an ex-Congressman. I wasn't sure which he was this year.

"An unfortunate lady made a mistake yesterday, Fortune. I would hate to see the same thing happen to Carter for no reason. A much more experienced and powerful lady found my friend too much to handle also, something young Carter should consider carefully, don't you think?"

He wasn't afraid of me or of anything I might tell. It would be my word against his, his "friend's" public image against a well-protected hidden truth that would be all but impossible to prove. The public is accustomed to rumors about their servants, accustomed even to truths no one cares about. It was Chief Justice Earl Warren who said there was no way the organized drug traffic could exist without protection from high officials.

"My friend will go this far: Evans was a small loss, it will take work to tidy up after the late Spic Queen, so he will overlook the annoyance, buy back the stolen goods and forget the whole thing if Carter will also forget. This thousand for you up front, another when you contact Roy Carter and make a deal: five thousand for him to go away. Take a cruise, see the world."

"If he doesn't want the deal?"

He stroked the bills gently. "I'll make it simple. There's a ten-thousand total. You can give the kid any part of it, keep the rest. Make him vanish permanently, you keep it all."

"I don't bribe, and I don't kill."

He stood up. If he'd been wearing gloves he'd have put them on carefully.

"Most commendable," he said, shook his head, "but probably a mistake. Carter is a dead man, and I'm not even sure about you. These people are hard to control, live in a very primitive world, eh? Not civilized like us. Be careful, and, of course, we never met, did we?"

"Never," I said, "but I don't think I'd vote for you."

"That's democracy."

Corruption, naked self-interest, always makes me feel cold, a little helpless. Even hopeless. So I sat there for a time and looked at the empty chair behind my desk where he had sat, listened to the heavy rumble of the city. The rumble of millions of people my visitor felt no connection to, no brotherhood with. Only himself and his friends. A world maybe more primitive than drug peddling.

Then I got up and went out into the October afternoon. I took my cannon this time. Roy Carter was in a lot of trouble, a lot of danger. Real trouble and real danger, and if I was going to save him from himself it was beginning to look like I'd have to be on the other end of the gun. I walked uptown.

The light was gray as I took the stairs to Anne Woollard's room. There wasn't much chance she would return now that they knew I could watch the room, but she had a cat she fed. It was my best chance, and the cat was the weakness. There was no answer to my knocking. I used my keys. Inside, the spartan room was even more spartan, the kitchen clean and unused, the window open and an automatic cat feeder and water dispenser set on the floor under the window. It had been a good theory anyway.

At the Rescue Mission her office was closed and dark, but the Reverend Davis was there. She hadn't been in since I lost her yesterday, and he was worried.

"She's missed more time the last week than all the years she's been here. I don't know what it is, Mr. Fortune."

"You think she went to her parents'?"

"No, the number she left is in a different area code. Long Island, I think."

Her weakness wasn't the cat, it was the middle-class upbringing, the Puritan responsibility. The telephone where she could be reached in an emergency had a 516 area code: Nassau and Suffolk counties. I didn't think she would be visiting Roy Carter's parents or Judy Lavelle, but I had my contact at the telephone company check for the address anyway. It was a private telephone in the Islip area.

I took a taxi down to Fugazy's Car Rental in the Village. It was still light when I crossed the Williamsburg Bridge, drove through Brooklyn to the Southern State Parkway and headed east.

35

IT WAS TIME TO take Roy Carter in. Or try to, anyway. Before anyone else got hurt, no matter what he was doing.

With the smell of the sea in the night, I passed the cabin on the narrow inlet of Great South Bay. The new gray Honda Accord was parked at the side. I drove on along the gravel road for half a mile, walked back keeping close to the thick growth of scrub pine and tangled brush.

There was a light in the cabin. There was no sound, and no shadows moved across the lighted windows. I had my hand on the old gun in my duffel coat pocket as I reached the window. From the lower right corner of the window, with my left eye, I saw no one inside the cabin. Light, a table, wooden chairs and wicker armchairs, rugs, a fireplace, wood, bureaus, a sink, but no one.

At the front door I listened. I could hold the gun against my left side, lower my right shoulder and hit the door hard at the high lock. This was a summer cabin, plywood and nails, the door should break open easily. But if Roy Carter were inside I wouldn't have a prayer. Not with a gun. I would have to talk, hope the chance for surprise would come. I knocked.

"Who is it?" Anne Woollard's voice.

"Dan Fortune."

There was a silence.

"The door's not locked, Dan."

She lay in a brass double bed in the corner of the single room out of sight of the window. The rest of the room was almost empty. A single worn couch I hadn't seen from outside. The empty cardboard of fast-food meals littered the sink and the kitchen sideboard.

"Roy said you were a good detective."

She looked like someone who had lain in the bed, alone, doing nothing, for some time. I sat on one of the straight chairs across the room from the bed. She sat up in the bed against the pillows, held the covers up to her throat. Her bare feet stuck out at the foot of the rumpled sheets and blankets.

"He's gone, Dan."

"Gone where?"

She reached for a cigarette on the bed table, lit it with one hand, the modest sheet still held to her chin with the other, looked disgusted with herself. "Reverend Davis gave you the phone number I left. I don't think I'll ever learn. Roy would be furious."

"You want to tell me about it now?"

She closed her eyes, moved her body under the covers as if remembering when she hadn't been alone there. It explained a lot about her and Roy Carter. But not all.

"I don't want to tell you anything, Dan."

"What's in it for you? What do you get?"

"I get to help."

"Help with what?

"Not what, who." She seemed to see a vision in the smoke of her cigarette. "He's got so much power. You wouldn't know what it can feel like to a woman, all that power, that drive inside you. What it feels like to hold all that force in your arms." She smoked and looked toward the window, but there was only darkness outside, the darker shadows of trees. "He's doing something, Dan. About Jackie and Rags and Jeanne-Marie and Coley Evans and MacKay and all of it. He's trying to change the way things are. *Doing* something so we don't have to live the way we do. All my life I've lived with the proper and weak. I went to the mission to help, but there was nothing I could do. I'm not strong enough, but he is."

She lay in the bed, smoked and stared at me as if defying me to say that what she was doing was wrong.

"How's he going to do all that? Change the way we live? By killing? By murder?"

She smoked, went on staring at me.

"Judge and jury and executioner?" I said. "Vigilante justice? One righteous man decides who is guilty? No one has that right, Anne. We fought thousands of years to escape one-man justice by king or lord or vigilante." It doesn't matter who's done what, we can't let one man be judge, jury and executioner."

She lay staring at me, the bedcovers up to her chin, her eyes, her whole face angry, telling me that whatever Roy Carter was doing, whatever his motive or his guilt, she would not desert him. I took my chair to the bed, sat down close to her.

"Listen to me, Anne. The police know Coley Evans used Jeanne-Marie to set up the killing of another drug dealer and white slaver named La Reina. They know Evans wasn't in business alone, there was someone else behind him who gave the orders. They think Evans and the man behind him had Jeanne-Marie killed because she knew too much. Coley Evans's woman, Hally Balada, told Roy who Evans' boss is. Roy was there when Jeanne-Marie was killed, I think he was there when La Reina was killed. Tell him to go to the police before it's too late."

She turned her face away, looked at the cabin wall. "Leave us alone, Dan. Go away. It's too late. He's gone. I couldn't stop him if I wanted to—and I don't."

I looked at her auburn hair loose and rumpled in the bed, at her bare back where the covers had slipped as she turned to the wall. Roy Carter was gone, and from the sound of her voice she was afraid he wasn't coming back to her any more than he was to Judy Lavelle. The difference was she still wanted him. It was there in her voice, in everything about her.

"Or do we have it all wrong?" I said. "Roy isn't doing anything except covering up a killing. All the big talk about Jeanne-Marie's killers just a smoke screen. He killed Jeanne-Marie, is trying to cover it up. Maybe he hired those two punks himself. Maybe he and his friends killed Hally Balada. Maybe he sent Jeanne-Marie to Evans. All part of a drug deal that went wrong."

She rolled from the wall, clutched the covers tight around her as she glared at me with angry eyes.

"He didn't send Jeanne-Marie to Evans! He didn't know about Evans until she called him! He didn't even know where she was until the night she was killed!"

"Then how'd he find her?"

"He followed Evans!"

"Who sent her to Evans?"

"Some Vietnamese people out here! She wanted to find Hoan, but it was Evans who—"

She stared at me the way a child does when he's said something he didn't mean to say and hopes maybe you didn't hear, somehow missed it, didn't notice the mistake.

"Who's Hoan, Anne?"

"No one!"

"He's the man Coley Evans worked for, isn't he? The big boss out in California Hally Balada traded to Roy for half the stolen heroin."

"No!"

"Hoan," I said. "It's a Vietnamese name."

She turned back to the wall, wrapped now like a cocoon in the blankets. "Go away, Dan."

"Is he making a deal? Jeanne-Marie went up to New York to find Hoan and make a deal and Roy didn't like that? He followed her, found her, killed her and Evans so he could deal with Hoan himself?"

Her voice was low. "He didn't kill Jeanne-Marie."

"You're sure? You know who did?"

Suddenly she was calm, her voice quiet and drained where she lay and talked not to me but to the cabin wall. "I had him for awhile. He was in my life. Whatever he does or did is to try to change things. That's enough for me."

"And if he did kill Jeanne-Marie?"

"It doesn't matter."

I stood up. "It matters, Anne."

I left her there in the empty cabin with the October wind outside. I knew now that she really didn't know where Roy Carter was or what he was doing. Carter wouldn't have told her. He would have known I'd find her, or the police would, and sooner or later make her tell us if she knew.

I went out into the sea wind and walked along the dark road to my rented car. If Roy Carter were out for vigilante justice, it wouldn't end with some man named Hoan, or with prostitutes and pimps. It never does, and I had to try to stop him before he killed again.

If he was a covering up his own crimes by going on to more crime, I had to stop him even more.

36

I PARKED IN THE night at the side of the dirt road near the big frame house of the Dhoc family, walked to the ramshackle house with its sagging porch. I knocked.

The big boat bobbed and creaked against the dock in the inlet, but no one answered my knocks. I sat on the porch, lit a cigarette cupped against the wind and watched the silvery reeds blowing flat along the creek inlet, undulating like the surge of the sea itself, the surface of the inlet rippling in the wind.

"One-armed mister?"

I saw no one.

"You are friend of Jeanne-Marie?"

A soft voice, nervous yet determined. I looked across the porch, through the darkness, at the house itself. She stood inside the dark room at the window that opened onto the porch behind me. A Vietnamese girl of maybe thirteen, dressed in a sweater and skirt like any American teenager.

"I saw you with Judy, but I was afraid."

"Afraid of what?"

"Just afraid."

"Can I come in?"

She stood for a moment, then walked to the front door and unlocked it. I went in. She went back to the spot where she had been standing, as if it were a sanctuary. Accustomed to the dark, she didn't turn on a light.

"Afraid of me?" I asked.

She nodded.

"Of your parents too?"

She nodded.

"Because they lied?"

Slender and even delicate, with thick black hair and soft eyes. Yet determined. Determined and unsure. The eyes you see on all refugees, on all those forced to learn a new life they had not sought or wanted. I remembered those eyes on some of my ships in World War Two. Eyes that had seen too much too soon, learned too much too soon. Like half the world today.

"What's your name?"

"I am Sarkin Van Dhoc."

"Who is Hoan, Sarkin?"

She smiled for the first time. "He was very great man in Vietnam, now he has a whole new life in this country. He helps all Vietnamese people. He helps people to escape from Vietnam, even those who were Vietcong in the war. He finds them jobs, gives many people work. My family was not doing so well, you know? Our boat was small and old and slow. Mr. Hoan helped my father buy the big new boat, with new nets and everything."

"Where is he, Sarkin? Where does Mr. Hoan live?"

"In New York, I think. I have not met him yet, but when it is time for college, my father will take me to meet him and then I will see him."

"Your parents sent Jeanne-Marie to New York?"

"She wished to meet Mr. Hoan."

"Where in New York?"

"I do not remember. She was excited. She thanked my parents very much."

"They were good friends, Jeanne-Marie and your parents?"

The girl shrugged. "My father said she tried too hard to be American, to forget Vietnam too fast."

"She didn't have much reason to remember Vietnam."

"I guess not." The shrug and the stubborn face combined. "Only she had a bad idea of America too. I mean, she thought America is all money and buying everything and having anything she wanted right away and being famous."

"That's not such an uncommon idea of America even for Americans," I said. "If they weren't friends, why did Jeanne-Marie come to your parents for help?"

I never heard a sound until they were in the room. I had the sudden vision, illusion, of them standing almost invisible in jungle shadows. The two older men, Tran Van Dhoc and his brother Li, again stood small and slender in front of the younger men, their lined, tired, stubborn faces unsmiling.

"She told me," I said.

The older woman I had seen in the kitchen the first time appeared behind the young men and stared at Sarkin. The girl's dark eyes were defiant. It was the older woman who looked away.

"So you did send Jeanne-Marie to New York," I said.

Tran Van Dhoc motioned. The older woman and two of the younger women walked to Sarkin. Sarkin's face was pale but still defiant. The women led the girl back behind the men, their faces neither angry nor accusing. They seemed to comfort Sarkin, as if they understood her need to tell the truth.

"To Hoan," I said, "the fine man who helps all Vietnamese. Who gets people out of Vietnam and finds them jobs in America. A lot of jobs for girls, I'll bet. The daughters of your friends, maybe of your relatives. Mr. Hoan who helped you get that big new boat. How many girls for a boat? For nets? A new house?"

Tran Van Dhoc said something in his own language. The brother, Li Van Dhoc, motioned to the younger men, and they herded the women and children out of the room. Only Tran Van Dhoc and the older woman remained.

Tran Van Dhoc said, "We send Jeanne-Marie to Mr. Hoan in New York as she wanted. That is all."

"Where in New York?"

He gave me the address of Coley Evans's hidden cellar office near Tompkins Square.

"Where does Hoan really live?"

"We do not know."

The older woman said, "Many people try to talk to Mr. Hoan. He wishes to be private."

"I'll bet," I said. "What did Jeanne-Marie want from Hoan?"

"For him to help her," the woman said. "She want Mr. Hoan to help her sell her story, make a motion picture, be rich and famous. A job, money and perhaps a return to Saigon."

"She was a nonperson in Saigon, a nothing."

"What was she in this country?" the woman asked. There was granite in her face. A cold determination, almost ruthlessness.

"I have to find Hoan," I said.

Tran Van Dhoc said, "We know only where we send Jeanne-Marie. Mr. Hoan want us, he come to us."

"I don't believe you."

"We know only where we send Jeanne-Marie," Tran Van Dhoc said. "You will go now."

"I'll find Hoan, but it could be too late."

"You will not find Mr. Hoan through us," the woman said.

"How many nieces?" I said. "How many daughters of friends? For a nice new boat?"

The woman looked at me from black eyes under the thick black hair peppered with gray. "There has been worse to our children. Much worse. From our enemies and our friends."

They stood together in their big living room, two small, thin, hard people. It's easy to condemn what you've never had to face yourself.

I walked out, drove to the first gas station and called Judy Lavelle. Roy Carter had not expected to return to Pine Dunes from the start, and now he was really gone, but there was an off chance he had seen Judy Lavelle one last time. At least called, said something I could use. It was a straw, but sometimes it's all you have in my trade.

Judy answered the phone herself. "I've been trying to reach you for hours, Dan! Roy came out to talk to his father! I just found out this afternoon."

I hung up and got back to my rented car.

37

THE SMALL CAPE COD cottage at 142 Hickock Drive in Pine Dunes sat on its single lot surrounded by lawn and flowers and trees and identical houses. There was light downstairs and upstairs. Judy Lavelle was waiting for me in front.

"When was he here?"

"Two days ago, I think. The day after we talked to him, I guess. Melanie told me this afternoon when I called here. She doesn't like me, wanted me to know he hadn't come to me."

She stood back as I rang at the front door. All the lights were on, but no one came. I went on ringing until a voice called, "Jerry? Someone's at the door already!"

The door opened.

"Guess I didn't hear you," Jerry Carter said. "Sorry."

"You didn't want to," I said, pushed past him with Judy behind me. "You haven't called in a couple of days."

The house hadn't changed since I'd talked to Debbie Carter and her girls, but with Jerry Carter in the living room it seemed smaller. There was light at the top of the stairs ahead, the sound of rock music from the second floor. Debbie Carter was in the dining room watching a small black-and-white television while corn popped in an electric popper. In the unseen TV room the big color set droned the same program.

"I was gonna call, you know?" Jerry Carter said. "I mean, I was gonna come in an' pay you tomorrow."

We stood in the living room of too much blonde wood and heavily upholstered furniture, flowered slipcovers on everything. He didn't sit down or ask us to sit.

"Why?" I asked.

"I don't figure I can pay you more'n I owe right now."

"I haven't asked you to pay," I said.

He waved at the air, those big hands that never knew what to do with themselves. "Money's gettin' tight, an' Roy's just helpin' catch the guy got Jeanne-Marie killed. Him an' the cops can handle it, right? Nothin' for you to do."

"Is that what he told you, Jerry?"

He looked at Judy Lavelle as if she had betrayed him by telling me Roy had been to Pine Dunes, stood uncertain in the room as if everything had betrayed him. A mixture of defiance and vulnerability in the confused blue eyes, the heavy face belligerent and defensive at the same time. Unsure and alone.

"What did he tell you, Jerry?" I said. "When was he here? Two days ago? You didn't tell the police? You didn't tell me?"

Someone had sold him—or Debbie—the perfect "at home" clothes. A gaudy orange and green jogging suit, loose on his legs, tight over his belly and thick waist, zippered everywhere from ankles to neck. He looked like a giant stuffed animal, a cartoon character, but his anguish was real as he sat on the edge of a flower-covered armchair, looked at his hands, looked up at me, looked around the bright room.

"He tol' me I shouldn't tell no one. He said he was okay, he just hadda stay out o' sight awhile." He shrugged. "I mean, he's my son, you know?"

"What else did he say, Jerry?" I said. "What did he talk about?"

"I don't know what he said. I mean, he talked, only I still don't know what he was talking about. I asked him what the hell he was doin', who those two creeps after him was." He shook his head in a kind of disbelief. "He said those two scum got born poor an' outside an' couldn't help bein' what they was. He said all we lets 'em do is pimp and con and hustle, gives 'em a little welfare to keep 'em quiet. I said what the hell was he talkin' about? It was bums an' misfits like them draggin' us down all over the country." He looked from me to Judy and back to me, astonishment on his heavy face. "He tells me I grew up poor in a slum an' I should know better! He tells me I been conned into buyin' a bag of shit! Been made to think what the big shots wants me to think!" In the dining room Debbie Carter had turned from her television to look at us as Jerry's voice rose angry and unbelieving. "I told him no one tells me what to think! It wasn't no slum where me an' his mother started. We was poor, sure, but we worked for what we got. Maybe I should go on welfare myself, 'stead of wantin' my job back."

"You couldn't live a day on welfare, Jerry," I said.

"Forty years I worked. Since the day I come home from the war. Now I'm laid off an' bums an' whores lives fat."

"Bums and whores we still put in jail," I said. "The rest we keep alive, but only barely."

"You sounds like him!" He flailed his arms. "He talks about all them people in Vietnam an' Africa an' South America like we owes them. Every damn stray cat from everywhere we lets in, an' what do we get for it? They take our jobs, eat our food, an' then tell us to go to hell!"

His voice echoed in the small comfortable living room, outraged and injured. But more injury than outrage, an uncertainty because his own son's words had outraged him. A man's son should agree with him, not tell him he'd been wrong all his life.

"He talked about Vietnam and South America?" I said. "How? What did he say?"

Debbie Carter came from the dining room, her television show unwatched behind her. "The stupid kid went to Vietnam, you know? With the Communists an' all. He saw Eller's grave! He's crazy. I mean, I'd like to see where Eller got buried an' all, but I ain't going to an enemy country to do it."

"You talked to Roy too, Mrs. Carter?"

"Ask him!" Debbie Carter said, tossed her gray ponytail at Jerry. "Does he tell me my son is here? Does he tell me my son is goin' away? Not him. Does my son come to me to say he's movin' out? You know, like maybe 'Good-bye Ma?' No! Maybe we don't see him for years, you know, but does he come an' say good-bye to his mother an' sisters?"

She raised her eyes to the ceiling, then sighed and shook her head. "He tells me what Roy told him, talked about, an' maybe it's better I don't talk to Roy. I mean, the way he sounds maybe I don't want to talk to him, you know? Carryin' guns, stealin' dope, shootin' people! That's not any son of mine. Like he's gone crazy."

There was something unreal about her manner, the way she spoke. She was playing a role. The solid, clear-thinking mother who knew right from wrong even if he was her own son. A role she had probably assumed long ago when she was a girl at home waiting for marriage. It was like watching afternoon soap opera. Only Debbie Carter's role was real. She thought she felt what she said. It was the role she played every day, and she had no idea what she really thought or felt, no idea who she really was. She had been playing her role so long she had no way of knowing what she really thought or felt about anything.

"Does the name Hoan mean anything to either of you?"

It was too sudden a shift, too much to ask, and they both just stared at me. I gave them some time, asked Judy Lavelle. "Judy?"

"I don't know any Hoan, Dan. Sounds Chinese or maybe Vietnamese or something. Is it?"

"Probably," I said. "Jerry? Mrs. Carter?"

"I wish we'd never heard of Vietnam," Debbie said. "Someone Jeanne-Marie knew maybe. Who knows?"

Jerry Carter said, "I never heard of no Hoan. Who is he?"

"I think he's who Roy's looking for. Coley Evans' boss."

"He the guy got Jeanne-Marie killed?" Jerry said. "I mean, the guy made that Evans kill Jeanne-Marie." He was beginning to find some kind of logic in his son's actions.

"Unless we've got it backward and Roy and Jeanne-Marie were in a drug deal with Evans and Hoan and something went wrong. Jeanne-Marie, Evans and Hoan double-crossed Roy, or everyone double-crossed everyone, and Roy killed Jeanne-Marie and Evans and now he's after Hoan."

"No way!" Jerry Carter hauled himself off the flowered chair. "No way, you hear? If he killed anyone it was just that Evans an' he was nothin' but a pimp an' dope dealer!"

Reality was reaching him. Roy and me and all the talk of killing and drugs was breaking through the numbness of the eleven o'clock news, the gaudy fake blood and violent special effects of *Dirty Harry* and *Rambo* movies. It was reaching Debbie too, but not as naked yet, and she had no way to react except in her lifelong role.

"Jerry?" She stared at him. "He killed that man. Maybe he murdered Jeanne-Marie. Mr. Fortune says he's going to kill more people. Jerry, what's happened to Roy? What's happenin' to us?"

"When he left, Jerry," I had to press, "where did he go? Where did he say he was going?"

Jerry sat down again. "He never said nothin' about where he was goin'. He just come because maybe he wasn't coming back for a long time. He said he had stuff he had to do. He never said what or where he had to go."

"He must have said something," I pushed. "A hint, a slip. Where you could reach him. Where to send his mail. How was he leaving? Air? Car? Bus?"

Jerry shook his head. "Nothin'. He had a car waitin' outside, some guy drivin' an' just waitin' for him."

"Who was waiting in the car?

"How do I know?" His voice was low, sullen. "He says the company'll get guys to work cheaper other places, the company gonna go into some other business an' got no more use for me. Forty years with the company, an' he says they don't need me no more so it's good-bye Jerry—so long, it's been good to know you. I told him forty years me an' the drill press been there. A guy works hard in this country he keeps his job. A man wants to work he always can."

He looked from one of us to the other. I heard the question mark at the end of his sentences. A week ago they would have been statements. Roy had made them into questions. I leaned down close to his heavy, confused face.

"Jerry? I think he's going to try to kill this man Hoan, whoever he is. We can still stop him, help him."

Debbie said, "He's gone crazy, Jerry. We got to help Mr. Fortune."

Jerry shook his head. "He's gonna be okay, you know? It's all some kind o' mistake. He's our son, Deb. The only son we got now."

I saw a flicker deep inside Debbie Carter's eyes. A moment of sudden reality. It was her son. She blinked at her husband, began to play with her gold necklace.

"Roy made a phone call."

The voice came from the stairs. I realized that the rock music had stopped on the second floor. Debbie Junior came down the stairs, accusing eyes fixed toward her father. Eyes that held a long-standing grievance, an ancient conflict within the family.

"He didn't even talk to Mom or us. He wasn't gonna say good-bye to us. Didn't think about us, that we was maybe even in the house. He forgot me an' Mel got phones up in our rooms."

I said, "You heard where he was going?"

"Deb—" Jerry said.

She ignored him. Her blue eyes looked only at me, her blonde head high, as tall as a short woman could stand, like a witness righting some great wrong. "He was talkin' to that guy out in Berkeley was a friend of Eller's. Gary somethin'. Said he was goin' out to Santa Barbara to find some guy named Hoan."

"Fortune—" Jerry said.

I went to the telephone. If there weren't mistakes we'd never catch anyone. It's the unconscious that does it, habits and reflexes. A middle-class boy has to say good-bye. He doesn't think about who will hear a telephone call from his own house.

"He says the guy's a monster," Jerry said. "Uses our bucks to murder his own people, sells drugs—"

Captain Pearce had gone for the day. If I was going to get the redeye to the Coast, I didn't have much time. I told the night sergeant on duty about Hoan and Santa Barbara, told him to get to Pearce and tell him to contact the police out there. Then I called Kay Michaels in Los Angeles. She wasn't there. I left a message on her answering machine: I would be out on the redeye flight from Kennedy to LAX.

In the small, bright living room of the house in Pine Dunes Jerry Carter still talked to protect his son, even if he didn't know what he was protecting him from, but sensed now that something dark and heavy hung over Roy.

". . . he says the guy got Jeanne-Marie killed, sells refugee kids to . . ."

I said to Debbie Junior, "Who's this Gary? Where does he live in Berkeley?"

She'd had her moment, her revenge on her arrogant brother, and now she watched her father uneasily as if some sense of reality had reached her too. This was real. She chewed on her lip. It was her mother who answered.

"Gary Winters. He was in Vietnam with Eller. Him an' Roy talked a lot on the phone. That's all we know."

She stood and looked down at her husband. She wasn't sure anymore, but her rules told her she should tell me. Jerry Carter sat and looked up at her. Debbie Junior looked at both of them—she was scared now.

"I'll stay here awhile, Dan," Judy Lavelle said.

I gave Judy my gun, they don't like a private detective to carry a gun in Los Angeles. Out in the night the tall daughter, Melanie, leaned against my rented car. Her Irish skin was pale, her dark hair black. She clutched something to her.

"Eller had a scrapbook, you know? Sent it to Roy from over there. Roy was always lookin' at it, puttin' new stuff in it. Crazy kind of junk from newspapers an' magazines and all that never made no sense to me. Roy burned it 'fore he went up to the city after Jeanne-Marie, only I'd swiped a couple pages before."

She thrust two sheets of heavy paper at me and vanished into the night back toward the small, neat house with its bright windows pouring light out into the darkness. She wasn't going to be upstaged by her younger sister. I got into the rented car, turned on the top light, and read the two pages of Eller Carter's scrapbook.

38

The first clipping from Parade, *was under the photos of five smiling Oriental gentlemen of various ages. It was dated November 26, 1972.*

Failure of a Mission

Why did the U.S. go to war in Vietnam?

For exactly, we are told, the same reasons we previously went to war in Korea—to afford Asian people the right to self-determination, to permit them to choose their own form of government.

As of last month, South Vietnam was under martial law, ruled by Gen. Nguyen Van Thieu. South Korea was under martial law, ruled by Gen. Park Chung Hee. Cambodia was under martial law, ruled by Gen. Lon Nol. The Philippines was under martial law, ruled by Ferdinand Marcos. Thailand was a military dictatorship under Field Marshal Thanom Kittakachorn.

Self-determination?

The second was only pieces of an article, without newspaper or date:

East German Jan Hoffman Edges Cousins for World Skating Title

DORTMUND, West Germany, (AP)—Jan Hoffman of East Germany and Britain's Robin Cousins have ended their figure skating rivalry after dividing the World and Olympic titles.

The next objectives of both super skaters are very different and reflect the difference in the sports systems under which they rose to the top.

Hoffman is heading back to Karl Marx Stadt to study medicine and become part of East Germany's athletics machine as a sports physician.

Cousins, however, is planning to reap financial rewards from his long years of expensive training under coach Carlo Fassi in Denver ... is expecting to join a touring ice show.

American Charles Ticknor, finishing third in both competitions, is also weighing professional ice show offers.

The third was from the Los Angeles Times.

Guard Gets 30 Days in Beating Death

LOS ANGELES, *Special to the Times*—A Pioneer Market security guard who pleaded no contest to involuntary manslaughter in the August 1981 beating death of a man was sentenced to 30 days in the county jail's work-furlough program on Friday.

The guard, Louis Sandidge, 52, who was also placed on three years' probation, pleaded no contest in the death of Roberto Chavez, a 34-year-old city maintenance worker. Sandidge was sentenced by Los Angeles Superior Court Judge David Aisenson.

Chavez had been drinking on the market's premises, and part of Sandidge's job was to keep drinkers away. Witnesses testified that Chavez offered no physical resistance but that Sandidge struck Chavez up to eleven times with a baton before chasing him from the lot.

Chavez was later found dead a block away. An autopsy found that he died of internal bleeding from blunt trauma to his abdomen.

The deputy district attorney who prosecuted the case said that the sentence was just. "There was no intent to kill."

The fourth was complete but unidentified:

Nixon, Ford Benefits Cost U.S. $500,000

WASHINGTON (AP)—It is costing American taxpayers more than half a million dollars a year to support former Presidents Richard M. Nixon and Gerald R. Ford with pensions, personal staffs and office expenses.

Nixon last year spent $163,329 in federal funds above his $85,000 pension, including the cost of five color television sets and repairs to his electric golf cart. His eight-member staff received salaries totaling $95,658 in 1978.

Ford received $106,000 in presidential and congressional pension benefits and spent an additional $291,685 in federal funds last year. Ford's expenses included $2,242 for plants in his personal office, plus $100 a month for a professional service to water them.

Both ex-presidents are asking for small increases in the next fiscal year.

I thought about the scrapbook all the way to Los Angeles. About Roy Carter's two years of wandering around the world, his anger at the world, of what he had told Jerry Carter. I was beginning to see a new picture. A picture I didn't like, that scared the hell out of me.

Kay was at LAX waiting for me. The almost-green eyes and easy smile on the tall, slim body. The dark hair and gaunt face.

"Trouble?" Her voice had that same deep, quiet quality, usually half-amused by everything. She wasn't amused tonight.

"Enough," I said. We held each other. Three thousand miles is too far. "I need some dinner and a drink."

I was tired but keyed up too, I hadn't seen Kay in almost a month, when she'd last been in New York. It wasn't midnight yet in Los Angeles. We had a favorite restaurant, La Farandole, in North Hollywood. It's Basque, the table cloths are made from peasant coverings, white with red and green stripes, and they have good beers. On the drive I told her about Roy Carter and the unknown Hoan.

"You did all you could," Kay said. She thought of me, not of Roy or Hoan.

"I'll drive up as soon as we eat, get a couple of hours' sleep."

"You didn't come three thousand miles to sleep," Kay smiled. "Tomorrow early I'll drive you up. You can rest on the way."

In La Farandole the owner, Sebastian, greeted us with hugs, insisted we have the *cassoulet basque* special and apologized for being out of Sierra Nevada Ale.

"I am sorry, Dan. A Beck's?"

"Beck's," I said.

That settled, Kay asked, "You don't think this Roy Carter is involved in drugs, Dan?"

The good beer was cool, with a bite. "I think he took the heroin to trade, and I don't think it's only a vendetta against Jeanne-Marie Johnson's killers."

"Did he murder the girl?"

"I don't know. I do know it's all got a lot to do with his dead brother and Vietnam."

We had one more beer and the *cassoulet*.

"The way Roy Carter talks," I said, "sounds like someone who wants to change the world. A leftover from the sixties."

"Maybe we've all forgotten too soon what we learned in the sixties, Dan. Not much has changed."

"Not much," I said. "Only us, our hopes. The sixties' ideas were too hard to live with."

"Let's go," I said, before dessert or even coffee.

We ate, had another Beck's. It's a superior beer no matter how many millions drink Miller or Bud. That's what advertising is all about. The intense advertising that sells beer or beliefs. Most of us like what we're told we should like. The supreme falsehood is that people know what they want. The truth is the few know what they want, convince the many to help them get it.

We left before dessert or even coffee. I was anxious to get to Santa Barbara, but I wanted Kay too. We went home to her ground-floor apartment in a narrow three-story building in the Hollywood Hills.

Afterward, I tried to sleep, but couldn't.

"Dan? Let's go now. We can be there by five."

Ten minutes later we were driving north to Santa Barbara in the small hours of morning.

39

The two small people in their sixties walked hand in hand along the secluded rural lane bordered by tall, ragged eucalyptus and gnarled old live oaks. They strolled easily, inhaled the pungent odor of the eucalyptus. Both wore starched white linen trousers, white cotton overshirts open at the collars. The man's sandals were a gold color, reflecting the last sun of evening. The woman's were plain leather.

A ritual evening walk, something they had done for many years, casual but not frivolous. The kind of ritual that maintained a unity. Substantial people not given to whim or impulse, they stepped firmly along the quiet road between its high walls and hedges of hibiscus and bougainvillea, trumpet vine and oleander. Between the big houses and stately palms, the Italianate fountains in glimpsed courtyards, the massive roofs above the sea of greenery and flowers. From time to time the man spoke, pointed to birds, nodded to certain flowers, indicated trees as if gently instructing the woman.

She was slender and deferential, walked a small half step behind so that the man could see her yet still have a clear view right and left. Her body was slim yet womanly, and her gray-black hair was coiled into a tight bun in back. She wore no jewelry beyond her wedding ring and a gold cross at her throat. She said nothing as they strolled, listened to the man, looked when he pointed.

The man was short rather than small. A thick torso, fleshy hands and heavy thighs under the starched white pants. White-haired, with an almost stately stroll. Hooded eyes and a broad nose, brown-yellow skin, the face of Southeast Asia. A full-lipped mouth that could have been a woman's, the short legs slightly bowed, his torso longer than his legs. He spoke to the woman in French. To the silent young man who walked behind them he spoke in Vietnamese.

The young man carried an Uzi submachinegun cradled in his right arm, his finger on the trigger, the gun almost hidden by a sport jacket. His eyes looked everywhere in slow sweeps. When an occasional car passed on the quiet lane, the Uzi slipped easily out of sight under the jacket, reemerged as the car vanished and the bodyguard continued his watchful walk behind the couple. Alert, and yet somehow not. Watching by rote, lulled by routine. Looked, but didn't quite see. Glanced at his wristwatch as the stroll neared its end.

A white Rolls-Royce stood in front of the enormous Spanish Mediterranean house where two more young Vietnamese men waited for the strolling couple. The work of a famous architect, the mansion was a local landmark lived in by old families and millionaires and, once, a notorious Hollywood star detested by the local gentry. It stood almost directly on the back road, its massive doors facing only a narrow parking area, its windows barred, a high wall enclosing its grounds.

One of the young men in the open doorway spoke to the approaching couple in Vietnamese, "Someone out back."

"Delivery truck," said the second.

The man in white nodded.

"Check it," the first young man said.

The second young man went into the house.

The white-suited couple chatted softly as they stood beside the white Rolls-Royce. The young Vietnamese guard returned.

"Jurgensen's. Cao is watching him."

The white-haired man led the woman into the mansion. He looked at his watch, spoke in French to the woman and went up a broad, sweeping staircase to the second floor. The woman went into the kitchen, observed the white-jacketed delivery man, who smiled as he carried a case of beer. She left the kitchen and sat down in a small side room in front of a television set, leaned her head back and closed her eyes.

The large house became silent. The guard who had strolled with the couple went to his small third-floor room and made a telephone call. It was to his girlfriend, he spoke for a long time arranging the night ahead. The *other two young men sat in the main hall where they could watch the front door while they drank Vietnamese beer. The man out at the pool watched the mountains and the lush greenery and read a book in the warm afternoon. The man at the gate dozed.*

After about ten minutes the woman got up and went up the wide stairs.

The white-jacketed delivery man left the house carrying a case of beer, returned for a second case, then drove off. The guard at the pool watched the van until it was out of sight, then went back to his book. The delivery van drove out the rear gate where the gate guard dozed. About six-thirty the cook and maid came down from their rooms to prepare dinner. At eight, when their dinner was ready, neither Monsieur nor Madame came down. They had not come down by nine. At ten, the cook and maid spoke to the oldest of the five young men, Cao Dong Van. Cao discussed the matter with the others, deciding not to disturb Monsieur and Madame. They had remained in their rooms without dinner before.

It was just after midnight when the deputy sheriff knocked on the mansion door and asked if Mr. Hoan was all right. Cao and the other young men were cautious. Why was the deputy concerned for Monsieur? The deputy explained that the New York police had warned them about some kid who might be on his way out to cause trouble for Mr. Hoan. Cao asked the deputy to wait, went with the others to Monsieur's room. They knocked nervously. Monsieur did not like to be disturbed. They knocked again, and again. Alarmed, they opened the bedroom door. They found the bodies lying under the covers in Monsieur's bed, their faces turned toward the wall. Both had been shot at close range with a .22 caliber pistol.

Later the young men found two cases of beer missing. That was all. Truong Duc Hoan, his wife and two cases of Vietnamese beer.

=40=

"I'M NOT SURE THOSE half-assed guards know what happened yet," the Santa Barbara sheriff said. "I'm not sure I do. What was Mr. Hoan doing with armed guards? I never saw any armed guards out there. What kind of nut is this kid your Captain Pearce warned us about anyway? Christ, I wish you'd all called a day earlier. Just one damned day."

The dawn was just breaking outside the bay window of the sheriff's office. The sheriff looked like a man who'd been up for hours and wasn't used to it. I told him what kind of nut Roy Carter was, and what Truong Duc Hoan had been. I told him I was sorry we'd been late with our warning, and I pointed out we didn't know for sure Roy Carter had been the killer of Truong Duc Hoan and his wife any more than he did.

"Prostitution?" the sheriff asked.

He seemed more stunned by Truong Duc Hoan's business than by his murder.

"Drugs and probably smuggling too. You didn't have any suspicions about Hoan? Nothing strange ever happened around that mansion?"

Gray-haired, in a rumpled charcoal-gray tropical worsted suit, the sheriff sat and studied me as if trying to understand what my angle was, what I was up to. He looked at Kay as if the answer to what I might be up to lay with her. She smiled reassuringly. I sat across the desk and waited while he thought.

He spoke slowly, carefully. "I'm not sure I'd have any suspicions now except the way they were shot. What you tell me is talk, hearsay. I'd need more than that most of the time. But killed like that? Silenced twenty-two caliber gun, three shots in the head for him, two in the chest for her. An assassin's M.O., terrorists. Planned. No sound, not even seen. Those two-bit guards saw one delivery man, but there had to be two. My assistant coroner says they were shot as early as five-thirty last night. They might not even have been shot in the bed. Some blood on the carpet near the bed and the door."

"No one saw or heard anything?"

He shook his head. "The delivery truck was stolen from Jurgensen's, but the driver never saw who jumped him and tied him up, and none of those guards took any kind of a real look. The man on the gate said the driver was a Latino sitting down and wearing a white hat so he couldn't give any height or hair color. The man at the pool says the same. But there had to be two of them, because everyone says the deliveryman never left the kitchen or pantry. That's why they suspected nothing. The deliveryman was downstairs the whole time where he could be seen, while the real killer was upstairs." He shook his head at the stupidity of Truong Duc Hoan's Vietnamese guards. "Tell me more about those two hired killers you say are after your Roy Carter."

I described Wilmer and Ernie. "They wouldn't have had anything to do with killing Hoan. My guess is they were working for Hoan. Out to get the heroin back, maybe to stop Carter before he caused Hoan any trouble."

"Why wouldn't Mr. Hoan have used his own men, if he was the gangster you say he was?"

"I think he relied on anonymity, a low profile, his personal guards. Hired any killers he needed, used middlemen so nothing could be traced back to him. In New York they think he murdered a competitor just last week, using hired hands."

The sheriff didn't like being given conclusions by a detective from New York, especially a private detective. "I'll look around for those two anyway, just in case." He looked out his window. "It's hard to figure. Mr. Hoan, I mean. Came here about ten years ago, maybe eleven. Bought the Old Harris place and showed up in that white Rolls. Didn't change a thing out there, kept to himself. They appreciate that in Montecito. A good neighbor, minded his own business. Took those walks with his wife every evening. Most people figured he was retired. Sometimes he seemed to be away for a week or so at a time, and sometimes he had some visitors. Not a lot, never more than one extra car out front there. Never heard any wild parties or anything like that. No trouble at all. Those young fellows never acted like guards. We thought they were houseboys and gate guards like a lot of places out there have."

"There's trouble now," I said. "Any idea where the killer is, what happened to the truck?"

"We found the truck right back at Jurgensen's where they stole it from. We're working on it for leads. Looks maybe like the FBI's interested, an important Vietnamese and all."

"But no leads to the killer?"

"Not so far," the sheriff admitted reluctantly. "But he's got to be crazy. I mean, what kind of nut kills a guy and takes the time to steal two lousy cases of beer? If they were thirsty, they could have gotten beer anywhere. They weren't any empties in the truck when we found it. They've still got the beer with them, and it doesn't look like they're drinking it. What are they saving it for, a party?"

"Vietnamese beer?"

The sheriff nodded. "Mr. Hoan had Jurgensen's import it special. They imported a lot of special items for Hoan, always out there delivering. That's why the truck got in so easily."

"You have any reason to think they're still around here, Sheriff? In the county?"

"We don't know they're not."

"Yeah," I said. "Okay if we go?"

The sheriff considered the question—and me. I knew more than he did about a murder in his county, maybe an international gang assassination, and he didn't like that. He didn't like that I knew one of his rich citizens had lived on prostitution and narcotics. But he didn't see what he could do about it or how I could be of use to him.

"Okay, I guess. Leave an address where we can get you if we need you. You want us to let you know when we get them?"

"Sure," I said. He wasn't going to get this killer, Roy Carter or anyone else, but I didn't tell him that.

Outside, the morning sun was just coming up in the east in a high and clear blue sky, the hills and fields brown as if it were summer. We walked to Kay's car.

"Did Roy Carter kill him, Dan?"

"It sounds like it. I hope not, but it'd be a hell of a coincidence if he didn't."

"The other one with him," she said, "could it have been that woman?"

"Anne Woollard? No, Hoan was killed early last night. Anne Woollard was in New York."

"Then who, Dan?"

"I don't know," I said, but I was beginning to get an idea. An idea I didn't much like, but one that made sense, explained a lot that had happened.

"Where do we go now?"

"To the airport. You drop me there on your way to L.A."

"I want to go with you."

"Life is unfair."

"I knew that already. You're going after Carter?"

"I think I know where they are."

"Do you have to go, Dan? Can't you send the police? Tell them what you know and let them go?"

"I'm working for Jerry Carter, Kay. He hired me to protect Roy as much as anything. I don't know what Roy Carter's done. Maybe nothing. I have to know what happened before I go to the police. I owe my client that much. Both clients."

She nodded in the sun, her dark hair like a hood over her high cheekbones. I imagined her dark hair on the pillow. Maybe it was guilt.

"That Judy Lavelle girl? You like her, don't you?"

"I like her. She's just starting out the hard way."

"When will you be back in L.A.?"

"As soon as I can."

"Be careful, Dan."

"Always."

We got into the car and drove to the airport. There was only a commuter plane to San Francisco before afternoon. I took it. I already could be too late.

41

ON THE RIDE TO Berkeley the water of the broad inland bay lay to the right until we passed Candlestick Park on its peninsula, drove on through San Francisco and out over the Bay Bridge. To the left, toward the distant open sea, the great bay was white and choppy all the way to the orange-red Golden Gate Bridge.

Across the long bridge, where Seventeen joins Eighty, the highway skirts the bay at water level and the whitecaps broke the surface on the wind, spumed over rocks far out, lapped at the shore. The airport bus got off on University. The Berkeley House Motor Hotel was only a few blocks up toward the hills of the campus.

I checked in and went straight to the telephone book. In it I found that Gary Winters lived at 24 Nolan Court. The man at the motel desk said it was around the hundred block of Hillegass. Hillegass was all the way up the campus hill across Telegraph, facing People's Park. The numbers here were 2500. It meant that the address I had was far over toward Oakland, probably in Oakland. I called a taxi.

Twenty-four Nolan Court turned out to be a gray frame house of three stories with a smaller cottage behind. An overgrown yard of brown grass, a cracked concrete driveway that led to no garage and three mailboxes on the porch to show that it was divided into three apartments. The bottom mailbox indicated that Gary Winters had the first-floor apartment. I rang and heard no bell. I knocked and got no answer. I tried the door and went in.

A shadow moved from behind the door. I turned with my lone fist ready, seemed to run into a wall, landed on my right shoulder in a green and red haze. I fought off the haze, saw two legs in brown slacks and shoes. A gun held toward the floor. I didn't try to get up, lay there on some kind of dusty carpet and silently tested my shoulder and arm to be sure I still had one. I did.

"Who are you?"

"Dan Fortune."

"From where?"

"New York."

"Why?"

"To talk to Gary Winters."

"Talk about what?"

"A case I'm working on."

"Case?"

I heard a hesitation. He was police.

"Private investigator," I said.

"Show me."

I held up my wallet. He took it. I tested my arm again. The shoulder was bruised, nothing more. My jaw was sore where he'd hit. I didn't touch that. Tough. He gave me my wallet.

"What happened to Winters?" I said.

He sat down in one of those high, circular-backed wicker armchairs they make in Indonesia or the Phillipines that look like the thrones of jungle pirates. One of the chair arms was smashed, and I saw that the whole room was a wreck. Furniture overturned and broken. Framed photos, beer bottles, figurines, vases, flower pots littered the floor. Windows were shattered and two mirrors broken. Blood on the rug near me

"Sorry about the muscle, but you came in uninvited."

He didn't put his gun away, just rested it on his lap. He wore a neat brown tweed sport jacket with his slim brown slacks. He nodded that I could sit up.

"We figured it was just another of Winters' flashbacks from Nam," he said. "What's your case, Fortune?"

"I'm tailing the younger brother of a friend of Winters' who was killed in Nam. His family hired me. The kid's involved in a killing in New York that was probably self-defense, but he won't come in."

"What's he doing in Oakland or Berkeley?"

"I'm not sure he is in Oakland or Berkeley."

"He got a name?"

"Roy Carter."

He thought it over, put his gun away on his hip, motioned for me to take one of the battered chairs. "Winters' landlady called us as usual. We found him on the floor, shot in the arm, the place busted up again. He gets these flashbacks, thinks he's in Nam, shoots the place up if he has a gun, busts it up if he don't. Once he got hold of an M-16 and shot two clips into the walls and furniture, was out in the yard skirmishing when we got to him. The judge put him inside awhile for that, but most of the time he's as normal as any of the street people around here."

"What did he say about this time? Lieutenant—?"

"Morgan." He lit a cigarette, gave me one, went on watching me. He wasn't that sure of me yet. "Two guys came and tried to push him around last night. Asked him a lot of questions about people he says he doesn't even know. He told them to get lost, they pulled guns and got nasty. He broke the arm of one, took the gun away from the other and threw them out. Got shot in the arm doing it. When we arrived he was alone on the floor so we figured he'd had another flashback."

"Did he describe the two?"

"A scrawny black guy and a fat Caucasian slob."

Wilmer and Ernie. I looked around the battered room. The broken and littered framed photos, like those in Roy Carter's room in Pine Dunes, were all of Vietnam: soldiers and Saigon streets. The figurines and mementos were all from Southeast Asia, the beer bottles had held Vietnamese beers.

"Can I talk to Winters?" I asked.

"Sure. We're just holding him in the hospital for his own protection. I'll drive you."

At the hospital, Gary Winters was seated in a wheelchair in an eight-bed ward with a uniformed cop guarding the door. He was a big man with wide shoulders and thick chest bursting out of a brightly colored vest from somewhere in Southeast Asia, massive upper arms protruding from an army camouflage fatigue shirt. One of the arms was in a sling and heavily bandaged. Below he wore ancient Army wool OD pants from World War II.

"Fortune here's a private from New York wants to talk to you," Lieutenant Morgan told him. "He says your story's even true this time, so you're loose if the docs say okay."

Winters looked at my empty sleeve. Then he looked up at my face. His eyes were neither friendly nor unfriendly.

"Talk about what?" He had a rough voice, thick and heavy and low. As if he didn't use the voice much.

"The two who attacked you," I said.

He looked at my arm again, at Lieutenant Morgan and at a doctor who walked up with his white coat flapping open over a trim, three-button suit.

"Can I roll out of here, Doc?"

The doctor shrugged. "You've been shot worse before. Follow the usual procedures, check in with me in three days."

"So we talk," Winters said to me. "Only first a bite an' a beer, right? Can't talk good with a dry throat and a empty gut."

The doctor gathered his white coat around him, spoke to an orderly and walked away looking at his watch.

Lieutenant Morgan said, "I can drive both of you back to Winters' place. I'll look around more for some evidence on those two. On the way Fortune can fill in what he didn't tell me."

The orderly asked Winters if he had any flowers, cards or candy he wanted to take.

"Shit," Winters said.

The orderly unlocked the wheelchair and pushed it out and along the broad hose-washed corridor toward the elevators. Morgan went off to get his car. I followed the orderly and Winters. The massive man seemed to enjoy the wheelchair ride, directing the orderly with sweeping waves of his good arm. On the street floor we went out the front door where Lieutenant Morgan waited beside his car.

"You take the back, Fortune."

The orderly locked the wheelchair. He and Morgan stood on either side as Winters raised himself out of the chair with his one good arm, held him as he let go and gripped the top of the car door and swung his whole body, the legs limp and useless, into the front seat. Then they folded the wheelchair and put it into the back seat beside me.

It explained why he had looked at my empty sleeve. It explained the massive arms and shoulders. He'd been building them since Vietnam, must have surprised the hell out of Wilmer and Ernie. They'd have figured a cripple was a pushover.

"Brought it home from Nam?" I said.

"All the way. The big one for you?"

"Juvenile delinquent."

"One mistake or another," he said.

Morgan drove, "Tell me all of it, Fortune."

I left out Truong Duc Hoan. I didn't want complications for Winters, and I didn't have the answers yet on Hoan. Winters and Morgan both listened and said nothing until we were near his apartment.

"Hey, Morgan. You come this far, how about you ride us on to Cruchon's? I always like to chow at Cruchon's."

"French?" I said. "How much is this going to cost me?"

"Not too bad," Lieutenant Morgan said. "A nice lunch place up by campus, cheap to a New Yorker. Okay, Winters, I'll look your place over alone. But you get your own way back."

Morgan was a decent cop and a decent man. For most, cops or men, Winters would be nothing but a lot of trouble. But Morgan drove us all the way back to the campus, dropped us in front of an open restaurant with a large redwood deck on Channing Way just off Telegraph. We steadied Winters as he lifted himself by the top of the door and one powerful arm into the wheelchair. He took the hospital sling off his arm, threw it away and rolled along the side path that led to the entrance of Cruchon's. Morgan held me back.

"I was in Nam too," the lieutenant said. "I believed in it. I believe in this country and what I do. But he paid his dues, and maybe I don't like what he brought back inside him but I understand how it got there. I think I'm right, but I can't tell him he's wrong. He can be dangerous. To you and himself. So be easy and be careful."

He got back into his car, drove off. I followed Winters into Cruchon's. The side door led up some steps into a high room of pale wood walls with a fireplace and doors that opened onto the redwood deck. Someone had already lifted Winters up the steps, he was out on the deck in his wheelchair, a bottle of Tsingtao Chinese beer half-empty. The waiter watched him.

"I'll have one, too," I said.

"Not bad beer," Winters said. "I like Vietnamese brew. The food too. Got used to it over there. A lot of their restaurants now in San Francisco, a big colony from Nam. Fine, tough, nice people. Friendly even after all we done to 'em."

I waited until he had finished his second Tsingtao and half his avocado and bacon omelet before I made him work.

"Tell me about the two gunmen."

He laughed. "They come looking for Roy Carter too, tried to push me around. I got mad, broke the fat one's arm, threw the brother out the door, got winged. Landlady called the police before we even started scuffling, fuzz got there fast enough to scare them away before they could regroup on me."

"Was Roy here?"

He finished his beer. "Nope."

"You were close to Eller in Vietnam?"

"Close enough."

"Was Eller mixed up in something over there, Gary? Drugs, smuggling, prostitution?"

"No."

"What did happen to him over there?"

"He got married."

He waved for a third Tsingtao, finished his ome-lette. He was evading. I needed to reach him.

"A man named Truong Duc Hoan and his wife were killed in Santa Barbara. I think Roy killed them, Gary. Roy talked to you from New York, told you he was going to Santa Barbara. What else did he tell you? Why was Hoan so important to him? What do you know about Truong Duc Hoan?"

He drank his beer. "Just that he was a slime, and Eller's father-in-law."

42

GARY WINTERS SAID, "TROUNG'S old man was a big landowner in one of them French-loving families up in the north in Hanoi. After Dien Bien Phu and the French pullout in fifty-three, old man Hoan had a lot of trouble with the new guys of Uncle Ho. While Ho and his boys was figuring out what to do with old man Hoan, Truong piled up all the cash the old man could give him and ran for the south. He made it to Saigon okay and set up his own business with Daddy's dough. The idea was to get the business going and bribe Daddy out. Then the North/South war started up, us Yanks came and it got awful hard to deal with the North. Daddy got lost in the shuffle and finally died still up in Hanoi, digging on a road gang with other unreconstructed capitalists."

A ragged street person wandered past below the deck where the well-dressed patrons were eating salads and omelets and other lunch delicacies. Winters waved to him, raised his beer.

"Dinh, that was Eller's wife, Dinh Bich Hoan, figured Truong was afraid the old man would want his money back if he came south so didn't try all that hard to get the old man out, and Truong liked being boss man and wasn't doing that good anyway. He'd taken on a high-profit business, but risky, and with the war heating up it went to hell. So he looked around for something profitable, spotted all us Americans coming over, opened up a string of joy houses for the boys."

He finished his beer. I waved for another. Two students in wheelchairs motored along Channing below the deck, one operating her chair with her mouth, the other with his forehead. Winters watched them, and then his beer as it came across the deck.

"Truong used his wife, sisters and daughters in the houses when he started up, Dinh told me and Eller. Dinh wouldn't touch it, stayed on up in Hanoi with the grandfather, got close to the Viet Minh. When she did come down and back to the family, they didn't really trust her too good in the south and that included her father. But no one did anything to her because Truong was the biggest white slaver in South Nam and carried a lot of weight with the ARVN and the Americans. He had a white Rolls-Royce and an old French colonial mansion and even cut all the red tape to get Eller and Dinh married. He wanted that marriage. Marrying a Yank took the Cong label off Dinh."

"She was a Communist, Eller's wife?"

Winters sucked the beer. "Let's say she hated the Saigon governments, all of them, and had friends up north."

"And Eller?"

"He married her. I'd of married her if he hadn't. She was a hell of a girl. He liked her, and he liked her ideas. We'd learned a lot over there. I mean, I never knew what the hell the kids here in Berkeley was fighting for before I went over. When I got back I lived two years out in People's Park and thanked those kids every day for saving it for me."

"She's still in Vietnam? Eller's wife?"

He nodded. "Truong got out with his money and his family, set up business over here. Dinh stayed, and so did Eller."

"What really happened to Eller?"

He emptied the beer. "No one knows for sure, except maybe Dinh. I guess she planned to stay on all the way even after the North came down, and Eller would of stayed with her. Maybe he was gonna desert and got shot by our guys, or maybe he was too American and got shot by the Cong, or maybe he was just in the wrong place at the wrong time them last days. Whatever, he died and Dinh's still there."

He turned the empty Tsingtao bottle in his big hands. He didn't seem to be thinking about another beer this time.

"Roy knows all this?"

He shrugged. "He knows."

"And then Hoan got Jeanne-Marie killed too."

He set the brown bottle on the table, went on touching it, stroking the surface. "I wouldn't know, Mister. Roy wasn't here. I don't know what he's doing."

"Then how come you lied to the police, told them you didn't know the people the two gunmen were asking you about?"

"I always lie to the police."

He was lying to me too, but I didn't have the muscle to make him admit it. I didn't think I was going to need his help to find Roy Carter anyway.

"You hated Hoan too, didn't you, Gary? Eller and Dinh hated him for what he did, what he was."

He turned the brown bottle around and around, but he said nothing. The interview was over. I waved to the waiter. He hurried over with the bill, not quite trusting me either. I paid it.

"You want me to take you home?"

"Push me along Telegraph."

Two waiters helped me lift him down the steps. I pushed him down to Telegraph as far as a grocery store where he went in and bought a bagful of groceries and two six-packs of Chinese beer. He let me pay. On the street again he let me push him up the hill to People's Park. Street people seated in an open clearing among the litter and scraggly trees greeted him. He distributed the beer and food.

"My friends thank you, and I thank you. I'll stay here awhile. Look me up any time you're in town."

I left them seated on the ground in the scruffy rectangle of grass and trees that had cost so much anguish so many years ago. Before I was out of sight, I stopped. Gary Winters was staring after me, looked away quickly.

I walked back down to Telegraph. It was getting dark. Winters expected me to stake him out, tail him. He wanted me to do that. I called another taxi, gave the driver the number of the house on the edge of Oakland where Winters lived.

43

THE WEATHERED GRAY PAINT of the big frame house glowed white in the dusk. I stayed in the twilight shadows, moved in as silently as I could. The upper floors were dark, the only light was in Gary Winters' ground floor apartment. The smaller house behind was totally dark and looked empty. There were no cars on the dead-end street, none in the driveway.

With Gary Winters back in People's Park, who was in his apartment? It could be Lieutenant Morgan waiting for Winters to return, but I didn't think so. I was pretty sure who it would be. The certainty that had brought me from Santa Barbara to Gary Winters.

City streets don't make you light on your feet, but I got to the house without making too much noise or seeing anyone. Low at the right-hand corner of the window, I looked in. The light was on, but no one was in the room. The floor was still littered, the furniture still the wreck it had been earlier. Nothing was changed. Then why was the light on? Who had turned ... I heard the step behind me.

"Told him you figures it out sooner or later."

I turned. The Chief stood in the narrow path of light from the ground-floor window. In eagle feather and war paint, the fringed shirt and Apache moccasins.

"Roy Carter was always a step ahead of me, wasn't he?" I said. "You knew about Judy·Lavelle being at my place. He found Hally Balada right after we talked to her. You had to be watching me and close to Roy Carter, both."

"I knowed you make me sometime."

"You took him to Hally Balada. Did you finger her, Chief?"

"That ain't us, Dan. Hoan's troops."

Roy Carter appeared behind him in the dusk, the last light almost gone. He had his Ingram in his hands.

"He made Winters, like I said he does." The Chief said to Carter. "He got to Santa Barbara, spotted that there Nam beer. If he know 'bout Winters, he got to know what we do with two cases Vietnam beer." He grinned at me. "We was watchin', saw you an' the cop. He come back alone, but I figures you be along."

Roy Carter had said nothing. A shadow in the half light in his voluminous black jacket, the camouflage fatigue pants, the paratrooper boots.

"The pad out back," the Chief said to me.

I could yell, but who would hear? I didn't think it would help, and it could hurt. I walked behind the Chief and ahead of Roy Carter. A weed-grown path led to the cottage at the rear. Painted the same gray color as the house, it shone under a ragged sycamore. Inside, it was small and dim. The usual secondhand rental furniture and a bare floor, a single lamp that turned on at the door. The Chief motioned me to a lopsided armchair. I sat. Roy Carter went into another room. The Chief sat facing me on a matching armchair that leaned the opposite way. He had a gun. A German P-38 from World War II.

"What's the rest of the heroin for?" I said. "Your pay?"

"This one goes down for free, Dan."

In the feeble light, with the Chief's feather and fringe and war paint, I could have been back a hundred years out on the plains in the flickering shadows of a campfire, hoping for the cavalry. But there would be no cavalry. Not even the police.

"Gunning down people?" I said. "That's what you do now, Chief? Innocent people. Cold-blooded killing? That's it?"

Roy Carter came back from the other room. He held two bottles of beer. Coors. The Vietnamese beer was for Gary Winters. The Ingram swung loose from his neck like a talisman.

"Is that what they told you in Santa Barbara, Mr. Fortune. What the police in New York told you?"

"What do you tell me?"

He handed me one of the beers, gave the other to the Chief. He sat down, watched me as impassively as any Indian warrior in that firelight on the plains a century ago. Young but not as young as he had been. The thin, boyish face not quite as boyish, the full mouth harder and tighter, the toneless voice darker and slower and heavier . . .

. . . *They arrive in Santa Barbara three days ago. Roy asks the innocent little questions of a youthful tourist. He finds the Spanish-style mansion with the white Rolls-Royce parked on the narrow strip of macadam in front. He learns about the evening stroll, sees the delivery van come and go through the service entrance where there is a single guard who sits on a folding chair and whose weapon, if he has a weapon, is not in sight. There is another man behind the big house near the pool, three more scattered around. Housemen more than guards. Truong Duc Hoan is a businessman not a gangster, does not want* to be conspicuous, offend the neighbors. He hires killers when he needs them, keeps his anonymity, is apparently unaware of any immediate danger.

Roy sees Truong Duc Hoan and his wife start out on their evening walk. He and the Chief steal the delivery van, tie up and stash the driver. The Chief, minus feather, fringe and warpaint, and dressed in the Jurgensen's white jacket and hat, drives. Roy is in back with the groceries under a plastic tarpaulin. It is after five, and the man at the service entrance is tired and bored. The gate guard doesn't want to get out of his chair, but he does and is a little surprised to see a driver he doesn't know. The Chief puts on his Chicano act, explains that he has worked at the store for some time but has just started driving, names the driver who he says has quit, explains that part of Mr. Hoan's order just came. Roy knows that all Mexicans probably look alike to the Vietnamese gate guard, that the man's English is likely to be poor, that he has had a long, dull day. Roy is prepared to kill the guard if he has to, but it would increase the risk and he hopes he doesn't have to. The man waves the van in, goes back to his chair, dozes.

At the pool behind the mansion the second man lounges on a chaise. The man at the pool looks idly toward the van. It's been ten years since they all came to Montecito, no one has had to use or even draw his gun in all that time. When only a dark Chicano in a Jurgensen's white jacket and hat gets out, the man at the pool doesn't even get up. The Chief goes inside into the cool pantry of the old house. He listens for the sounds of the other housemen/guards. He knows one is with Hoan and his wife on their walk, and now he hears the remaining two open the front door and speak to Hoan. He hurries back to the delivery van.

For an instant the entire house is empty. Roy slips out of the van, into the pantry, and up the back stairs of the old mansion. Built in the days of many servants, these old mansions always have back stairs. On the second floor Roy easily locates the main bedroom where a French-educated Vietnamese gentleman of Truong Duc Hoan's age should sleep alone. There is a four-poster double bed with a canopy like mosquito netting. Delicate French provincial furniture and some white wicker for hot climates. The large desk tells Roy that he is right—this is Truong Duc Hoan's private room. He knows that after his walk Hoan will take a nap, perhaps do some work, before a late dinner. The customs of a rich man in a hot climate. In the silent bedroom, Roy waits.

Down in the pantry, the Chief carries bags slowly into the house. He stops to smoke a cigarette. Yawns. Stays in the shadows. One of the housemen from the front comes back to look. The Chief, in the pantry, holds a case of the Vietnamese beer, smiles. The Vietnamese goes back to the front of the house. The Chief returns to the delivery van, sits behind the wheel, talks on the CB radio as if discussing his next deliveries with the shop.

Upstairs, Truong Duc Hoan enters his bedroom, closes the door, sits on the four-poster bed to remove his gold-colored sandals, yawns and sees Roy Carter.

Hoan understands the situation instantly. He smiles.

"So? Very skillful, young man. I do not know you, but I know what you want. You want money. We all want money, eh? You will kidnap me, frighten me, for money. So, I will give you money. I have it here in this room. You may tie me up. I will not attempt to alert my men. No risk to you, no risk to me."

Roy says, *"I'm Roy Carter."*

Truong Duc Hoan, on the edge of his four-poster bed, one sandal in his fleshy hands, white hair catching the late evening sunlight through his bedroom windows, frowns. Hoan is puzzled. The name means something to him, but he cannot think what. He tries to think, aware that it could mean his life.

"Jeanne-Marie Johnson's friend."

Hoan smiles and sweats, but it is no use. The ambushing in New York, the death of Coley Evans, are minor incidents in his worldwide business operations, he does not remember the details, makes no connection of the names.

"Eller's brother."

Hoan is confused. He blinks. His eyes flicker around the room as if the answer is somewhere there. Roy understands at once. Hoan has many daughters, many American friends.

"Dinh's brother-in-law."

Truong Duc Hoan goes pale. He is an intelligent man. He knows what his youngest daughter thinks of the world and of him. Perhaps he makes the connection between his daughter and the girl decoy in New York. Perhaps he remembers the name now: Jeanne-Marie Johnson. Whatever, Hoan spreads his fleshy hands, smiles again, negotiates, is ready to do business.

"Very well, you and Dinh win, so? Take me to prison. I will go peacefully. None of my men will harm you."

Roy draws the pistol from where he has been holding it under the white jacket. A Smith & Wesson .22 LR with a silencer.

"Too many dead," Roy says. "You've used too many people. Your own people. Jeanne-Marie."

Hoan looks at the pistol. It is an assassin's gun. Not a thief's gun. Or a kidnapper's gun. Or an extortionist's gun. He holds his hands out in front of him like a shield.

"I will pay you anything you want! I'm rich. Don't be a fool like my daughter, like your brother. I will—"

The long-barreled gun makes almost no sound. The small-caliber bullets are inaudible. Truong Duc Hoan still holds his hands out as if to stop the bullets. Hoan is already falling, already dead, but his hands are still forward and up as if to stop death in mid-air.

Hoan lies on the floor. Roy bends over him. The three bullets have left only small blackened holes in Hoan's head and almost no blood. The body is heavy as Roy drags it to the bed, lifts it up, turns the head to the wall, draws up the covers.

He hears the footsteps, is behind the door when the woman comes in, moves toward the bed. Something— Roy will never know what—makes her turn. She stares at him. Her mouth is open. She knows. In a moment she will scream. He shoots her. He has no choice. He puts her into the bed next to Truong Duc Hoan and slips out of the room.

He reaches the pantry unseen. The Chief is watching the front hall and the rear yard. They each pick up a case of Vietnamese beer and walk *out the side, one at a time in case the man at the pool is watching. He isn't. He's reading. The guard at the service entrance is dozing.*

They leave the van where they stole it, check that the driver is secured, transfer the two cases of beer and drive north in the car Roy rented.

No one has really seen them.

At worst it will be four hours before Truong Duc Hoan and his wife are found. With luck it could be morning. In four hours they are in San Jose. In six they are in San Francisco.

44

"WHY?" I SAID IN the small cottage.

Roy Carter walked into the other room, returned with his own bottle of beer. He sat on the bare floor with his back against the wall. His forearms rested on his drawn-up knees. His left hand rubbed his eyes, his face. In the black jacket, camouflage fatigues, boots, he looked like a soldier in the ruined room of a captured village, tired, the battle over for today.

"He got rich on the pain of his own people. He preyed on the world. Him and everyone like him." He raised the beer, seemed to read the label before he drank. "Over there they suffered and he got rich. They died and he lived in mansions, drove a Rolls-Royce. He got champagne, they got Agent Orange. Their villages burned and he got fat. And we helped him. We defended his comforts, his privileges. Because we're just like him. Eller knew." He drank. A long drink of the cold beer. "He and all like him live off the work and sweat and pain and death of others. Eller saw. They con us, exploit us, use us. Use my father, use the Chief, use me and you. Use all the poor of the world."

"Use Jeanne-Marie?" I said.

His thin face, the bright dark eyes behind the glasses, looked straight ahead as if he were alone in the room, as if he were on his bed back in Pine Dunes, staring up at the ceiling after reading one of Eller's letters.

"She thought America was a flashy car, glamorous clothes, a penthouse in Las Vegas. Hollywood, money, fame. What she heard from the soldiers when she was little, learned from the American magazines they still read over there, from listening to the old Saigonese who made a good living off the Americans. Everything would be a Hollywood movie when she got to America, and it looked to her like it was going to happen without her having to do anything, not even learn English."

"You tried to tell her? Set her straight?"

He nodded, but not to me. "I was away when Dinh sent her over from Nam. When I got back it'd already started falling apart on her but she wouldn't give up. I told her what she wanted didn't exist, never had existed. Not for her or anyone like her. Not for my father, or Eller, or me. It was all a big lie. She wouldn't listen to me. She had no skills, no education, but she went on trying, scheming, wanting everything she was never going to get."

The Chief got up and left the room. I finished my beer. I was being cool and calm, drinking beer. But still my throat was dry. He'd killed at least three people, maybe four, maybe more, and he sat there on the floor, his back against the wall, talking to himself as much as to me. The Chief returned with three more beers. The only door I knew about was behind me.

"When she came back from California the last time, she was broke. My father told her to go to school, learn English, study some trade she could use to make a living. I told her to open her eyes to what the world really was, maybe go back to Vietnam. She couldn't face the reality. She came up with a scheme to sell herself and her story to some magazine, centerfold nude and all, went back to New York again. That fell through too. My mother said she was too foreign to make it in America."

It didn't look like he had the Ingram under his black nylon windbreaker, but where was the silenced .22? Both his hands were in sight, hanging loose from wrists resting on his knees, the beer bottle on the floor. The Chief sat a little behind me, to my right, the P-38 stuck into his beaded belt.

"She went crazy. She was going to make it. She'd be *big*. Rich. Famous. An American." He picked up the beer, wiped his mouth hard. "That's when she went to the Dhocs. I didn't know what she was doing. Not until she called me from New York." He leaned his head back against the wall. Held the bottle in both hands on his drawn-up knees. "She was happy. Excited as a kid with a new doll. She'd gone to the Dhocs to contact Hoan. Every Vietnamese in this country knows about the great benefactor, Truong Duc Hoan. They only had the address of that basement office in New York. She went there and met Coley Evans, told him she needed

help, had a proposition for Hoan. He put her off.
She slept in a doorway that night, just like she had
in Saigon. When she went back to Evans he was all
over her, said Mr. Hoan wanted to help her, had an
important job for her to do in New York, then
they'd talk about her future."

If Carter had the pistol under the jacket, how
fast could he move with his eyes closed, his
knees drawn up, a beer bottle in both hands?
How fast could the Chief get the P-38 out of his
waistband? If I made the break, made it outside,
how fast could I run? Which way? It would all
depend on how much start I got, how well they
knew the area, how much luck I had.

"A small but important job helping the police.
She'd be paid, of course, and then they would talk.
The only thing that bothered her was they had her
staying in a whorehouse, dressed up like a whore,
and wouldn't let her leave or call anyone. She was
calling me from some office down on the basement
floor. They said it was to fool the crook the police
were trying to trap, but the other whores seemed to
know Evans, and that surprised her because he
worked for Hoan."

His eyes were smaller and harder behind the
thick glasses. "It didn't surprise me. I tried to tell
her about Hoan, but something must have scared
her and she hung up. I went up to New York,
watched Evans, but he didn't go near the brothel
until the last night. About eight o'clock Jeanne-
Marie came out dressed in that Chinese dress and
high heels, made up like a Saigon hooker. They
drove to the river and uptown maybe ten blocks.
Jeanne-Marie got out, walked back south four
blocks and went into this boarded-up store on the

river block. I paid my cab, stayed way back up at the corner across the avenue."

The Chief got up again. He was restless. It was getting late, and talk wasn't his idea of fun. If he went for more beer, it might be my only chance. He went. Roy Carter looked at me. The dark eyes were magnified behind the glasses. He put his beer bottle down. I smiled. The Chief returned. We all had a beer.

"I watched for an hour, then this big Lincoln limousine showed up, parked, circled again toward the river, came back after a while, left again. Around ten it came back and parked outside the store. Someone went in. Another car parked on the other side of the avenue from me where it could see the store and the Lincoln. Five minutes and Jeanne-Marie came up the block. She got to the corner, looked back, and all hell broke loose. I couldn't see what happened, but I could hear shooting. Jeanne-Marie screamed and ran. The other car drove off. It had to be Hoan, or someone he sent to watch and report. I ran after Jeanne-Marie, but I lost her."

He took a long drink of his beer. "I lost her, Fortune. If I hadn't, maybe—" He drank again. "I ran those streets from the river to Eighth Avenue all the way south past the brothel. I saw Evans there, but I didn't find Jeanne-Marie. Until I went into that diner and they told me she'd been there only a few minutes before." A long, slow drink. "I heard the shot, found her in the alley. I ran through that stinking alley all the way to the street at the far end, but I didn't see anyone. When I got back she was naked, stripped by the poor who live in that slum. I looked for clues until I heard the police. All I found was a metal button could've been dropped any time."

I took the pin emblem in its plastic bag out of my inner coat pocket. "You lost it again in Evans' basement."

The emblem no longer interested him. The alley no longer interested him. "It doesn't matter. I know who killed her. The world that made her want what she couldn't have. The world that made Truong Duc Hoan. A world based on the few having more than the many. The incentive, the carrot for the donkeys, the con. Maybe it can produce more, but it has to produce unequal. Some have a lot, many have little and most have nothing. A system based on hopes that fail. For every winner, a million losers."

I knew then why self-defense didn't matter, why witnesses didn't matter once he'd made his escape. He didn't want safety, he wanted justification. He didn't want to be protected, he wanted to be understood. He didn't care about witnesses because he wasn't going to be caught. Not alive. And if by accident he should be taken alive, he wouldn't need any help to tell why he had to do what he had done. Prisoners of war need no defense, can only show the truth and wait for time to do them justice.

I said, "You can't blame a man like Hoan on the system. He's an aberration, a corruption of the system."

"He *is* the system," Roy Carter said. "The naked truth of the system. Even at the end he tried to make a 'deal,' con me."

The Chief was listening, no longer restless. His beer was empty, but he wasn't going for another. Not now.

"What do you want instead, Roy?" I asked.

His fingers whitened on the beer bottle. "A world where my children don't start with advantages and expectations yours don't have. Where one man doesn't work until he drops while another lives in comfort on that work. Where the poor don't sow and the rich reap. Where one man doesn't live on another's misfortune, use another man's desperation to profit himself. The end of a world where I use every force from the police to the church to keep what I have and you don't."

"Yeah," the Chief said.

The corruption, self-interest, cynicism and exploitation can become too much for some people. A disillusioned soldier in Vietnam and his socially conscious wife. A boy who worshipped that soldier, blamed his death on the exploitation of the rich and powerful. A half-Irish, half-Italian street hustler who identified with the dispossessed Indians. A privileged girl who saw too much pain and injustice. They have to do something, and then they become dangerous. Very dangerous.

"You can't force people to change," I said. "You can't tell them to think. They've got to think for themselves, Roy, make their own choice."

"Democracy?" he said. "Free enterprise?"

"Something like that."

"Who says equality isn't democratic? Who says community isn't free? Don't confuse capitalism with democracy, Fortune, or democracy with free enterprise."

I heard the anger grow in his voice the certainty. I was Fortune now, the "Mister" gone. I was losing him all the way, and I didn't know how to get him back, how to reach him.

"Did Eller say that?" I said. "Or did his wife say it when you visited Eller's grave? Does she like the new Vietnam? A Soviet satellite? Cambodia? Maybe Thailand soon? Freedom by the sword? For those who do what they're told?"

"It's still war, Fortune." The anger was colder. "It takes time to change centuries. You break eggs to make an omelet. Eller knew that. He died trying to bring change."

"How did he really die? Did Dinh tell you when you were there?"

He turned the beer bottle in his hands. "He'd decided to stay when the Cong came. She doesn't know if he told anyone besides her or not. After the North had most of the city, she found his body in a street near the American Embassy. He'd been shot. She doesn't know if it was the Cong, the ARVN or us." He finished his beer, stood up.

"You can't free people by repression and conquest, Roy."

"We can't go on with a world ruled by Hoans and Hitlers, Nixons and Somozas."

Too much had happened. He'd taken the step, crossed the line from dreams of justice into the shadow world of war for the people, but the people had no faces. He no longer cared who had killed Jeanne-Marie, if he hadn't killed her himself. He had his own needs now.

I asked, "Who really killed Jeanne-Marie?"

"What does it matter who pulled the trigger, Fortune? Hoan killed her. Used her the way his kind have used millions of others, and killed her as sure as if he'd pulled the trigger. I knew who he was and what he was. I didn't know where he was." He turned his eyes full on me. "But I found where he was, and I killed him."

"And his wife?" I said.

"I didn't want to kill her. I had to."

"The way someone had to kill Jeanne-Marie?"

He didn't have anything to say, but he didn't flinch either. He looked me straight in the eye

There was a difference between Hoan's wife and Jeanne-Marie Johnson. The difference between his right and Hoan's wrong.

I said, "The trouble with terrorism is it can be used for bad causes as well as good causes. You end up with armed camps killing the people they say they want to save. The people caught in the middle again, suffering and dying."

He looked at his watch.

"There has to be a better world than we have, Fortune."

"I know," I said, "but I'm not sure there is."

He watched me in silence for a time. Young and thin and pale, not much more than a shadow. "Then nothing matters. All I can do is kill all the Truong Duc Hoans I can find."

He walked from the room. The Chief stood up, motioned. I walked ahead of him into another room at the rear of the house. It was a bedroom not much bigger than a closet. The Chief locked the door. I checked the single window. It was barred.

I lay down in my clothes. The bed was comfortable, I hadn't had much sleep the last two days, but I didn't sleep. I lay there as rigid as a hostage locked in a silent room. But the body has its own defenses, even against fear, and sometime toward morning I fell asleep.

45

THE CLICK OF THE lock woke me up.

I lay without moving. I didn't like what Roy Carter was doing, but I understood how he felt, what he wanted. It was a cause I could sympathize with. But a cause becomes a lot less noble when you are one of the eggs going to be broken. I lay with my eyes closed but alert, ready to make one last attempt. Surprise was the only chance for a one-armed man against younger men with two arms.

"He's gone."

I opened my eyes. The Chief stood over the bed against the first cold light of dawn, dressed in single feather, warpaint and fringe.

"Gone where?"

"I got some coffee outside."

He had the P-38 in the waistband of his ragged jeans, walked ahead of me to the kitchen. He didn't look like he'd slept at all, drank his coffee in silence, the single eagle feather erect, his black hair heavy in its two thick braids, his war paint in three bright red lines under each eye.

"Where has he gone, Chief?"

"Where his people sent him."

The coffee was good and hot. A damp October chill rested on the grass and trees and back yards outside the window of the small kitchen.

"People?"

"Where you think he got the Ingram? How he got trained so good?"

"They're getting him out of the country?"

He looked at his watch. "Already got. *Sayonara.*"

"Vietnam? Eller's wife?"

He shrugged. "Managua to Manila, Nam to Naples, they got lots of places he can go. Hell, he don't got to go no farther'n San Juan."

He drank his coffee, hunched at the narrow kitchen table.

"Is that why, Chief?"

"What why?"

"Why you helped him? Joined him?"

He drank his coffee. "I hear, I see. He was one guy ain't gonna sit no more on his ass takin' shit. He's one guy hittin' back. That's the only weapon we got 'gainst this here world got no fuckin' place for us. You think 'cause I know how to live down where I got to live I like it? You think I like to con an' cheat an' steal? Shit, man, I like to live nice an' clean an' safe like any white man. So when you sends me lookin', an' I run into him, I sign up. He doin' something. Doin', not talkin'."

"Killing?" I said. "Murder and violence?"

"They ain't no give, man, only take."

The sun was almost up, and the coffee was almost gone. The cold dawn light began to turn yellow through the haze of smog and morning fog. We were both a long way from home. My cup was empty, even if his wasn't.

"Do I walk out?"

The P-38 was in his waistband under the beaded belt. He drank coffee. He drank slowly, as if he didn't want the coffee to end. He didn't seem to be thinking about whether I would walk out or not. Maybe he didn't want to think, or have to. I could wait, or I could act. I smiled.

"Do we talk—" and lunged for the P-38 in his waistband. The coffee flew out of his hand, he fell with the chair to the floor. I had the gun in my solitary hand, we were on the floor. He held the gun, grabbed at my lone arm with his other hand.

We both heard the sound at the same time.

Someone crashing through the brush toward the cottage. More than one man. The Chief let go of the P-38.

"You keep the sucker," he said. "Take a look."

The windows of the cottage had no curtains. I saw them across the yard. Wilmer and Ernie crashing through the trees and bushes like two city dogs who had never seen grass or real dirt. Stumbling. Bushes tripped feet, caught sleeves and gun barrels, made noise. Ernie had a dirty cast on his left forearm.

"They want Roy Carter," I said, "not us."

"You gonna go out and tell 'em he ain't here?"

I wasn't and I didn't have to.

The police appeared on both sides of the big gray main house behind the two thugs. I could see them in the other yards on the flanks, too. Lieutenant Morgan stood on the weed-grown path between the houses. He had his gun out.

"Hold it right there! Police!"

For most of us the reaction to that command is to stop in surprise and some anger and a little fear and wonder what the police could want with us. For Wilmer and Ernie, having heard it all their lives, the reaction was something else. Cut and run. Open fire. Escape however they could. Resist, evade, vanish.

Wilmer fired.

Ernie ran.

Lieutenant Morgan dove to cover. The uniformed policemen opened fire on Wilmer. Detectives ran among bushes and over fences after Ernie. I watched from a corner of the window, P-38 ready. The Chief sat under the window. It was over in three minutes. Firing, shouting, ducking and running. Then silence.

Wilmer lay in the grass and weeds. The uniformed police reloaded. The detectives returned, breathed hard and shook their heads. Lieutenant Morgan looked somewhere toward the hills. Sirens began in the distance, the uniformed policemen spread out to hold back the neighbors, the detectives stood around the body on the ground.

Gary Winters appeared around the corner of the big house in his wheelchair. He rolled up to look down at Wilmer. Lieutenant Morgan walked toward the cottage. I went out to meet him. The Chief came behind me. Morgan stared at the Chief's feather, braids, fringe and war paint. The Chief folded his arms, leaned against the door frame, inscrutable.

"Dead?" I asked.

"Dead."

"The other one? The fat one?"

"We lost him. We'll find him," Morgan said. "We've had the place staked out. I figured if they wanted to talk to your Carter as bad as it looked like they did, they might try here again. My men saw you show up last night, meet a guy who fitted your description of Roy Carter and some Indian, waited to see if those two would show and they did."

"You figured right."

He nodded, satisfied with his thinking. "Where is he?"

"Who?"

"Roy Carter."

"Gone."

"Gone? When? Where?"

"Last night. I don't know where."

He watched me, not so friendly. "My men never saw him leave."

"I suppose he didn't want to be seen."

He watched me like a policeman. "There's talk of some killings down south your Roy Carter could be part of. You know about that?"

"I know about it."

"Was it Carter?"

"I can't prove it. I'm not sure anyone can."

"And Carter's gone?"

"He's gone. I don't know where."

"Does he?"

He nodded to where the Chief leaned against the doorframe. The Chief's dark, war-painted face showed no expression. I didn't know if he had been going to let me walk away before Wilmer and Ernie and the police arrived, or if he'd been going to finish Roy Carter's work, eliminate another witness. He would have done what he had to. It was something I would never know for sure.

I didn't care a lot about the death of Truong Duc Hoan or Coley Evans or La Reina, and the Chief hadn't been part of the last two anyway. But I cared about Truong Duc Hoan's wife. I cared about the innocent bystanders caught in the explosion, the nameless eggs broken to right the wrongs.

"He knows," I said. "He was there in Santa Barbara. I don't know if you can prove it, but he was there."

I told him all I knew about the killing of Truong Duc Hoan and his wife, gave him the P-38. They'd get my statement and send the Chief down to the Santa Barbara police and let them take it from there.

The Chief said, "Shoulda snuffed you, man."

"The wife, Chief. I can't let the wife slide. All the wives who get killed while Roy Carter's saving them."

"We got wives too. They dies too."

"He could have taken Hoan and Evans to the police, told his story, let them handle it. That way Hoan's whole operation could have been shut down, now it'll just go on under someone else."

"Shit, man, they gets out in a hour on bail. They gets a slap, 'n back in business sellin' shit."

"What was Roy Carter selling? Ten kilos of H."

"Everything cost."

Even revolution costs money, and the money has to come from somewhere.

"There has to be another way," I said.

"They ain't. Not no way gets nothin' done."

The detectives took him to a waiting patrol car. Lieutenant Morgan left some men to comb the area for fat Ernie, for any leads to where he'd run, took me and Gary Winters downtown to get our statements. We gave them, signed them, left our addresses and took a taxi back to the big gray house. Winters talked me into taking him and what was left of the Vietnamese beer to People's Park.

I called Kay Michaels from a pay phone on Telegraph, told her I had to go back to New York before I came down to Hollywood. She wasn't happy, but she understood. Or she said she did. I told her I'd think a lot about the three thousand miles always between us, and she told me to get

my damned business done in New York, and then I
headed for San Francisco International.

46

IN MY LOFT I got a night's sleep, made a stop at the
library and went across to the Rescue Mission. The
door was still open. Three wary kids in the recreation
room to the left watched me with the same hostile
eyes. The Reverend Davis was in his office. Anne Wollard wasn't.

"She's quit," Davis said. "What do I do without her?
Where do I find someone else like her? Do you know
how long it took her to adjust, to become effective?
All thrown away. Why?"

"You ask her?" I said.

He waved a hand angrily. "Some nonsense about
wanting to do more." He glared up at me. "Talk to
her, Mr. Fortune. She's at her apartment packing.
Maybe you can talk some sense into her."

I left him looking through worn resumes that had
probably been in his files longer than Anne Woollard
had worked for him. There wouldn't be many candi-
dates for the job, selfless dedication to the poor and
unfortunate is a rare commodity.

At the rooming house up the street Anne Woollard
opened the door to my knock, went back to packing
her two suitcases on the bed. The black-and-white cat
ate under the window.

"It'll miss you," I said. "The cat."

"That's all I feel bad about."

"Where to?"

"Why? Are you going to have me arrested too?"

"You heard from Roy Carter? From his friends?"

"The Chief had a call, he called me. Why, Dan?"

"Hoan's wife. An innocent bystander just to protect himself, his cause. That's how it begins, justification of any violence because it's a means to the end. The cause becomes more important than the people it's supposed to be for."

"Will he go to prison? The Chief?"

"He knew the risk. It won't be easy to prove he was part of it all."

"You'll testify against him?"

"Yes."

"And me?"

"You weren't part of the killings as far as I know."

She packed some underwear. There was little left on the bed to be packed. She held a white summer dress, stared at it.

"You going to join him?" I said.

"I hope he sends for me, but I don't think he will."

"You know the 'Cause' will always be first . . ."

She closed a suitcase. "I know that, Dan."

"Then where?"

"Managua. El Salvador. Havana. Pick coffee, plant corn, purify the water. Somewhere I can do something to help."

"You think they're right in Managua?"

She closed the second suitcase, looked slowly around the room to be sure she had everything she wanted to take with her. She looked at the cat, still eating, indifferent to us.

"It'll find another free kitchen," she said. "Cats are adaptable."

"Almost as much as people."

She went to the door, looked back. "A time comes when you have to do more than bind the wounds, pick up the pieces of the victims. I don't know if they're right in Managua, but I know that we're wrong."

The cat turned to look as she left. It stared at the open doorway. Then it turned back to its food, and I went down to the street and caught a taxi down to Fugazy's. I rented a car, drove across town, through the Midtown Tunnel, along the Long Island Expressway to the Southern State Parkway.

Gray October was moving rapidly toward the snows of November and December. The traffic was relatively light this weekday mid-morning, and I reached Pine Dunes faster than I'd expected. Judy Lavelle's house was in an older part of the Island a mile from the Pine Dunes tracts. It stood on more land, with more trees and less lawn, was a three-story white frame from the Twenties with a large shaded porch around three sides. Judy came out of the house as if she'd been watching for me, stood on the porch and hugged herself in the chilly air.

"The police called Mr. Carter," she said. "That's what Roy wanted? To kill that man because of Jeanne-Marie?"

"Jeanne-Marie was the trigger," I said. "The last straw. Vietnam, Eller, injustice, the whole world the way Roy sees it was the reason."

She shivered in the chill. "Is he sick, Dan? Crazy?"

"I guess that depends on where you stand and how you look at the world."

"Killing people he doesn't even know?"

"Governments and soldiers kill people they don't know every day," I said. "He's obsessed, over the edge of what we call normal, but he's not crazy."

"We won't see him again, will we?"

It was "we" now, all those who had known Roy Carter in his life, not "I." He wasn't hers anymore, he was gone from more than Pine Dunes. She had come through and out into her own life.

"Probably not," I said.

"It's going to be different," she said. "College, what I want, everything. I'm not sure what I want to do, but I'm going to find out. I think I want to get married, have a family, settle down. I think I'd like to stay around here."

She smiled at me. We'd had one night we'd both remember. With luck it wasn't the kind of night she'd need again. It had come from fear and confusion and loss. Growing up.

She came close and raised up to kiss me. "I'm glad I met you anyway."

I smiled. "Me too."

She went into the house, got my gun for me and was still on the porch when I drove off toward Pine Dunes. A thin sun was trying to break through the heavy gray sky when I reached the house on Hickock Way. I didn't really want to talk to Jerry Carter, but I owed him a full report and he owed me money. Debbie Carter and Melanie were coming out as I walked across the neat little lawn surrounded by its now-bare flowerbeds.

"You talk to him," she said when she saw me. "He's just sittin' there. No job, now he just sits. I feel bad about Roy too, what they say he did. I don't know what's happened to him, you know? I never knew what got into Eller. I don't know Roy no more. Killing people, the cops after him. I don't know what he's doing, what he wants."

She wasn't cold or unfeeling. Neither she nor Melanie, who shifted from foot to foot, looked at her watch. If Roy had come home after murdering someone, she'd have mothered him, helped him, comforted him. But she could never understand him, and he was gone and she didn't want to think about what he had done or what was going to happen to him. She wasn't selfish, but she had her own life and her daughters, and that was hard enough to handle when there was nothing she could do about something she didn't understand.

"We got to meet Debbie Junior," she said, pulled on her white gloves. "We're all shook up, Melanie don't even feel like working. We're gonna have a nice lunch, try to forget about it. You talk to Jerry, tell him it ain't none of his fault. Tell him we got two girls, we got to go on, right?"

The house was gray and silent inside. No lights, no voices, no television, no sound at all. Jerry Carter was in the small flowered living room. He sat there doing nothing. His big hands rested in his lap, folded one over the other. He didn't even have a can of beer.

"I guess I owe you money," he said.

"I'll send a bill. No hurry."

"You done your job." The big hands moved in his lap.

"They ain't callin' me back. He's right, Roy. It's okay, I got the money, only Roy he's right, you know? They don't need the drill press, an' they don't need me. They got a robot now, they got a new plant way down in the boonies. Jap robot, you know? Like who won the war, right?"

He tried to laugh. His mouth, face made the right shapes, but his eyes couldn't. They held all the fears that come to someone who has just seen his certainty of a lifetime, the foundation rock of his world, crumble under him.

"Forty years an' I don't know nothing about the company. I ain't no part of it. Just a hunk of equipment like the drill press."

"They won't offer you something else? A different job?"

"Sure. I could push a handtruck for the robots, maybe sweep the shop. I mean, I could do somethin' like that if I want to move to the new plant out in Nowhere, Utah. No guarantee, they got a lot o' younger guys needs jobs, too."

"You can pay me in installments, Jerry," I said.

"It ain't the money. We're lucky, we're okay that way. Pension, social security, money in the bank. It's the other part, you know? I mean, what the hell am I? Forty fuckin' years."

The big hand fluttered over his belly. The forty years of his life seemed to hang one by one in the house where he'd lived them. The dream house of the boy from Brooklyn—his own castle.

"You talked to him? I mean . . . after he . . .?"

I told him everything Roy had said, everything he had talked about. What had happened to Truong Duc Hoan and who he had been. The woman and the Chief. Where I thought Roy would go, what he would do from now on, how he was going to live and how he would probably die.

"A terrorist?" He could barely say the word, his voice hoarse.

"He'd say a guerilla, a freedom fighter."

He blinked at me. "Whose freedom?"

"Everyone on the outside looking in. From Harlem to Honduras. Eller taught him that. When Eller died, Roy blamed Vietnam, the injustice of the world, everyone in power. Call him one more victim of Vietnam."

His hoarse voice was almost inaudible "He's my son, Fortune."

"They're all someone's sons."

He moved one big hand as if to protest, then let it drop. He raised it again, rubbed his eyes. His belly hung over his wide leather belt. He looked down at his belt, at his belly.

"I can't do nothin'," he said. "I couldn't do nothin' for Eller, an' I can't do nothin' for Roy."

"You can hope he finds a different way."

"Nobody gives up nothin' they don't got to. There ain't no other way. Not how he sees what he got to do."

I had no answer.

"He's on his own. We's all on our own. That's the bottom line."

I had no answer to that either, turned to the door. It wasn't what Roy would have said, but, in the end, what Roy was going to do might not be so different.

"Jeanne-Marie," Jerry Carter said behind me. "He kill her too?"

"No," I said.

"You know who did?"

"I know."

47

IN HIS DESK CHAIR he looked at the small metal emblem in its plastic evidence bag lying on his desk. He looked up at Captain Pearce, then looked at me. He said nothing.

"It's a clan hat badge," I said. "The clan crest in silver worn on a bonnet. I looked it up in the library this morning after Roy Carter had told me where he found it. I'll bet you've got a display plaque on the wall of your study out there in Great Neck. Maybe in the living room. The clan crest and tartan and war cry, a framed certificate of authenticity with the whole history of the MacKays."

George MacKay watched me the way an exterminator watches a cockroach. He was back in his white suit. He'd pulled some strings, called in some favors, paid some incentive money, crawled a little and been allowed to open again. The white suit was in celebration.

"Roy Carter found it in the alley beside Jeanne-Marie Johnson's body. Probably had it on your key chain, loose in your pocket, on a watch chain, something. How many MacKays you think walked through that alley this year?"

"She stole it from my desk," MacKay said. "I caught her down here one day. Must've stole it right then."

I sat down. His eyes said that if I'd been alone I wouldn't be sitting. I'd have been out on the street ten minutes ago. Or dead. Or worse.

"Roy Carter saw Coley Evans here after the La Reina massacre, before Jeanne-Marie was killed. You told the police you didn't have anything to do with the trap on the Spic Queen, and you didn't see Evans that night."

"I didn't have nothing to do with La Reina. I forgot Evans come here later. We talked, that's all."

"About what?" Captain Pearce said. He was behind me, to my left, against the wall.

"Business."

In the gloom of the old pantry floor the street sounds were the same as on any night. The squeal of tires, the anger of horns and voices, laughter, a baby crying. An ordinary evening in late October, growing cold, but warm in MacKay's small office.

"You hired those two gutter punks," I said, "Wilmer and Ernie. I thought it was Hoan who hired them, but they were still trying to kill Carter after Hoan was dead, and then I knew you'd hired them. Roy was in the alley that night, you'd seen him. When you missed the badge, went back to the alley but didn't find it, you guessed Roy had to have found it. And he was nosing around too much. He didn't know you'd killed her, but he might find out. A good businessman doesn't take chances if he can do something about it."

His eyes weighed his chances of doing something about us. If it was necessary to make a move. Pearce mostly. He wasn't too worried about me.

"That gonna be hard to prove, Fortune."

"No it won't. Wilmer's dead, but Ernie'll talk."

He said nothing, turned the plastic bag with the badge in it in his scarred hands, his face almost pensive. There were ways of dealing with the testimony of a punk like fat Ernie. There were ways of dealing with fat Ernie himself. In or out of jail.

"She knew her killer, MacKay. She walked right into that alley. All along you gave me information free. I wondered about that. That's not the way it happens down here. You give nothing away, never get involved if you can help it. But you wanted to find Roy Carter, hoped I'd lead your hired killers to him."

"That all you got? Hunches an' guesses?"

"No, you made one real mistake. On the record too. In front of the police. Jeanne-Marie left here around eight o'clock with Evans. You said that was the last time you saw her. But when you described what she was wearing to the police and to me you were too accurate. You described the advertising button from Aldo's diner. She got that button from the counterman ten minutes before she was killed. The only way you could have known about the button was to have been in the alley when she died."

His face showed no expression. The only sign of a reaction was the faint purple of his dry-shave scars, a tightness to the welts of his other scars.

"You didn't have any connection to La Reina or Hoan except to let Evans stash Jeanne-Marie in your place so La Reina would believe she was one of Hoan's prostitutes. But when Evans came here that night he told you Jeanne-Marie had panicked, was so scared she might even go to the police. It wouldn't worry him, he had a complete alibi, no one could connect him to the ambush or Jeanne-Marie."

"No one ties me to that ambush neither!"

"No one's trying," I said, "but you realized if she ran to the police, told them everything, they'd be sure she was one of your stable and close you down, maybe for good. If you killed her, who'd know she'd ever been in your place? Evans? Your girls? None of them would talk. She wouldn't be identified for weeks, maybe months. Just another runaway girl dead in New York. So you sent out your connections to find her. That kid who came into Aldo's, used the telephone, forgot to drink his coffee, was calling you. You killed her and made your train. You killed her in that alley because you were out of business if she talked."

I don't know what I expected from him, but I got nothing. He only sat, toyed with the hat badge.

"What you didn't know was she'd called Roy Carter. He changed everything by finding the MacKay badge and by identifying her. The police and I came around, and you were in trouble. You had to disassociate yourself from her, hope her connection to the La Reina killings didn't come out. And you had to get rid of Roy Carter." I shrugged. "But the La Reina thing came out, your punks couldn't get Carter, you dropped the hat badge and you remembered a diner button you weren't supposed to have seen."

Pearce had his handcuffs out. MacKay didn't look at him. He didn't look at me. He didn't move. He sat and looked at the MacKay hat badge in its plastic bag.

"A man got a right to climb out of the snit. You fight an' claw out. You kill if you got to. You never let nothin' send you back. I got a business, I got a family. I made me a good business in the gutter and it got me out and I don't let nothing take it away. I take care of my own." He looked at me now. At Pearce and the handcuffs. "You ain't got enough. I'll beat it."

He stood up, turned with his wrists behind him. Pearce put the handcuffs on. There was a brilliance to MacKay's eyes, not a lot different from Roy Carter's. Maybe they'd both beat the charge and the odds.

"You got out," I said, "but you got out alone, on the backs of those still down there."

He showed his teeth, walked ahead of Pearce out of the office. A uniformed policemen came to take him to Pearce's patrol car. The usual crowd that gathers around New York police cars was there. One of the curious had somehow gotten down into the garbage area. He suddenly stumbled from the shadows, lunged at MacKay, his head turned as if flinching, the big .45 caliber automatic held out in both hands. He shot George MacKay five times before Pearce and his patrolmen swarmed him under in a chaos of uniforms, garbage and crashing cans.

MacKay had been hit all five times, flung against the wall like a soggy rag, dropped dead on what was left of his face, throat and chest. The white suit looked like it had been washed in blood. I turned away, leaned on the wrought iron railing with my head down. I thought about his family out in Great Neck. He'd have had good insurance. It would have been important to him.

Pearce swore at length. It was the second death in custody this week. A policeman hates to have a prisoner killed while in his custody more than anything on earth except the death of another policeman. The patrolmen dragged fat Ernie up to where we stood over MacKay. The gutter gunman breathed harder, his rags torn, the cast on his forearm cracked and filthy, his fat face bloody but almost happy.

"He dead?"

"He's dead," Pearce said, "and so are you."

"Shit, second-degree tops." He stared down at MacKay in his blood and white suit. His pig eyes violent and unforgiving. "Wilmer he got dead and the son-of-a-bitch says no scratch 'cause we didn't get the fucking kid. Wilmer's dead. He oughta have paid."

"His troubles are over," Pearce said. "Yours are starting. I'll personally see they throw the book at you."

Ernie laughed. "Shit, the joint's better'n any place I ever flopped in. Least I eats good."

The morgue wagon came, and more cops, and a phalanx of eager and suspicious reporters, and the high civilian brass, and just about everyone except the mayor. They took MacKay's body and Ernie and Pearce's on-the-spot report to the Commissioner. The civilian brass handled the reporters, ordered Pearce to keep quiet and advised me to do likewise, and after only a couple of hours the sidewalk was clear again, the passersby hurrying on their usual way.

"Let's walk." Pearce said.

Pearce sent his car away. We walked up to Eighth Avenue in the late night. It was a lot colder. I pulled up my duffel coat collar. Pearce didn't seem to notice the temperature. He didn't say anything, just walked. Up one side of Eighth Avenue, down the other, the pimps and tricks and hustlers and peddlers and thieves giving us a wide berth. All except the boy hookers showing their erections in doorways, and out-of-town customers on the cruise, who didn't know enough to recognize a police captain. There are more boys on the streets these days than girls, but I don't know what that means. Maybe the girls have gone indoors, are better organized. Or maybe it says something about us, not them. On Forty-second Street Pearce pointed to an elegant older black man dressed like a diplomat.

"He is a diplomat," Pearce said. "Three nights out of five he's on that corner looking for boys. He doesn't speak English or know the city, but he found the Strip. As long as men like him buy, the poor and desperate will sell. Sex or drugs or anything anyone wants."

We passed a video arcade. One boy, fifteen at the most, stood playing a violent video game and arrogantly displaying his tight, lean body in sequined lavender jeans, a short fur-trimmed purple velvet jacket, white ankle boots, pink silk shirt and black tasseled gaucho sombrero. He had a cigarette holder, delicately chewed a small cake from a box on top of the video game machine. Furtive older men and younger boys watched him.

Pearce said, "He eats well, lives high, and when the johns look him over he's being noticed by someone."

We walked on to Broadway and uptown again with the hordes who seemed to have nothing better to do than walk shoulder to shoulder in the glitter of neon that is Times Square.

"Two arrests," Pearce said, "and lucky to get two. A cop does what he can in this cowboy country. The arrest on the Chief probably won't stick. Your testimony is hearsay and guesses. Unless they get some real witnesses out in California, he'll be back here hustling in a month."

"You ever find out if anyone killed La Reina's man Madero?"

"It goes down as suicide. We'll never know for sure. On the Balada woman and her mother we know it was ordered by that Truong Duc Hoan. Outside killers.

Maybe we'll pick up one of them someday on another charge and he'll tell us about Balada."

"Roy Carter?"

"San Francisco says a man answering his description flew out of San Jose on a private jet to Mexico around midnight. Had a passport, the airport knew the pilot. That's where the last five kilos of smack went. The Mexicans say he took a flight out of Mexico City to Managua. Or to Rio. Or maybe Tokyo."

"How do we stop him?" I said. "Them? The terrorism?"

"We kill one here, jail one there," Pearce said. "It stops when they have more to live for than to die for."

We walked on in the cold of the crowded and gaudy streets of the Minnesota Strip until the captain finally said good night and took a cab for home, wherever that was. I walked on down to my office/apartment and went to bed. In a day or so I'd fly back to California. I needed the vacation, they wanted me in Santa Barbara to see if any case could be made against the Chief, and I wanted Kay Michaels.

The three businesmen hurried from their official limousine through the crowds in the airport of Santiago, Chile. From France, England and Peru, they were ranking members of a copper consortium negotiating a new trade agreement with the Pinochet government, were escorted by two deputy administrators of Chile's International Trade Ministry and two armed soldiers. They were hurrying because their limousine had been unexpectedly delayed by an accident that blocked the road on its way to the airport.

Formalities were dispensed with, tickets quickly validated as the copper negotiators waited almost alone in the VIP Lounge where the other dignitaries from all over the world, in Santiago to secure profitable agreements from the struggling Pinochet regime, had already boarded the last flight of the day to the United States. Four men came through a rear door of the VIP Lounge that was always double locked. They had submachine guns, shot down the three copper negotiators, the Chilean deputies, one soldier and two bystanders. The surviving soldier killed one gunman, the other three jumped back through the door, locked it behind them, eluded all airport security and escaped.

The dead terrorist was identified as Roberto Fanon, a former Grenadan bodyguard of Maurice

Bishop, two of those who escaped were thought to have been well-known Chilean guerillas who vanished back into their mountains and the fourth was described as a young Anglo suspected of being an American wanted in the United States for the murder of a Vietnamese businessman.